HOOK

AND

SHOOT

Published 2016 by Jeremy Brown
Cover design by Michael Nagin

Printed in the United States of America
ISBN 978-0-9983933-3-9 Paperback
          978-0-9983933-2-2 eBook

10 9 8 7 6 5 4 3 2
Second Edition

For Ellen

HOOK AND SHOOT

CHAPTER 1

YOU CAN'T PUNCH A GUY IN THE FACE IF HE ISN'T AROUND. I've tried it.

At first I thought Banzai Eddie Takanori was just waiting until I healed up after the Burbank fight. I had a sixty-day medical suspension with thirty days of no contact to let the scar tissue clump together into some kindergartner's idea of eyebrows. Docs cleared me after five weeks, and I got back to light sparring and rolling, my trainer Gil watching for blood like a vampire shark.

Seven weeks after the fight and still no Eddie. We saw him on TV at Warrior events, so he was alive despite my earnest voodoo doll attempts; naming a taco Eddie and eating it doesn't always work. Every day Gil left him messages and threatened it was the last time he'd call. I didn't panic until Roth and Terence and the other guys at the gym quit busting my chops and asked how I was doing.

Opportunity was toying with me. Finally thought I'd caught the bastard, got a good grip, but it was pulling away. When it snapped I'd be left with a limp chance just long enough to make a noose.

I was staring out the front windows of The Fight House, Gil's gym, thinking about getting a degree—maybe they'd look at my résumé and give me an honorary doctorate in wasted potential—when a black stretch limo floated to a stop in the parking lot.

The driver got out and frowned at the sun, pulled his white shirt away from his chest, and stepped inside the lobby. "Mr. Wallace?" British accent. If it was fake, a nice touch.

"I don't care what these assholes said, I still have a job. I'm not washing that thing."

He glanced at the car. "Ah, no, I—"

"Who's here?" Gil shouted from the sparring cage, took his time on those stumpy legs of his getting to the front. He sipped his barrel of coffee and looked the driver up and down. "Who's this?"

"Driver."

The guy was lean, mid-thirties, just under six feet with a relaxed smile and eyes that tried to look soft but didn't quite remember how. He tolerated our scrutiny for two seconds. "I'm here to pick up Mr. Wallace for Mr. Takanori."

"Sweet Jesus, finally," Gil said. "Where we going? Do I need to change?"

The driver considered Gil's sweaty gi top and stained cargo shorts. No shoes. "Mr. Takanori was clear: the invitation is for one."

Gil's jaw clenched. "He's out there?"

"Mr. Wallace, if we could."

Gil found his cell phone on the counter. "Does Mr. Takanori have his phone with him?"

"I can relay any message."

"Tell him to call me. He owes us a fight contract, and I'm tired of this waiting bullshit."

"Call Mr. Hobbes. Done."

Gil looked at me. "You tell him too. You have your phone?"

"Yeah."

"Call me and give him the phone."

The driver said, "It will be handled."

"I'm right here, phone in hand. No time like the present."

The driver opened the front door. Heat boiled in off the black-top. "Mr. Wallace."

I waved to Roth and Terence, standing in the boxing ring with their mouths hanging open. "Peasants."

"Don't sign anything," Gil said.

"Won't even take my crayons."

I walked to the limo thinking Eddie had waited this long because he wanted the perfect matchup for my next heavyweight fight. Something that would take full advantage of the KO win over Burbank and the eleven new fans I'd picked up.

Serves me right for thinking he'd give me what I deserved instead of what he wanted me to have. He'd waited until he had something to hold over my head, despite being short enough the two of us would make a decent ventriloquist team—might have to rip his spine out, but he never used it.

The driver opened the door.

I waved at Gil and got in.

The next time I saw him was a day later. I had my next fight lined up and a fucking blow dart sticking out of my face.

CHAPTER 2

THE LIMO SMELLED LIKE NEW LEATHER AND DIRTY laundry.

I didn't see any piles of clothes and mine were clean, which left one source. I sat in the rear seat and faced Eddie. He had his back to the closed driver panel. Just him, no typical gaggle of yes-men and gophers.

The last time I'd seen him in person he was standing outside the Golden Pantheon Casino with someone else's blood spattered on his face. Maybe mine—it was dark out. That was almost two months ago. Since then, I guessed he'd had about seven minutes of sleep. His charcoal suit sagged. Even his little blue faux hawk was wilted.

The limo rolled to the street, and a small speaker clicked next to Eddie's head.

He leaned into it. "Just drive around." He spent a few seconds staring at me or something halfway between us. "How you doing, Woody?"

"Good."

"How's your lady?"

"Marcela."

"Sure, I know."

"She's fine," I said.

"Sorry she can't come with us today."

"Don't be. She's in Brazil."

His throat did some tricks. "Since when?"

"A week after the Burbank fight." Remind Eddie of that little earthquake, case he forgot. "Her, Jairo, everybody."

"They're okay?"

"Yes. Why?"

"When's the last time you talked to her?"

"Yesterday. What's going on?"

Eddie stared out the window. "Nothing, brah, just making sure my superstars are happy. You happy?"

"Oh yeah. I love it when somebody dumps bullshit in my ears."

He smiled, and I heard the skin on his face crinkle. Stress made him look his age, closer to forty instead of his usual thirtyish. I waited for my Burbank spark to get a blaze of contract talks going. It hit Eddie's ear and fizzled.

For a few days after the fight, the MMA press had been all over me coming from nowhere to knock Warrior's poster boy out. They wanted interviews, life stories, thoughts on the Middle East.

I missed it. Too busy checking the mainstream media for stories about a Brazilian woman named Marcela Arcoverde getting kidnapped so Kendall Percy could mess with my head, make sure I lost the Burbank fight to get him a huge payday. The piece of slime needed that money to pay the Yakuza , debt he'd taken off Eddie's back. All Eddie had to do was find a chump to get mangled in the Warrior cage, and everything would work out fine.

Kendall said so.

I've seen crocks of shit before; his reassurance was a masterpiece. Marcela was dead unless I found her. Her cousin Jairo would make sure I was dead if I failed, so he came along and we hunted.

Not a word of it was ever reported.

No mention of Kendall Percy and his crew—Lance, Big Jake, Steve—going missing from their illegal bookmaking hub in the back of a bakery.

No coverage of an El Salvadoran gang's garage hangout—Tezo's kingdom—where he'd kicked me and Jairo into a cesspit to fight to the death. Until he got bored, shot Jairo, and tried to drown me in a stained claw-foot bathtub. I made it out and turned him and his boy Parasite into autopsy photos. I hadn't taken a bath or soaked in a hot tub since—showers were safer and didn't give me the cold shakes.

No breaking news about a shoot-out at the desert compound built by a gun nut called Chops, me and Marcela dragging Eddie over warm bodies on our way out. Or the mass grave Chops dug and filled with scraps of Big Jake, Lance, Steve, Tezo, and his thugs—but no sign of Kendall. You could spend weeks combing through the land mine crater on the slope behind Chops's stronghold, maybe come up with a burnt fingernail or a bolt from Kendall's Caddy.

Good luck making it out of Chops's rifle scope with that evidence.

There were five people still breathing who could give eyewitness accounts.

Marcela and Jairo: They're proud of wiping those stains off the planet. Jairo shows off his bullet wound, tells people it's from cross fire in Rio de Janeiro's Cidade de Deus. Marcela never mentions any of it when we talk, only wants to know if I'm okay. My stomach still bounces when I think about her. I do it dozens of times a day.

Chops: A career criminal who thinks badges are targets and carries a cyanide capsule in a hollow tooth. I don't worry about him going to the authorities.

Me: The record of self-destruction is impressive, but I'm not big on confessions.

Eddie: Show him a picture of a fork, and he'll squeal like a stuck pig.

I watched him in the back of the limo, staring out the window at nothing, the stress a black hole pulling him smaller and tighter into himself. He needed some empathy. "Are you gonna open your fat mouth and talk to anybody about what happened?"

The leather seat squawked from his spin toward me. "Happened? Maybe it's past tense for you. For me it's *happening*."

"Semantics."

"Yeah, that's what I need right now: investigations and bad press."

"You say right now. I'm talking about forever."

"My forever is right now. Day to day. You been waiting to hear from me. You think I've been poolside this whole time, just sipping daiquiris and getting jerked off?"

"Daiquiris?"

"Besides all the shit piled on me, I still have a company to run. You caused chaos when you beat Burbank, turned the whole division upside down. Yeah, keep smiling. Even with the huge mess, I still got your next fight lined up."

"When?"

"You don't wanna know who?"

I shrugged.

Eddie leaned toward me, spent some time scanning the lumps and lines around my eyebrows. "Cuts are healing nicely. Which ones are from Burbank?"

"The new ones. When's the next fight?"

He sat back. "Two weeks. That enough time for you and Gil?"

"Two minutes, same answer. But you couldn't let us know sooner?"

"I've been a little busy. Delegation's tough when you can't trust anybody."

"What, the debt thing?"

He laughed, a dry bark. "Yeah, the debt thing."

"They reach out to you?"

"No. And that's bad, man. The Yakuza's like a snake. You want to be able to see and hear it. You can't—any rock you turn over, you know?"

I peeked under my seat.

"Relax," Eddie said. "They won't come at me until after your fight."

I looked up.

"Now you want to know who you're fighting?"

———

Eddie pushed a button on the driver's panel. "I need some coffee. Woody, you want something?"

"Answers."

Into the panel: "Two coffees." He opened a hidden cabinet and pulled out a package of wet wipes, used one on his neck and face. It came away a different color. He stuffed it all back in the cabinet and looked at me. "Answers. Maybe we can share some."

"I don't know anything about the Yakuza."

"Strip away the tattoos and traditions. They're just violent criminals."

"Oh, then you should read my dissertation."

"Even better," he said, "I saw it live."

"I can't help you."

"Listen first."

"I don't want to help you."

"What if it's close to the same thing as helping yourself?"

"How close?"

He let his eyes roll around, like he hadn't thought about it yet. "It's the exact same thing."

———

The driver's panel slid down. Eddie took the two coffees in thick white paper cups, and the panel slid back up. He handed one to me so I could put it in the cup holder.

"What do you think of Mr. Burch?"

"Who?"

"My driver. He's British."

"Does he have anything to do with my next fight?"

Eddie flapped his suit jacket. "Not really."

"Then I don't give a shit about Mr. Burch."

"I won't tell him you said that. You familiar with the MMA scene in Japan?"

"I know of it. I assume they punch and kick each other. Some choking."

"Fighters are built up into folk heroes. We're talking about the land of the samurai, the birthplace of Bushido. Some of the fighters stick to that honor code, would rather die in the ring or cage than fail."

"Dying kind of sounds like failing."

"Not to them. All that 'die on my feet rather than live on my knees' shit." Eddie took my nod of appreciation for agreement. "And the Yakuza is balls deep in all of it."

"Good thing organized crime stays out of combat sports in Vegas."

He waved a hand at the city outside the window. "Not the point. I'm talking about the Yakuza making a move on Warrior specifically. Not an invasion of the sport. It's a precise attack on me and my company."

"Well, don't you owe them a shit ton of money?"

Eddie sniffed. "You wanna get technical, Kendall took on that debt."

"And they didn't just let it all slide after he blew up? Huh."

"So, yes, I owe them."

"What did you do?"

"Doesn't matter. What matters is they're going to take my company. Which also happens to be your employer."

"Yeah, about that."

He put a hand up. "We'll get to it. And any contract we put together won't mean shit if they have control."

"So don't sell them the stock. Or shares, whatever they're called."

"They aren't sending accountants. They're sending a fighter. Do you own a suit?"

I frowned. "A suit?"

"Much like the one I'm wearing now."

"No."

He pressed the panel button. "We need to see Dorian first. Then the meeting. But don't call until afterward." Came back to me without waiting for acknowledgment.

"Why do I need a suit?"

Eddie looked at my jeans, shirt, and tennis shoes like they were dead relatives of mine. "The fighter's a heavyweight, thirty-one years old. He's a catch wrestler with Olympic gold medals in judo, made his way up to MMA super fights in the promotions over there legitimately. Well, what passes for it. Got a record of twelve and three, two draws. Now his management is saying he's ready to challenge the big boys over here."

"Tell them no."

"Doesn't work that way. We take on all comers if they're worthy. This guy is. But he's a fucking seed. Once he gets in our system, the Yakuza has roots. From there it's just a matter of time. They'll grow and push me out one way or another."

"Sell it. Get out on your own terms."

"That's what you'd do?"

"No, but I'm stupid."

Eddie nodded.

I'd have smacked him, but his skin still looked filmy.

"I got one move left," he said. "That's why you need the suit. If this doesn't work, you need to beat their guy in the cage. Two weeks from now, send him home crying."

"Why me?"

"Because I believe in you."

"Eddie."

"If he's any good, I don't want him to beat anybody important."

Glad I pushed that one. "What's his name? Maybe Gil's

mentioned him."

"Goes by one name: Zombi."

Nope. I would have remembered that.

CHAPTER 3

THE LIMO SLIPPED INTO A SMALL COVERED PARKING area notched into a three-story building. We were somewhere northwest of the Strip. Lots of trees and flowers probably got bottled water while the landscapers drank from the hose.

Burch opened the door for Eddie and the heat clamped down on us. Eddie didn't seem to notice. Burch led the way to a thick, unmarked steel door in the corner of the parking area and pushed a button set in the frame.

We waited, Burch checking the corners behind us, then his watch.

Eddie stared at the door, leaning forward on his toes.

I checked my phone to see if my provider was allowed within this property value.

A black guy about my height and age opened the door, all smiles. He wore a dark suit and a shirt and tie I knew were a shade of lavender, but I'd call them purple if anyone asked. It moved on him like feathers on a peacock. "Mr. Takanori, welcome back."

"Dorian, sorry for the drop-in."

"Please. Come on. Get out of this furnace."

Burch turned to me. "Okay here?"

"For what?"

"Be right back." He stepped past Dorian into the building and left Eddie with me.

Dorian said to Eddie, "Something wrong?"

"He's very careful."

"Needs to be more careful with those shoes. Drier than a Mormon funeral." Dorian examined me. "Dumpster's around the corner."

Eddie said, "This is one of my guys. We need something for him to walk around in today and half a dozen or so fitted as soon as possible. Head to toe."

Dorian cocked an eyebrow. "You take a shower today?"

Burch came to the doorway. "All clear, Mr. Takanori."

We stepped into a short hallway, then through another unmarked door and down a set of narrow stairs. Pushed through a heavy black curtain into a cool, round, semidark room of solid wood panels lined with suits and angled shelves of ties, handker-chiefs, shoes, and socks. Everything glowed with indirect lighting, the kind that requires engineers and technicians and Mayan calendars to dial in.

Dorian nudged me. "First time?"

"How'd you know?"

"This is gonna be fun, man. Lighten up. Enjoy it. My suits can't do a thing for you, walking around with that look on your face."

"What look?"

———

"Put your arms down. Relax your shoulders." Dorian checked his work so far. "Why are your hands so big?" He came back in with a tape measure, pins, and chalk.

Eddie sat in a leather chair and knocked back an espresso, staring at the recessed plasma screen showing financial news with the sound off.

Burch patrolled the suits and rubbed a few ties before he finally stopped in front of me and got down to it. "Mr. Takanori tells me you've worked executive security before."

"That was a while back. And security might not be the right word. Security wants to avoid trouble. I usually got hired to make some."

"So you know what it looks like."

I checked one of the six mirrors in front of me. "Pretty much."

"We're going to a meeting after this. Just do what I tell you. Anything seems off, don't keep quiet about it."

"You got a phone book? Only a couple pages of guys better qualified than me."

"That's not an option right now."

"Why not?"

Burch glanced at Dorian, who kept working and said, "With these acoustics, I can't hear a thing. Never do."

Burch came back to me. "We don't know why yet, but no one will help us."

"You mean no one will help Eddie. Why are you here?"

His eyes were ice chips. "I'm a soldier, mate."

I made sure Eddie wasn't listening. He was miles away. "What's he got on you?"

"Just do what I say, leave the stories for Valhalla. Dorian, how much longer?"

"How good does he need to look?"

"No arrests for exposure."

Dorian stood, touched a white cloth to his forehead. They both stared at me. I felt like a piece of bad furniture.

"I'll cover him up," Dorian said, "but he's going to look like a side of beef in a potato sack."

"Twenty minutes?"

"Fifteen. I have another client coming." To me: "What are you carrying?"

I looked at my hands.

Burch opened his coat, showed me the pistol holstered against his ribs. He let the coat fall and the tailoring made the rig disappear—no bulge, no shadows. He tugged a pant leg up so I could see the strap around his ankle but not what it held.

"Nothing," I said.

Dorian looked at Burch, who shrugged. "Boy likes to get his hands dirty."

Likes to stay out of prison, too.

Burch said, "Mr. Takanori, we can be at the meeting in thirty minutes."

Eddie stared through the TV, the wall, the city. "Make the call."

CHAPTER 4

THE SUIT DORIAN PULLED OFF THE RACK FOR ME FIT like a layer of oil. I sat in the back of the limo and didn't have to push the coat out of my face or shake the legs down so my knees wouldn't show. It was a new shade of black with a gray shirt and tie, matching socks, black shoes. The knot in the tie was so big I had to feed it every half hour.

Eddie stared out the window at everything starting to brighten up as the sun went down.

I said, "Where we going?"

"I don't know. Mr. Burch handles that."

I kinda missed the old Eddie. At least brash assholes aren't boring and depressing. "Who's the meeting with?"

"Just shut the fuck up and let me think, will you?"

I kinda missed the new Eddie. I checked my suit, made sure I hadn't gotten anything on it yet. Dorian said he'd call when the six custom fits were ready. My old clothes and shoes were in a plastic bag in the trunk. Burch didn't want to sully the rags he used on the tires.

Eddie said, "Sorry about that. No offense, but I'm not thrilled I had to come to you for help."

"So it's unanimous. You can let me out here."

"Brah, you been listening? Warrior is on the endangered list. If it goes, you got no fight contract, no promoter, nothing."

"Sounds terrible. Wait, that's exactly what I have right now."

Eddie opened another cabinet, took out a stack of papers, and set them on the seat. "This is your four-fight contract. It includes the fight against Zombi."

Ring that bell, Pavlov. "Gil's gonna go through that thing with a microscope. I'm not signing anything until he likes it."

"You can get John fucking Hancock to autograph it, won't mean a thing." He tossed the stack in the cabinet, left it bent and creased, closed the door. "I haven't signed it yet." He crossed his arms and waited for my reaction.

I chewed my tongue and ran the options.

I could strangle Eddie before he pushed the panel button. Even if he got to it, I'd have his head off before Burch stopped the car.

The other option was to sit here and take it.

I checked the seat for a coin to flip.

Eddie said, "If this meeting goes well, I'll sign it soon as we get back in the car. You and Gil can take all the time you want, get a pre-nup, whatever."

"We're meeting the Yakuza?"

"Don't be naïve. Listen, you see any Asians besides me, set the place on fire and get me into this fucking car. Clear on that? We're meeting one guy. His driver, if he has one. Guy's a clown, though, probably leases a Fiat."

Now Eddie wanted me to dig at him, pry the information out

so he could feel important and show off a bit. I looked through the moonroof and picked at something in my teeth.

He got impatient. "Say you get bit by a snake. Zap, right on the hand. The venom is potent, spreading toward your heart. What do you do?"

"Immediately regret shaking hands with you."

"Play along. You might learn something. You chop the hand off. Maybe the whole arm, make sure you get rid of every drop of poison."

The limo turned into a narrow lot that cut the city block in half. I didn't know where we were. All I could see were cinder-block walls and service doors.

Eddie said, "But check this: what if you knew you were gonna get bit before it happened? What would you do?"

"Kill the snake."

"Kill the entire Yakuza? Not an option."

He waited again. Typical Eddie. He had a point to make but wanted me to do the heavy lifting.

"I'd get a suit of armor. Let the snake dull his teeth trying to sink in."

"Not bad. But there's no armor against these guys. The correct answer is what I'm about to do: buy an extra arm."

CHAPTER 5

BURCH LED US THROUGH A SERVICE DOOR, PAST SOME cooks too busy to notice us, and down a hallway. It was an Italian place, garlic and wine heavy in the air. We stepped into a closed-off room, a space reserved for wedding receptions, first Communions, and contract killings.

A man sat alone at the middle table, hunkered over a basket of bread and a tumbler of whiskey. Clinks and conversation came from the other side of curtained glass doors. The man was in his fifties, too old for how long his hair was in back. It was gone on top, sidling away from a bloodhound face that made me want to give him a smack, tell him whatever it is, it can't be that bad.

He looked up, nodded at Burch like he knew him, and started to say something to Eddie. Then he saw me in the suit. "You said no lawyers."

Eddie gaped. "Him? How drunk are you?"

"So what? You brought muscle."

Guy didn't recognize me from the Burbank fight or otherwise. I started drafting a valentine to my new suit.

"He's my bullshit detector. My other one's out of juice from the last time we talked." Eddie sat down across from the guy, a second glass of whiskey waiting there, and waved me to the next table over. Burch stayed by the door.

The guy said, "I'm not the one pulling all this last second cloak-and-dagger crap. I had to ditch my wife to get here."

"You're welcome. So let's get it done."

"I told you last time what I need. Otherwise we got nothing to talk about."

"Lou, I've seen your books. You're hemorrhaging faster than an Ebola clinic. You want—no, you need—to off-load Elite as soon as possible. I know this. I already won. All that's left is the pillaging, and I'm willing to work with you on that."

So this was Lou Gerrone, owner of Elite Combat Sports. Five years ago it was a major player in MMA. Now guys went there to get careers started by beating up on guys who didn't know theirs were over.

Lou plucked a piece of bread out, tugged the crust off. "You gonna change the name?"

"Don't see why. It's a recognized brand."

"I just figured you might call it Warrior Triple A or some shit. Banzai Eddie's Personal Developmental League."

I expected the nickname to get Eddie screaming. He either didn't hear it or pretended not to. Distraction or diplomacy, I got a better grip on the significance of this sit-down.

"Doesn't matter what the name is," Eddie said. "It's never gonna be on the same level as Warrior. No offense, but when this is done, at least your guys won't have to slog through a shitty contract before they get a chance to fight for me. If they show me something, I'll bump 'em into Warrior right away. Regardless, the name is staying."

"You gotta treat my fighters right."

"I told you everybody's safe. Nobody's getting cut until he deserves it. Or she. I'm keeping the women's divisions too. For now."

"And the tax thing."

Eddie nodded. "You're staying on as vice president—"

"Now see, we're right back where we were."

"Jesus, all right. President, okay? And you don't have to do shit. Just collect your check and stay out of the press."

"No bullshit shareholder meetings, any of that?"

"How about I tell security not to let you in? Case you happen to wander into the building during a bullshit meeting."

Lou barked at that. "Ain't gonna happen, trust me. I'm getting my ass down to Mexico, see some real water. Not this blue chemical shit. Any of you guys ever smell the water in these fountains? No? I'll save you the trouble, just piss up your nose."

There was a moment of awkward appreciation.

Eddie said, "I'll have the papers drawn up, get them to you Monday."

"First thing?"

"Monday."

Lou stuck his hand over the table. Eddie shook it.

"You got a big debut planned?" Lou said. "Hey, don't give me that face. I'm just curious, one promoter to another."

Eddie eased down in his chair, took his first sip of whiskey. I watched the tension roll off him. "I have something working, nothing official yet. There's a Japanese fighter wants to jump into Warrior. I'm gonna let him dip his toe into Elite first, see if he squeals."

"Oriental guy? Huh." Lou killed his drink. "Man, I don't know if that's gonna draw for you."

"And that's why I'm leaving here with your company." Eddie winked and stood up.

I nodded at Lou and got the droopy lids from him.

We walked down the hallway, Burch on point checking the kitchen, doorway, parking lot.

Eddie put an elbow in my ribs. "Nice work. Looks like you're off the hook for the Zombi fight."

Funny thing about hooks: when you drop back onto them, they go twice as deep.

CHAPTER 6

E DDIE STOPPED WITH ONE FOOT IN THE LIMO. "SIT UP front with Burch. I need to make some calls back here. And one of you guys open this moonroof, huh? Air this bitch out."

"If Zombi's going to Elite, who am I fighting? And when?"

"Easy, brah. Call Gil and tell him we're on the way. You wanna do Guy Savoy again?"

The restaurant where Eddie had signed me to the Burbank fight and dumped me into the mess with Kendall. "No offense to the chef, but that place left a bad taste in my mouth."

"Good point. We'll figure it out."

He got in and Burch shut the door, popped the driver's.

I didn't move.

Burch eyeballed me. "I ain't opening your door."

"I got that."

"Oh, your feelings are hurt. Don't wanna ride up front with the help? How about the boot?"

"Boot?"

"Fucking trunk."

"Open it. We'll see who goes in."

He stepped close. "Look, mate, you oughta know by now. We're condoms to Eddie. He uses us to keep him safe while he fucks about, then tosses us in the bin. It's on you to make yourself comfortable in here with the coffee grounds and banana peels."

"You're comfortable?"

"Places I've been, this is a bubble bath. Get in."

My suit didn't seem to mind the leather in the passenger seat, so it was high quality.

Burch started the limo. There was a click from somewhere in the panel behind us.

"What's the fucking holdup? Moonroof." Eddie clicked off.

Burch pushed a button on a screen set into the dash between us. It had a digital sketch of the limo and showed the moonroof sliding open. There were two ghostly figures in the front seat, one in the back in the middle of the seat behind us. They all had blank faces and round heads, no gender details. The passenger ghost was blinking red.

"Seat belt," Burch said.

I buckled up. My ghost turned green.

"Not so bad up here, is it? If you want to make rocket ship sounds, I won't tell." He got the limo moving.

I called Gil and told him about the contract and Eddie buying Elite Combat. I left out Zombi and the Yakuza—no need for false hopes or fears—said we'd be there to pick him up for dinner in forty minutes, according to Burch.

"We're talking contract?" Gil said.

"Eddie has it with him now. Unsigned, far as I know."

"I'll wear my negotiating boots." He hung up.

I said to Burch, "You want me to tell Dorian to cancel the suits?"

"I'll take care of it."

I ran a hand down my tie. "Maybe I should get them anyway. How much we talking?"

"You could trade that one in for a compact car."

"Yeah, let's cancel the other six."

We hit a red light and stopped next to another limo. Thin white hands holding neon-green shot glasses flapped out of the windows. The driver slid his down and saluted us. We nodded. His passengers let out a collective screech; shot glasses were emptied. The driver winced, made a gun with his finger and thumb and blew his brains out.

The panel behind us clicked. I expected Eddie to order a commandeering of the other limo, at least a closed moonroof, but he didn't say anything. It clicked off. The light turned green and we rolled away.

Burch said, "You did well at the restaurant."

"I didn't do anything."

"Guy your size, I thought you might work the room like a dick-swinging contest, frothing at the mouth and bird-dogging everyone. But you played it right. Professional."

"How'd you end up in this kind of work?"

"You make it sound like a last resort. You're a fighter. Did you end up doing that? I'll wager you found out you were good at it, even liked it, and sought the path to make a living at it."

"Okay, so you started out as what, a crossing guard? Then hall monitor, security guard, cop?"

"SAS. Familiar?"

"SEALs from England."

"I know some lads who'd slot you for saying that, but it's close enough. I pulled the trigger a bit over in the sandbox, harassed the IRA boys, protected the Royal Family. Capitalize that when you say it, thank you."

"From royalty to Eddie? Steep drop."

Burch squinted. "Less incest."

The panel clicked. We waited. Again, Eddie clicked off without saying anything.

I said, "I ran into a few guys from the IRA. Said they were, anyway. About eight years back. Met up so they could take a look at a piece of equipment a maintenance guy took off a surveillance plane out at Nellis. They thought it might let them know some of our spying capabilities."

"Did it?"

"It was part of the coffee machine. Never saw those IRA guys again."

"I likely shot them in the face at some point."

I glanced down at the display panel and saw two red figures in the back of the limo, moving from seat to seat. Then none, then one, two. "Burch."

We both frowned at the screen for a few seconds.

Burch said, "Fuck me."

I braced and he swerved across a lane of traffic into a strip mall parking lot. As soon as the limo cleared the sidewalk he stomped the emergency brake and let the car slide into a double row of empty slots. He was out the door before we stopped.

I mirrored him on the passenger side, opened the back door and saw Eddie on the limo floor with a wiry Japanese guy sitting on his chest, choking him and trying to shove a short sword under his chin. Eddie had blood streaming from his nose.

Burch dove in and grabbed the guy's sword wrist, shoved it an inch away from Eddie's throat. I hauled on the guy's shoulders, tried to pull him out of the limo. He was welded in place.

"Hit the fucker," Burch said.

I knelt on the guy's right and clipped an elbow off the base of his skull.

He didn't even blink. He was staring at Eddie and muttering in Japanese; it sounded like a prayer or a curse.

I hit him again, put everything behind it.

He stopped talking long enough to spit out the piece of tongue he'd bitten off, then went back to it, bright blood running out of his mouth onto Eddie's chest.

Eddie stared at me, trying to talk. His eyes were glassing. I tried to pry the fingers off his throat. The guy could climb mountains without using his feet.

Burch said, "Hold the blade."

I locked on the guy's arm and planted a foot against Eddie's seat to keep my hands from moving. Little bastard was probably one forty-five, a featherweight, and he was shoving me around. If this ended well I'd give him Gil's card.

Burch closed both doors in the back of the limo. The street noise cut off. Now it was just Eddie's legs drumming on the carpet, the muttered prayer, heavy breathing, and teeth grinding.

Burch snatched something out of a cabinet, flicked his wrist, and opened a black heavy-duty garbage bag. He spread the mouth wide.

"What are you doing?" I said.

"Hold him still." He lifted his pant leg and pulled a six-inch fixed blade out of the sheath strapped to his shin.

I said, "Wait, take his hands. I'll choke him out."

"No time."

The guy didn't seem to notice any of this. He kept talking to himself, shoving the sword closer to Eddie's throat.

"You got him?" Burch said.

"For what? Put your gun on him."

Burch pulled the black plastic bag over the guy's head and past his shoulders as far as it would go. The praying got louder.

"What's he saying?"

"Fuck if I know," Burch said. "Get ready to roll them."

"Wait."

Burch slipped his knife hand under the plastic, felt around, then his teeth showed and his hand pumped.

The arms twitched three times.

"Roll them," Burch said. His hand came out, blood on it and the blade. He slammed his shoulder against the guy.

I twisted the sword away from Eddie, letting the guy tip over until he was on his back, and held his wrists above him.

Burch got under his legs and lifted him, stuffed his whole torso in the garbage bag, and held him there while he bled out.

He didn't kick and he wouldn't let go of the sword.

Eddie scrambled onto the bench and pulled air in, tugging his collar open. Blood and spit flapped off his lips. "Fucker came in through the moonroof." He sounded like someone had scrubbed his windpipe with a wire brush.

I felt the tension go out of the guy—one second he's marble, the next a noodle—and pinched the sword blade between my palms, dropped it on the floor.

Burch said, "Grab the tape."

Two rolls of duct tape were stacked next to the trash bags. I handed one to him. "You buy the whole serial killer kit?"

Burch wrapped the tape around the mouth of the bag and tightened it against the guy's waist. "Do this long enough, you know what's good to have around. Hand me another bag."

Burch kept that one closed and threaded it between the guy's thighs, flattened it against his belly and lower back like a diaper, then wrapped more tape around it and the first bag to make a fluid-tight seal.

He dragged the guy toward the back of the limo and dumped his feet on the rear bench. The trash bag trailed away from his head and sloshed like a black jellyfish. Burch used one of Eddie's wet wipes to clean the blood off his hand and blade, dried them on the guy's pants, and returned the knife to its sheath. He checked the windows on the driver's side away from the street. Some parked cars but no pedestrians.

"I'm out first, then Mr. Takanori. You follow, close the door immediately. It'll be tight in the front seat, but I don't think either of you wants to ride back here with stink pants. Ready?"

"I'll find a cab," I said.

"Sorry?"

"I'm out of this, whatever it is. Eddie, sign my contract and fax it to the gym. We like it, we'll sign it, and I'll see you at the weigh-ins."

Burch stared at me with a face that belonged behind a sniper scope. He glanced at Eddie and something went between them.

Burch said, "We need to talk."

"We just did."

"Hear me out or hand me another trash bag."

I rolled my neck.

Eddie said, "Woody, please."

His voice made everybody wince. Even the guy on the floor

felt sorry for him.

I pulled my phone out. "You have until the cab shows up."

———

Burch helped Eddie into the front seat, handed him a bottle of water, and closed the door on his wheezing. Burch wasn't even breathing hard. Between the two of us, you couldn't tell which one had just chopped up a man's throat.

We took a moment to enjoy the fresh parking lot air, then Burch got to the point. "I'd rather have your help than your corpse to deal with."

"You're getting neither."

"Look, I pegged you sharp enough to realize something's amiss, but maybe the dead bloke with a fucking ninja sword is too subtle for you. Mr. Takanori needs you around while we figure out what the hell's going on."

"Did Eddie tell you what happened the last time he and I rode around?"

"No."

"So you're not stupid, just ignorant."

Something flashed across his eyes. He blinked and was back into calm waters. "Mr. Takanori filled me in on what you were up to before he pulled you out of the shit pile."

"Yeah, so he could throw me to the wolves. I already sent him a thank-you card."

"My point is, after all you got away with, it'd be a shame to end up in prison now." Burch set his feet, ready.

I quit watching for the cab. Somebody pulled the plug on traffic noise. "Why would I go to prison?"

He nodded at the limo. "Accessory to murder. Saw it myself."

"You don't want to go down that road with me."

"Haven't put a foot on it yet. Just standing on the corner, looking down at the thorns and skeletons. Needs irrigation, looks like the path to fucking Mordor. But you should know this: push me to it, I'll bring a parade of shit to your door."

"By blackmailing me as an accomplice to a murder you committed? That's insane."

"Good, so we're on the same page. Now at first I thought Mr. Takanori wanted you around just to look the brute, what with the scars and all. But talking about your dodgy past, I get it. You want me to step away while you make the call?"

"What call?"

"Come on."

"Oh, sorry. You can stay right there. This won't take long." I raised my phone. "Ring, ring. Hey, Burch? Fuck you."

"Good one. I've seen two police cars drive past. Now call somebody who can help us before they pull over to see how much blow jobs are and find a dead body wrapped in a garbage bag."

Between Burch and Eddie with his unsigned contract, I was walled in with the lid pressing down. The only daylight came from the crack Burch was holding open for me.

Daylight, or the glare from an interrogation room.

Too soon to tell.

I remembered the phone numbers. The men who answered—if they were still breathing—would remember me. "You want the body burned or pieced out and sold?"

"Nice try. Don't worry about the body; it's going to a safe place. I'm naming him Collateral. Nice Asian name, yeah? You call around to your friends in the security game, see if anybody knows who Collateral is and who sent him."

"Aren't you all in the same union? You call them."

"I'm new in town. Nobody knows me."

"Who the hell are you? What makes you Eddie's last hope?"

"Nah, you're here now. I've been demoted to second-to-last hope. Make the calls."

CHAPTER 7

IT TOOK THREE CALLS, BURCH DRIVING AROUND WITH A closed moonroof and the lights in the backseat off. Four if you count the one to Gil to tell him we weren't picking him up.

"Why not?"

"I'll explain later."

"Oh, fuck me."

"What's that mean?"

"Are you still with Eddie?"

"Yes."

"Don't say or do anything else. Just get dropped off and let me deal with him tomorrow."

"Okay."

"I'm going to sleep. Please, please don't let me wake up to bad news."

"Sweet dreams."

"I mean it. Don't trust him." Gil hung up.

Burch said, "You'll explain this later, huh?"

"I'll come up with something." I looked out the window and caught a weak reflection. We were both disgusted and looked away.

Eddie was glazed, staring through the windshield and rubbing his throat.

"Need me to dial?" Burch said.

I poked the first number in and wondered what would happen to Burch's head if I punched and kicked it at the same time. The phone rang while I considered the shape of his skull, where it might come apart. The first two calls were a few minutes each of catching up, apologizing, convincing that I was actually very sorry for whatever it was I did.

Really, I mean it.

The third went to Walt Burrell, head of Vegas operations for Gauntlet Security. Gauntlet specialized in close-quarters VIP protection—moving sheiks and princes and celebrities around without any grubby civilian fingers getting near them. Walt was close to fifty, a retired Marine with lines on his face from years in the weather and thinking just about everything he said was hilarious.

I apologized to Walt, then went through the dialogue that drew a blank from the first two calls. "You know I'm fighting for Warrior now?"

"Yeah," Walt said, "congrats on that. You got the face for it, might as well."

Eddie watched me. He knew the next line.

"Heard some talk they might be under new management soon."

Walt spent a few seconds breathing into the phone. "I heard that too. Pisser, huh? All our jobs are going overseas."

"My phone's about to die. You at the office?"

"You're coming by?"

"I can be there in twenty minutes."

Burch held a finger up.

"Make that one hour," I said.

Burch nodded.

Walt's breathing stayed slow and level through the phone. "You and who else?"

"I'm with a couple buddies. They won't break anything."

"Where've I heard that before?"

"I said I was sorry."

"See you in an hour."

I put my phone away.

Eddie sipped his water. "Who's this guy?"

"I worked security for him. Off the books, protecting assholes his company wanted to bill but didn't want to be seen with."

"Which company?"

"Gauntlet."

Eddie kicked the dashboard. "Fuck that." It sounded like skin was flapping inside his throat. "I called them after the whole thing with Kendall. Did everything but beg them for security. They said they couldn't help me."

"Not even off the books?"

"No. Same shit as all the other companies."

"Man. All the scumbags I had to protect—one of 'em turned out to be wanted for genocide—and Walt won't come near you."

"Hey, fuck you and fuck Gauntlet."

"All right. I'll call back, tell him to forget it."

"No," Burch said. "Mr. Takanori, if it helps me keep you alive, we need to talk to this man."

Eddie pouted into his water. He closed his eyes and worked on breathing through his bloody nose.

I leaned forward and looked at Burch. "What are we doing for an hour?"

"You like riding around with your felony? We're stashing him."

"I know a place just over the side of the Hoover Dam. It's perfect."

"Sorry. We're keeping your boy nice and handy." He smiled and winked.

I imagined squeezing his face through the steering wheel and doing donuts in the street, so I smiled back.

———

We were miles off the Strip, rolling through an industrial complex tucked away from the tourists and cameras in the northwest corner of the city. Lots of food prep and suppliers, some fabrication shops. I saw blinking neon and perked up at the sign of civilization, but it was only a blinking neon sign manufacturer.

Burch wasn't searching for a spot; he knew where he was going. He pulled into a short asphalt drive that ended at a chain-link gate ten feet high. There was a hooded steel keypad next to his door. He snapped a latex glove on while his window slid down, then punched in a number, the keys clacking like an old pay phone.

The gate shook and rolled to the side. Burch drove through and idled between the long, low storage buildings with narrow garage doors set a few feet apart. Buzzing overhead lamps and boxed fixtures along the walls knocked all the shadows out of the place and gave everything a cold, alien facade.

Burch went to the end, about a hundred yards from the gate, and cut left across two more aisles before taking another left. He eased toward the doors on the right and watched the numbers, stopped the limo halfway down the row.

"Here we are." He put the other glove on and got out, walked around the back of the limo.

I said to Eddie, "Have anything to say?"

He scowled. "Hurry up." His voice was crusty. He sipped his water.

I slapped it out of his hand.

He scrambled to save it from glugging empty. "Come on. Asshole."

I got out of the limo and closed the door. The night air still made sweat pop on my forehead.

Burch said, "What's he saying in there?"

"He said I'm in charge now."

"Keep your sense of humor. It's important in situations like this."

He pulled his coat aside, the butt of his pistol hanging there, reached toward a stainless steel disc on his belt, and came away with a single key attached by a cable. The key fit into a heavy padlock on the storage unit's overhead door. He opened the lock and let go of the key. It zipped back to the disc on his belt, gone. The lock sounded like an anchor when he set it on the asphalt.

Burch rolled the door up and hit a light switch for the single bulb in the middle of the ceiling. The storage space was bare plywood walls and exposed rafters, maybe twelve feet wide and twenty deep. There were three things inside. Near the light switch and close enough to smell were a stained box spring and mattress set.

"Eddie makes you sleep here?"

Burch gave me a face I was getting used to. He walked to the back of the space toward the last item.

I wanted to throw another dig at him, make him stop and turn around—anything to stall—but I couldn't breathe. My throat was clamped shut, and my ribs wouldn't expand. I couldn't pull my gaze off the floor to look at what was back there.

I've won fights during the stare down. Bored into the guy's soul, measured him up, found him lacking. He knew it, then fought like it.

I wanted to stare at what was at the back of that storage unit, beat it into a corner of my mind, and stomp it out.

My eyes stayed on the floor.

"Are you fainting?" Burch's shoes were at the edge of the frame in front of the thing taunting me. The shoes turned. "Catching up to you, eh? Deep breaths, get that blood smell out your nose."

I straightened up, stared at the rafters, the walls, the bare bulb that left a spotlight when I blinked and forced air into my lungs. Then I looked at the back wall.

A white box freezer as big as a sofa squatted there.

I don't mind freezers. They sometimes hold ice cream and I appreciate that. But it reminded me of Tezo's bathtub, that stained trough in an obscene room used for drowning beasts who failed in his death pit. Looking at that freezer, I heard the faucets open above me, saw the black spots creeping in, felt the cold walls clamping my arms while the filthy water sloshed into my mouth and nose.

I didn't want to be anywhere near it.

Burch shook his head, used the belt key to open another padlock. He lifted the lid and tipped it against the back wall. Frozen vapor folded over the lip and came toward me, then disappeared in the heat before I had to kick it away.

Burch tugged the box spring out and leaned it against the

unit's door frame, set one end against the limo's rear fender just behind the back door. He pointed. "Mattress."

I thought I would enjoy looking in that direction, even at the dorm Dumpster mattress, then realized that was exactly what the freezer wanted. It crouched behind me and waited.

"Today," Burch said.

I cleared my throat. "Gloves."

"One of the points of this exercise is to get your fingerprints on as much as possible. So that's a no on the gloves."

I studied the shades of brown and yellow on the fabric. When I squinted, the pattern turned into hieroglyphics of the history of the plague. I made a pact with it: if I have to cling to you in order to stay out of that goddam freezer, don't fall apart and I'll spread your spores to the seven continents.

I stiff-armed the floppy mattress to the other side of the garage door. Dust and mold coughed from the seams, saw my new suit, and drooled. The tang of damp cat urine lashed out, and the dust and mold bowed with respect. I kicked the mattress into place against the limo, just in front of the back door, and let it sag against the storage opening. Now we had a narrow chute that kept us hidden from eyes at either end of the aisle. If there were eyes above us—say in a helicopter—I could throw the mattress into the rotor and destroy the earth.

Burch opened the limo door. "You take the head."

"When did you set this up?"

"What, the freezer?"

"Yeah."

"Soon as I got into town. Let's go."

"Which was?"

Burch pushed his tongue against his bottom lip. "Mr. Takanori called me seven weeks ago."

"Let me guess—I'd just left him standing outside the Golden Pantheon."

"Don't know about that. He called. I got on a plane."

"Why?"

"Take the fucking head."

He stepped aside so I could duck into the limo. It smelled like hot wet pennies and shit.

"Get under his shoulders there. Don't let the bag burst."

Burch grabbed the ankles and pulled, spun the body, got the legs through the door. The trash bag sloshed between my feet. I tried to lift the shoulders and shuffle the torso out, stepped on the bag, and almost tore it.

"Nope," Burch said. "Out here. Now."

I had to straddle the body getting out. My next shower needed to be two things: soon and long. We each took a leg and slid the body until we could get our arms under the lower back, then the shoulder blades. I gripped Burch's forearm to make a sling, squeezed as hard as I could, and felt a wave of satisfaction when he clenched his jaw.

We walked the body through the mattress chute into the storage unit. I tried to turn so Burch would have his back against the freezer.

He stopped walking. "You think you can shove me in there? Lock up and be on your way?"

"Sounds even better out loud." I was sweating way too much for the work. The freezer opened wide for me.

Burch popped his forearm out of my grip and slid down the body toward the feet. I had to get under the shoulders, the trash bag sagging over my arm and wrapping it in a lukewarm sleeve.

I quit breathing again. We eased the body into the freezer, and I stepped back like it was made of cobras. Burch tucked the feet in so everything would fit.

I looked at how the bag of blood was folded around the guy's face, how it would freeze and lock his head in, cover his mouth, nose, eyes. I took a deep breath for him. "How'd he find the limo?"

"Followed us from the restaurant," Burch said.

"You saw him?"

"No, but what's the other option? He dangled from a light post hoping we'd drive by? My guess—and I'm fucking tired of guessing—is this wanker was following Lou, hoping he'd bump into Eddie. The Elite deal's been in the works awhile now. Somebody talked."

"So we need to talk to Lou. If they kill him, the deal's off and Eddie's stuck with Zombi."

"You mean *you're* stuck with Zombi. Can't worry about everybody on the planet. Lou's on his own."

Burch got the sword out of the limo. He showed me my palm prints and finger smudges on the blade, smiled, and dropped it in the freezer. Closed the lid and locked it.

"I don't need that key to get in here," I said. Sounded like I actually wanted to.

"No, you don't. But as of right now, the only way you're getting out of my sight and coming back here is if I'm dead. So I won't give much of a fuck, will I? How far are we from your mate's office?"

"Half hour, if you can avoid traffic and people falling through the moonroof."

"We might be a bit late. Been starving since I saw Lou tearing up all that bread. Need to get something down my neck.

You hungry?"

I glanced at the freezer, the mattress and box spring chute, the open limo with the stench of death still floating around in it. "Yeah, I could eat."

———

Burch and I got burgers and fries, Eddie a vanilla milk shake. He alternated between spooning it into his mouth and pressing the cup against his swollen nose. He didn't want to ride in the back even with the moonroof shut.

I told Burch where we needed to go. He did a decent job skirting the edge of traffic to get us onto the 215 Beltway, which we took almost to the Las Vegas Freeway. Just before the cloverleaf we cut north into a business complex and parked in front of a gray corrugated metal box about the size of a football field. The only access we could see was a windowless steel door with a tiny plaque mounted next to it and a small roof above.

I opened my door. Almost midnight and could still smell the hot tar from the parking lot. "Wait here."

I hit a button under the plaque, which had Gauntlet Security, Inc. etched into it.

Walt's voice came through a speaker somewhere in the over-hang. The cameras were everywhere. "Let me see you smile first."

"I am smiling."

"You look like you have to take a shit."

"Make sure your desk is clear."

The same tepid script from years ago. I'd found it boring the first time; he was probably falling out of his chair.

Walt said, "Who's in the limo?"

"Eddie Takanori and his bodyguard, guy named Burch."

"Burch. Never heard of him."

"He's British."

The speaker hummed. "Well, bring him in anyway."

I waved at the limo. Burch and Eddie joined me at the door. We stood there feeling stupid, then a low buzz came from the wall and something heavy clicked. I opened the door and let Burch lead the way.

The lobby was painted light gray and had recessed lighting on the artwork. Plush couches framed a glass table with bottled water and a bowl of mints on it. Eddie took one for his throat. An open hallway in the back wall led into the building. I saw three doors on the left and one at the end of the hall, all closed.

There was one door along the right side, open, and Walt stood in it with his left hand hidden by the frame. "*Hola.*" As soon as he smiled I remembered his eyeteeth were too big.

"Walt, this is Eddie Takanori and Mr. Burch."

"Nice to meet you. Mr. Burch, what are you carrying under your left arm?"

"Sig Sauer P226."

"Good choice. Am I an idiot if I let you keep it while you're here?"

"No."

"Good. I hate taking guns away from friends. Very demeaning. Mine's going to be on the desk, so let's not make any sudden moves toward that holster. Mr. Takanori, it's a pleasure. And *you.*" Walt stepped into the hall and held his arms out toward me, palms up. The chunky .45 in his left was pointed somewhere along the wall. "Look at you. Jesus. Last time I saw this guy, he had a shiner and one ear about cut off. And that was before he clocked in for the day."

"Thanks for seeing us."

"Come on back. I like that nickname you got for yourself. Woodshed. Better than what we used to call you."

"Aaron?"

"Psh. It wasn't to your face, buddy. We ain't morons."

We followed Walt into his office. It was the same gray as the lobby and hallway, with dark wooden bookshelves holding tomes on business and security and a row of small digital clocks showing international times. No photos or personal items. His desk matched the bookshelves and was wide enough for the four chairs in front of it. It had a multiline phone and a blank notepad with a pen next to it. Walt set the .45 on the pad.

Burch sat closest to the door. Eddie went next to him, and I gave them a one-seat buffer.

Walt said, "Mr. Takanori, do you need to clean yourself up?"

"I'm fine."

Walt looked sad about the way Eddie sounded. "I want to apologize for not taking you on as a client."

"I'll let it slide if you can start now."

"Well, things are still somewhat complicated. Did someone attack you tonight?"

Burch leaned forward. "How do you know about that?"

"All three of you smell like murder. There's dried blood on his shirt, in his nose, and hand marks on his throat. He sounds like a talking lawn mower. Unless he's into S and M, somebody got serious with him."

I said, "A Japanese guy jumped into the limo and tried to choke him. And stab him. Not sure about the order, but you get the idea."

Walt leaned back in his chair. "You're sure he was Japanese."

Burch and I looked at each other. Racism hovered.

"Yes," Eddie said.

"Huh."

Burch said, "Expand on that, please."

Walt asked me, "Your ass on the line here?"

"I suppose."

"All right, then. The way it started, I get a call from a Japanese gentleman who would not give his name. Says we might hear from Mr. Takanori, asking for personal protection, and we should decline. Now, you tell an ex-Marine he shouldn't do something, guess what he does first chance he gets?"

"But you turned me down," Eddie said.

"Let me finish, please. I tell the guy we already have client consultants, and he's welcome to go screw a garbage disposal. He informs me that anyone we put on the job will be killed, guaranteed, along with the client. Meaning you."

Eddie sniffed.

Walt said, "Again, that kind of statement only pushes me in the other direction. He says that, I'm ready to strap on a vest myself and tuck you in at night just to prove this shithead wrong. Then he says, in addition to keeping its employees alive, Gauntlet will earn ten thousand dollars a day, every day we don't protect you."

I could hear the digital clocks tick.

Eddie said, "These guys offered to pay you to stand down? Let me get killed?"

"Offered and paid. Every day ten large goes into our coffers."

"From who?" Burch said.

"Traced it back through four dummy companies before we gave up. Far as we know, we're being paid ten grand a day to consult on security for the transportation of floating bath toys."

"Bath toys," Eddie said.

"Primarily ducks. That's what our taxes will show."

Burch knocked on the arm of his chair a few times. "And you're okay with this?"

"Me personally, no. Makes me sick. But the folks who sign my checks see free money, no risk. And I'm willing to bet we aren't the only shop that took the offer."

"No one will help us," Burch said.

"Except Woody here. What brought you on board?"

"Blackmail."

"Ah. Hope they're covering expenses."

Eddie started to talk, had to bow his head and rub his throat.

I said, "On the phone we talked about new management for Warrior."

"This town, you never know what's pure bullshit or just plain horseshit. But some guys are talking about a debt Eddie owes to the Yakuza. A debt they've come to collect."

"Which guys?"

Walt shrugged. "Just guys. It's funny—some of them are heavy in the stock market, and they're hung up on whether to buy or sell Warrior. I tell 'em Eddie dying would be bad for the company, but they aren't so sure."

"That's hilarious," Burch said.

Eddie slumped in his chair. Blood trickled out of his nose. He left it alone.

"This doesn't make sense," I said. "If they want payment on the debt, what good is it to kill him?"

"Maybe they figure his death is worth more than the cash," Walt said. "A statement."

Eddie cleared his throat, like unclogging a drain. "Stop talking around me like I'm a goddamn lamp. They want my company, and they're attacking on all fronts to take it. They sent a fighter to get a man inside, and now they know I'm working a deal to keep him out. So they're going to kill me and make sure the last thought I have is of them destroying everything I've built. Pissing on my legacy."

Burch said, "Boss, let's stick with what we know."

"That's what I do know. That asshole in the limo told me."

I said, "What, the prayer? You don't know Japanese."

"I know enough. And it wasn't a prayer. He was reciting my epitaph."

CHAPTER 8

WALT WALKED US TO THE DOOR. BURCH CRACKED IT, looked out with his hand near the pistol. A hot breeze kicked into the lobby.

"It's clear," Walt said.

Burch ignored him and went to check the limo.

Eddie shook hands with Walt. "Thanks for being straight with me."

"Hey, wish I could do more to help. But I follow orders, whether I like them or not."

Eddie didn't look impressed by the loyalty.

Burch stepped inside. "Ready."

Eddie followed him to the car, moving like he was getting stiff from the tussle in the limo.

Walt waited until they were out of earshot. "You serious about the blackmail?"

"Yeah."

"What is it?"

"You got enough over me."

"True. But you're in this for real?"

"Until I find a way out."

"I think you and Burch are outnumbered," Walt said.

"How bad?"

"Over one hundred thousand members."

I did the math. "This is terrible."

"Yeah, but that's worldwide. Here in Vegas, maybe a couple hundred Yakuza, tops."

"Oh, that's it?"

"How bad is it for you if they get him? Hey, don't give me that look; you've thought about it."

"If Eddie dies, I'm right back where I was. Worse, actually, because I've seen how good it could be."

"That hope thing, huh? What a bitch. This doesn't work out the way you want, I could use you."

"Legit?"

Walt looked at my shoes and suit, winced at my scars. "We can't have anybody with a criminal record on staff."

"I never did time."

"I never been caught jerking off, but guess what? Everybody knows I do."

"Everybody?"

"The work you were doing before, that's always around."

"Protecting scumbags so they can be bags of scum in safety."

"Hey, it's money. Whether they're our clients or gunning for our clients, scumbags are job security."

"Thanks."

"Some free advice: they come hard for him, get out of the way."

"I thought that cost ten grand a day."

"I'll call you if I hear anything more about Eddie." Walt smiled as the door closed.

I could see the halo of the Strip to the northeast, shimmering past the blacktop and roofs still giving up the day's sun.

Burch waited at the limo, scanning the parking lot and the shadowed doorways. "You're in back."

"Get on 215 and head east, then—"

"We aren't going to your gym."

"Where are we going?"

He opened the door and stared at me until I got in.

——

I couldn't tell a man had been murdered in the limo. The smell was gone, back to the baseline of leather and Eddie's body odor. I wondered how many murder scenes I'd been in without knowing it. Add them to the ones I was aware of, and I deserved an honorary homicide badge.

Eddie was in his seat, studying the damage in a shaving mirror. I sat across from him. The limo rolled out of the complex and headed west, backtracking toward the storage facility. I strained to hear anything from the front seat, like Burch ordering another box freezer.

Eddie tossed the mirror into a cabinet, slapped it shut. "I'm gonna have to wear fucking turtlenecks for a month." He crossed his legs and looked me over. "Things have changed since I picked you up this afternoon."

"Just a bit."

"I thought the Yakuza wanted to battle. Turns out they're looking for war."

"I always assume the latter, work back toward battle, then a tiff.

If anyone's still around afterward, it's good for laughs."

"Explains why you've had to apologize to everybody tonight."

I let him think so.

"Who do you trust?" he asked.

"Marcela. Gil. Jairo. The guys at the gym."

"Not me?"

"The only time I'm sure you told me the truth is when I had a foot on your throat. You wanna do that every time we talk, I'll trust you."

Eddie tugged his collar away from the bruises. "Don't even talk about my throat right now. The Brazilians are out of town. Who can we count on?"

"For what?"

"We need numbers. We need an army."

"You think I'm gonna bring people I care about into this to save your ass?"

"Our ass. I equal Warrior; Warrior equals you. You equal success for Gil and his gym."

"Yeah, put my face on the sign out front. See how many people stop in for Halloween masks."

"What's more important to a fighter than money?"

I stalled, hoping it would turn into multiple-choice. He waited me out. "Respect."

"Reputation, which includes respect. You go up against a guy who's five hundred lifetime, but everybody he's fought says they never been hit harder. His record says he's so-so, but his reputation says he'll knock your ass out. Expand on it from the fighter to the trainer. The team, the gym. You go out as a massive underdog and beat Burbank. Fighters tend to notice that kind of thing. What's enrollment like at Gil's place since that fight?"

"It's up."

"How much?"

I didn't like getting tugged along toward his point, but he was right. "A lot. Only one or two have what it takes."

"Doesn't matter. It's the nerds and poseurs who pay the bills, and for every guy who has a shot, you'll get twenty hobbyists. They want the secret. They want your workouts and Gil's training. All of them coming through the door because you're winning in Warrior."

"Am I? Did you sign that contract yet?"

Eddie judged the distance between us. No chasms or moats close at hand. "No."

"Burch uses a frozen corpse. You use a pen."

"Weapons of choice, man."

"Puppet strings work both ways. I pull back, you're coming all the way down."

"Along with Gil, his gym, his students. That's the way you want to go, I'm sure he'll understand."

"Jesus. You're a fucking oil slick."

He shrugged. "All I want is to keep Warrior. And stay alive, which goes without saying, but just to be clear."

The limo turned west off 215 onto Flamingo Road and accelerated. We were climbing into real estate with multiple commas. Looking out at the luxury and comfort—the entitlement—did not improve my mood.

"If you want me to keep you alive, that's all you get. Me. Nobody else. I've caused them enough grief."

"If they can help—"

I leaned forward and thrapped his purple Adam's apple.

"Gack!" He flopped over and kicked the door. I sat back.

The limo rolled through a twelve-foot wrought iron gate that looked like a wall of black ivy.

Eddie survived, sat up, and almost fainted. "Shit, all right, calm down." He sounded like he'd swallowed a Muppet.

"I'm quite relaxed."

The limo floated through another gate, this one with thicker steel bars and a few swirls, not trying as hard to look nice.

Eddie said, "I need a shower. Then we need a strategy."

"You'll do what I tell you?"

"If it keeps me alive."

"Let's start with you shutting the fuck up."

———

We went through two more gates, serious heavy gauge steel with concrete abutments, the houses getting bigger and farther apart. Maybe they were mansions, like once boats were big enough you have to call them yachts or people get upset. Somehow, through the tires and suspension and leather seats, I could tell the asphalt was plush. There were signs for golf cart crossings and par five holes in front yards, and I wondered what the line was between mansion and palace.

Eddie's place was on or over that line. The limo pulled around a cul-de-sac and through a final gate into a parking lot that turned out to be Eddie's driveway. I got out and saw six garage doors, curved multilevel roofs, corners at all angles, and enough glass to make the place a mission statement at Windex.

I saw four chandeliers through the windows but had no idea what rooms they were in. Maybe the same room. The landscape had hidden lighting tucked everywhere, showcasing piles of rocks and flowers, the ten-foot stone wall surrounding the place, a gurgling fountain that looked like a naked woman standing under a waterfall.

Burch said, "I'll check the house."

"See you in two years."

He disappeared along a stone path.

Eddie got out and tried to take a deep breath that caught halfway through. He bent over and coughed, spat something onto the textured concrete. When he was done he straightened, smoothed his jacket. "What do you think of the place?"

"It's all right."

"Please. You ain't been to a museum this nice."

"I've never been to a museum."

"Brah, you gotta get some culture."

"What happened to you keeping your mouth shut?"

He muttered something about his house and he'd do whatever he wanted, but I lost most of it with him scuffing his shoes around.

Burch came out and waved us in. We followed him along the path that curved through bushes and cactus, over a short bridge that spanned a dry, narrow creek bed, finally to the front door. The entrance was recessed stonework and two eight-foot doors made of thick, dark wooden planks banded together with black iron.

"Did these come with battering ram insurance?"

Nobody answered.

Burch and Eddie walked into the foyer, polished marble tile on the floor and walls. From the door I could see all the way through a perpendicular hallway and a dim living area to the back of the house made of glass walls, beyond that a glowing pool and more concrete and landscaping that spread into darkness.

Burch and Eddie didn't see the man standing inside the door, wearing some kind of armored helmet and holding a samurai sword. I braced and lunged and realized too late it was a statue.

Burch and Eddie turned. I tried to play it off as a stretch, but nobody stretches with the war face I had going. Eddie sucked a tooth and went left down the hallway.

Burch spent a few seconds appraising me and the statue. "Want me to put that in the closet?"

"It's fine where it is."

"Let's take the tour."

"I've seen enough."

"Not by my standards. We'll start with the security room."

"Wait, what do you think I'm signed up for here? Eddie wants my help keeping him alive; you call me when you need something. And I mean really need it, like oxygen need."

"That's not my understanding."

"Update your software."

He put his hands in his pockets. "Remember what I said about the only way you'd get out of my sight?"

"Something about you being dead. I remember it made me happy."

"You're with me 24/7. You know the 'or else' bit, so let's skip it and get on with the tour."

———

Burch and I took a right at the hallway and entered the kitchen, a long room with high ceilings decked out like a Viking dining hall. Exposed beams, cookware, and cutlery hanging on the walls and a huge slab of carved wood for a table. The appliances were stainless steel and commercial grade. The wall along the left was made of panels that could fold on each other to make the kitchen and living room one huge space. The far wall was more glass, looking out on the pool.

We cut across the kitchen and went through a door, down some steps into a sunken hallway.

Burch stopped at one of the doors and punched buttons on a keypad. "Code's 12-07-41."

It sounded familiar. "Pearl Harbor?"

"Our Eddie's a student of war, warriors, battles. You'll notice a theme throughout the home. I'll warn you when statues are imminent." Burch opened the door.

The room was ten by ten, white walls with a desk and one wall covered in flat-screen security monitors. It crashed me back to Kendall's bookie room at the bakery.

"I didn't need to search the whole house just now. I came in here and checked the screens. If a camera had picked up any movement, there'd be a red light blinking in the corner of the screen and the time it happened. See, now we have red lights in the foyer, hallway, kitchen, and the hallway behind us. I clear those." Burch punched buttons on a keyboard, and the red lights disappeared. "Those lights for the staircase, upstairs hall, and master suite are Eddie going up to take a shower." He pointed at one of the monitors. "That's the master bathroom. And . . . there's our guy."

Eddie padded in bare feet over the bathroom tile in high-definition. He took off his jacket and let it puddle on the floor, went to work on his belt.

"I'm good," I said.

"Anytime we leave, we clear all alerts and hit this button. It gives us thirty seconds to leave the house before the alerts start up and the alarm is enabled."

"How do I get back inside?"

"Don't worry about that. You need in, I'll let you in."

"Fine. Let's just get out of this room."

"Don't want to see the boss's penis, huh?"

I headed for the kitchen.

Burch yapped from the security room, "What if it makes you feel better about yourself? Not taking a chance?"

———

Burch led the way upstairs. The wide stone steps had a plush runner up the middle and made a quarter turn clockwise to the second-floor hallway. We turned right and stopped on a railed bridge that looked down on the foyer and the living room with the pool outside.

Burch pointed at a set of double doors at the end of the hallway. "Eddie's suite. Door just before it on the right is mine, with access to the master suite through the closet."

"You put that in?"

"Original construction. I believe it's called a mistress hatch." He continued across the bridge into the enclosed hallway and opened a door on the right into a room bigger than my entire apartment. "This is you, for two reasons. If somebody comes down this hallway, I don't want all three of us cornered at one end. Either way they go, one of us will be behind them. And if they head your way, I hope you can entertain them long enough for me to get Eddie out. That reminds me." He hit some buttons on his phone.

I heard a recorded voice, then a beep.

"Dorian, Burch. Those suits for Mr. Wallace need to be let out under each arm. Call me if you need to see him again." He put the phone away.

"I'm not carrying anything," I said.

"You'll come around."

"You already have a dead guy to put on me whenever the mood strikes. I'm not giving you a weapons charge too."

"Then you can carry spare clips for me. Be my pack mule."

He dragged me through the rest of the house, pointing out escape routes and choke points and dead ends.

I ignored him for the most part and stared at the weapons hanging on the walls—everything from crossed stone axes over the living room fireplace to a Russian sniper rifle that pointed at a guest bathroom. There were tapestries of knights laying siege to cities, statues of gladiators in victory and defeat, and paintings that ranged from David vs. Goliath to Ali vs. Foreman. One showed an entire Roman legion fighting a dinosaur. I squinted at it until Burch noticed I'd stopped walking.

"Don't ask," he said.

He pointed out more things, and I stuck to my plan of should anyone invade the home I would throw Eddie out a window into the pool, then improvise.

"I saved the best for last," Burch said.

"Just say you're done, I'll agree."

He stopped with his hand on a doorknob. We were in the back left corner of the living room, the lights from the pool coming through the glass wall and making everything ripple. I recognized shapes out there—an outdoor kitchen and bar, furniture, a roiling Jacuzzi that made my throat want to clamp shut, but no invading

Yakuza army.

The living room was large and square with sunken couches in the middle around a block of obsidian that was either art or a table. The hardwood floor we stood on framed the room and made another ledge to sit on and stare at the art table.

Or the giant flat screen mounted opposite the fireplace.

Or the fireplace. Hell if I know.

Burch's door led to something between the garages and the backyard. He took his hand off the knob, like he wasn't sure I deserved it. "You need to get it through your head that you and I are in a foxhole together. Whether we like each other or not, we need to coexist. All I ask is be professional. I'll do the same."

"So far your blackmail and coercion have been top-notch."

Burch bowed his head. "Thank you for noticing." He opened the door and hit the lights.

I tried to keep my jaw from dropping. It landed somewhere near that goddamn table.

━━━

The gym looked like a showroom. The glass wall continued on the right and was made somewhat opaque by the banks of lights that ran the length of the room. There were stretching stations all along the glass, individual yoga mats with Swiss balls, bands, foam rollers, and lacrosse balls for masochists.

The wall on the left was adorned with pull-up bars, heavy bags in all shapes and sizes, free weights and kettlebells, and a squat rack with an Olympic lifting platform next to it. Gymnastic rings and a thick climbing rope hung from the ceiling. A wide opening in the far wall led to a white-tiled recess. I could see a glass door with a digital panel next to it—steam room—and the edges of solid doors with silhouettes for men's and women's bathrooms.

I came to the middle of the gym and couldn't help but smile.

Thirty-two feet across, four feet off the floor, made of metal and padding and canvas and vinyl. A full-size mixed martial arts cage as approved by the Nevada State Athletic Commission.

"Thought you'd like that," Eddie said. He stood behind us in the doorway wearing silk pants and a white V-neck shirt, a towel around his neck. His voice sounded better but still painful.

I put my hands on the apron, smelled the canvas. "We can't fit a full one at Gil's place."

"It's from the first Warrior event. See that bloodstain looks like Alaska? That's Badger Curry's blood from the war with Martin. And that's Martin's blood over there."

"Guys were fountains," I said.

Burch made a face. "Seems unsanitary, having it in your home."

I looked at the steps and the open gate above them.

"Go ahead," Eddie said.

I kicked my new shoes off and dropped my socks in them, took my time up the steps and onto the canvas. It was cool, a little rough from wear and exposure. There were other stains like fisherman's islands around the legendary mass of the Curry/Martin drainage.

I asked Eddie, "You train in here?"

"I get my time in."

Burch tugged on his lower lip and looked at the yoga mats.

Eddie strolled to the weight pile and picked up a kettlebell, started doing curls with it for some reason. "You think this place will suit your training in case you have to fight Zombi?"

"No."

The smirk dropped with the kettlebell. "You're joking."

"The equipment's great, long as Gil and the rest of the guys come with it."

"Not possible," Burch said. "The three of us are the only people allowed through the door."

Eddie said, "What about Vanessa?"

"And Vanessa. Once she's here tomorrow, she stays until this is over."

"Who's Vanessa?" I said.

"She takes care of the place, cooks, does laundry."

"So we stop by the gym and grab the guys."

"No," Burch said. "Too many loose ends, too much exposure. If they get spotted coming and going, they'll get the same offer as the security firms. Money or pain. Your man Gil leaves here one night and the next morning we get his ear in a box with a note telling us to send Eddie out. You want that?"

"Did you see Gil's ears?"

"We don't need those guys," Eddie said. "I'll coach you and you can spar with Burch."

I took a moment to savor the situation. Rarely am I in the same position logically and physically, and I looked down upon the poor, naïve crowd. "Burch, how much you weigh?"

"A bit over thirteen stone."

"English, please. Wait, American."

"Hundred eighty-five."

"Right. Don't take offense—I've seen you with your knife and I'm sure you're just as good with your gun—but in here with that gate closed, I'll destroy you. You're a warm-up."

He took his jacket off.

"Hold on," said Eddie.

Burch loosened his tie and unhooked the shoulder rig, staring me down the whole time.

I wiggled my toes and figured I could knock him out without getting blood on my suit.

Eddie waved the towel around his head. "Guys, think about me."

Burch froze with the rig half off and glared at him.

"If one of you gets fucked up tonight—I'm not saying who it would be—my security team is cut in half. Now come on. Let's be smart."

"Be a professional," I told Burch.

He took a deep breath and clipped the rig back on, stayed busy with his tie and coat. "Mr. Takanori, whatever you need me for, I'm here. If you need me to be a training partner for an oaf, I promise I'll hold back and not retaliate. I think half my normal physical output will suffice."

"Nice," I said.

Eddie stared at us. "Let's calm down a bit, maybe get some sleep. You two can spar tomorrow."

"Right behind you," Burch said.

"Do we need to set up some kind of night watch schedule?"

"The security system will handle it. I've got the iPad in my room; anything gets tripped I'll know right away."

Eddie hesitated, probably waiting for us to start barking and chewing each other through the chain link, then he looped the towel over his neck and left.

Burch smiled at me. "Sleep tight. You haven't any fucking idea what you're in for tomorrow." He kicked my shoes and socks under the cage and walked out.

———

I found the door to my room. There were four more doors along and at the end of the hallway, but I was done looking at Eddie's things for the day. I hung my new suit up on the outside of the closet door so I could keep an eye on it and stepped into the full bathroom, all tile and glass.

The window overlooked the landscaped front yard and low hills to the north. Because of the angle of the house I couldn't see the driveway or anybody creeping up it, but once I turned on the shower I quit worrying.

The day boiled off. I fell onto the bed, comfortable as cleavage, and dreamt about a warehouse of frozen claw-foot bathtubs with voices coming from them, black plastic wrinkling through the ice like rotten scabs.

CHAPTER 9

MY OLD CLOTHES WERE WASHED AND FOLDED outside my door in the morning. I put them on without making eye contact with my suit. My phone showed calls from Gil and Marcela, no messages. Wanting to hear her voice, I got her number on the screen but didn't know what to tell her. I killed the screen and went downstairs.

Burch sat at the slab of wood in the kitchen, drinking coffee with his sleeves rolled up. He looked at his hockey puck watch. "Vanessa, Mr. Wallace is awake. Please call the assassins and let them know it's okay to come after Mr. Takanori now."

Vanessa was at the stove moving something around in a pan. She was midtwenties, tall and lean with blonde hair pulled back, looked like she played a lot of beach volleyball. A red tattoo, some kind of flower petal, peeked out of her collar at the back of her neck. She smiled without turning around. "Got it. Should I cook enough for them?"

"Nah. I get the feeling those boys eat blood and misery." He nodded at the seat across from him.

I took the next one over.

"Coffee?"

"Water's fine."

"Vanessa, water, please."

I stood. "I can get it."

"Sit. It's why she's here." Burch frowned at my clothes. "That suit really does you a lot of favors."

Vanessa put a glass of water with a paper towel wrapped around it in front of me, then a small plate with a thick omelet and strawberries.

"Hey, thanks. Did you wash my clothes?"

"Yes, they feel okay?"

"Great. Thank you."

She touched my shoulder and went back to the stove.

Burch said, "All right lover boy, that's enough. First thing, no more sleeping until ten. I let it go this morning because Mr. Takanori doesn't need to be anywhere until noon and you had a big day yesterday. Very exciting, yeah? Today we do it all over again."

"All of it?"

"Hopefully we'll stay out of the freezer section." He winked over the coffee mug. "And we need to figure out your training schedule. Woulda been nice to get a session in before we head out."

"About that. You and me sparring and rolling isn't gonna work."

"Scared already?"

"What do you bring to the table other than a mobile punching bag? You know any catch wrestling?"

"Nope."

"Jiu jitsu?"

"Seems a bit gay to me. No offense."

"So you're pretty much worthless as a training partner. No offense."

"We'll see."

"We'll see what?" Eddie walked in wearing shorts and a sleeveless compression shirt, a towel wrapped tight like a scarf around his neck. I could see the tip of one finger bruise peeking out the top. He stood inside the doorway and tried to wipe sweat off his face with a corner of the towel without disturbing his drapery.

Burch and I settled in to watch.

Eddie realized he was onstage. "Fuck you guys." He pulled the towel off and Burch whistled. The bruises were two perfect hands wrapped around Eddie's throat, thumbs crossed over his Adam's apple, the whole thing like a purple butterfly.

Vanessa hissed air in. "You want some ice?"

"I'll take a Diet Coke. Thanks, sweetheart." He walked to the end of the table, splayed his fingers on the scarred wood. "You guys talking training?"

"I need Gil and the guys. I need my gear. I need footage of Zombi fighting. Most of all, I need to know if I'm actually going to fight him."

"I'm working on it," Eddie said. "For now, just assume it's on. My team is writing up the papers for Lou today, but if the Yakuza gets to him with money or otherwise, we have to plan for that."

I glanced at Vanessa.

"Don't worry about her," Eddie said. "Vanessa, you know all my secrets, huh?"

"I hope not." She put the can of Diet Coke in front of him with an identical paper towel wrap. I'd thought my glass was special. Marcela popped into my head and rolled her eyes.

Burch said, "Vanessa shows up this morning, I tell her she's staying here for the foreseeable future due to an ongoing effort to kill Mr. Takanori. Guess what she says."

Vanessa had her back to us. She cocked her hip a bit.

"She says, 'We're going to need eggs.'" He slapped the table. "Fucking cheers."

"Jesus," Eddie said. "With her around, what do I need you clowns for?"

"Eye candy," Vanessa said.

Burch pulled a long face. He and Eddie nodded at each other, acknowledging their qualifications. I drank my water.

"Shower time," Eddie said. "Woody, Burch is more than qualified to train with you. Make it work." He walked out.

Burch finished his coffee, smacked his lips, and grinned at me. "Right. Time for some fun. Vanessa, want to watch?"

Burch went upstairs to change. I followed the glass wall into the gym. No hand wraps and the only gloves I could find looked like they were for a third grader, so I put some Thai kicks and light jabs into the bags, got a light sweat going. I tried one head kick, and the crotch of my jeans threatened divorce. Chuck Norris does it in tighter jeans and cowboy boots, and good for him.

I went through a quick circuit of bodyweight exercises—push-ups, pull-ups, burpees, squats, planks, and jumps. It worked but it wasn't fun. Nobody pointed out that my burpees look like a mastiff trying to get off a skating rink, and if I shook any harder during the planks I'd need an exorcist. I could hear Gil saying it, but without the coffee breath it lost impact.

I grabbed a bottle of water out of the full-size glass fridge and dropped onto a yoga mat to stretch. The sun was in front of the house and put half the pool in shadow. In the daylight I could see that the landscape from the front yard wrapped around both sides and continued beyond the stamped concrete patio, with sculpted hills and dry creek beds all the way out to the back wall, a couple hundred feet away, the top of it barely visible. Statues waited in the sun for someone to walk past.

My phone buzzed and I winced, looked at the screen. The last thing I'd said to Gil was a promise to get dropped off by Eddie last night and not get into trouble. Technically I'd only broken half so far.

"Where are you?" he said.

"Eddie's place."

"The casino? What did you sign?"

"No, his house. I didn't sign anything. Take it easy."

"Eddie's house?" I could picture him trying to put it together, hunched over his desk and curling the phone into his ear. "You stayed the night there?"

"Yeah."

He paused. "Is it pretty nice?"

"It's not bad." The statues heard me through the glass and raised their eyebrows.

"Well, this can't be good. What's he selling?"

"Actually, he needs my help."

"What, moving furniture?"

"Don't get mad."

"Oh, Jesus. Hold on. Okay, tell me."

"You recording this?"

"I got a paper clip ready to stick in the electrical outlet. It's the only way I'll learn. I'm ready."

"Stop it. Eddie needs extra security for a while, asked me to do it."

"Is this connected to the thing from before?"

I wanted to lie but knew he'd see through it. "Yeah. The Yakuza's after him. For more than money."

"Come on."

I told him about the possible fight with Zombi and the four-fight contract Eddie would sign if he lived long enough.

"I'm going to kill that bastard myself," Gil said.

"You heard of this Zombi guy?"

"Don't change the goddamn subject. No, I haven't."

"We're gonna need some tape on him, see what he brings. Oh, and Burch says we can't have anybody coming and going, so you'll have to train me remotely."

I smiled into the silence. Gil was probably staring at his phone, wondering why it had stopped making sense.

"Who the fuck is Burch?"

"The driver. English guy who picked me up yesterday."

"That prick. He's kidding, right? He understands that if you're fighting I'm training you wherever and whenever I want. Right?"

"I think he suspects it but doesn't fully grasp what he's dealing with."

"I'll have a chat with him."

"He wants to be my sparring partner."

"Tell me which hospital he goes to. I'll visit him there. Jesus, these guys. Marcela called."

"Yeah?"

"I told her you were out running. She said she'd watch for it in the news."

"Hilarious. I'll call her back."

"And tell her what?" Gil said.

"Everything is fine."

"I can lie to her. You can't."

"That's not a lie."

"Well, it ain't the truth. Be careful. I'll start digging on Zombi. Hey, see what I did there?" He hung up.

The statues peeked over berms and around shrubs to see what I'd do next.

I got Marcela's number on the screen. The numbers were a symbol for her, the curves and angles and straight lines. There should be more numbers; these aren't enough to represent her. She requires decimal points and commas.

I still didn't know what to say.

I canceled the call.

The statues looked away.

———

Burch walked into the gym with a cardboard box that almost hid his face. He dropped it near the steps to the cage. "Sponsor gear. See if anything in here gives you the grapes to fight me."

He bounced up the steps and started doing jumping jacks. He wore running shorts and a sleeveless white shirt. He was lean, bands of muscle and sinew strumming under pale skin. I'd fought wiry guys before and didn't enjoy it very much. They're strong and have too many sharp points. As far as I knew I'd never sparred with a wiry trained killer, but I expected the same.

I poked through the box, found some shorts and hand wraps that looked like they'd fit, a boil-and-bite mouthguard still in its package. No luck on cups or supporters. "No kicks or knees."

"Those are for girls anyway. You and I shall be pugilists today. Peek under the apron. Should be more gear."

I lifted the heavy draping and saw three storage tubs with no lids piled with boxing gloves, focus mitts, and headgear. I dragged them out. "This stuff needs air and sunshine, otherwise it breeds."

Burch ignored me and stretched his legs by bringing his toes up to the opposite outstretched hand. Once, twice, that was enough for him. He started wheeling his arms around. "We had a bit of fun in the SAS called the hooded box drill. You stand in the middle of a dark room with a black hood over your head, and when you least expect it they pull the hood off and you're faced with between one and three blokes set on ruining your day. Your job is to treat them likewise."

"Bare knuckle?"

"Nah, small gloves and headgear with face shields." He didn't seem to appreciate the face I made. "How many press-ups can you do?"

"What the hell's a press-up?"

He dropped to the canvas and started banging out push-ups.

"Oh. I don't know."

"You don't know? Thought you trained."

"Not for a push-up contest."

I changed in the men's room off the gym, white tile and indirect lighting with stainless fixtures and two shower stalls with frosted glass doors. The only color was a glass mosaic in the wall across from the sinks that showed a scene from the Trojan War, Hector getting dragged around the walls. Achilles looked slightly Asian, and there was a single blue tile in his black hair. I ran the mouthguard under hot water and let myself get upset over the fact that the second-best bathroom I'd ever been in was Eddie's locker room shitter.

When I came out Vanessa was sitting on a yoga mat, her legs crossed at the ankles. She cheered my walk to the cage with a very quiet, "Yay."

I dropped my clean clothes in a heap onto the mat next to her. "Boooo."

Burch had his gloves and headgear on. He had to take his mouthguard out to whistle at my shorts. "He's a big one, ain't he Vanessa? Watch out when he topples. He might take the fence down with him."

Eddie walked in wearing a thick black bathrobe, a phone pressed to his ear. "How soon can we get that done?" He rolled a finger at us to keep doing whatever we were doing.

I put headgear on and found the biggest gloves in the bin, carried them up to the threshold. It's not a casual act, entering a fighting cage to do work. I took a moment to show respect.

"Quit stalling and get in here," Burch said. "Water's nice."

I stepped in and felt the cool grip of the canvas under my feet. Pulled the gloves on and tipped back into the fence, let it take my weight and bounce me upright. The gloves had thick wrist straps with Velcro. I used my teeth to tighten them.

Burch was across the cage hopping from one foot to the other, his arms hanging loose. "Ready, sunshine?"

"I'm ready."

Behind me Eddie said into the phone, "Hold on a second."

Burch said, "Vanessa, if you would be so kind."

"Ding-ding."

Burch skimmed across, leading left. Decent head movement. I held my left hand up near my shoulder. He glanced at it and kept coming, flicking a jab out like a snake's tongue.

He closed the distance, jab-jab-jab.

When he was close enough I threw the left hook. Gil calls it The Dumpster Filler because of all the equipment I've busted with it. Burch pulled both gloves in to take the blow. My fist crushed his gloves against his head, split them, and drove through to meet his temple. His legs gave out on the first impact. The second sent him tumbling sideways until he hit the fence and dropped onto the canvas like a sack of gravel. He didn't move. Then he started snoring.

Eddie spoke into his phone. "Can I call you back?"

———

Vanessa knelt next to Burch with her eyebrows pulled together, looking from him to me and back like I'd shat on her birthday cake. Eddie stared at Burch through the cage, possibly trying not to smile.

Me, I was grinning like I was getting paid by the tooth.

"I think he's peeing," Vanessa said.

Eddie ducked and looked between the cage frame and canvas, made a face. "Get him outta there. We need some bleach."

"Well?" Vanessa stood and waited for me to do whatever I was supposed to do.

I raised my hand in victory.

"Asshole. He's hurt."

"He's fine," I said. I kicked Burch's foot to prove it.

"Stop. Eddie?"

"Woody, just pick him up. Make sure he isn't choking on his tongue or anything."

Vanessa kept the sour face going and moved so I could tug

Burch away from the fence and roll him onto his back. He was made of rubber. I took my gloves off and pulled his mouthguard out, a string of drool chasing until it broke and fell on his chin. I slipped his headgear off and set his head on the canvas.

"Burch." I slapped him for a while.

Vanessa said, "Isn't there another way to wake him up?"

"Plenty."

Burch's eyes opened. He looked at the ceiling, the windows, me. "What happened?"

"We sparred."

"You look okay."

"Thanks."

He squinted and smacked his lips, saw Eddie through the fence. "Hey, boss."

"What day is it?" Eddie said.

"Hold on. Ash Wednesday? That's the only one I can think of."

Eddie glared at me. "Goddamn it."

"My bollocks are wet."

"We're gonna sit now. Ready?" I pulled him up and spun him so he could sit back against the fence. He enjoyed it.

Vanessa said, "He needs a hospital."

"This happens all the time at Gil's. Get him some ice and water. He's good as new."

"You're a moron," Eddie said. "I told you not to fuck each other up. Now we need a doctor to come here, and who can I trust?"

"I'm a doctor," Burch said and kept a straight face. "Of love."

I stood. "This is my favorite version of Burch so far. I vote we keep him this way."

Eddie said, "Fix him."

"It looks hard to be serious in a bathrobe. Is it? Okay, Burch, ready to stand up? Here we go."

He wobbled a bit but stayed on his feet. I removed his gloves.

"My mobile's ringing," he said.

"Take it easy. Deep breaths."

"Wait." Vanessa turned her head. "I hear it too. Where's his phone?" She ran out of the cage and dug into Burch's shoulder bag on a chair just inside the door. She took his gun out and set it on the next chair over without a second glance, then came out with his cell phone. It chirped while she looked at the screen. "Complete Secure Storage. Should I answer?"

Eddie shrugged, frowned at me.

I recognized the name. There was a dead guy in a freezer on their property. "Last night."

Eddie touched his throat and turned gray. "Answer it."

"Hello? . . . Yes, this is Mr. Sheridan's number, but he's in a meeting right now."

"That's called an alias," Burch told me. "And I'm not in a meeting. He didn't even call my number. It's a forwarding system that—"

"Shut up."

"Right." He nodded and winked, our secret.

"Okay, thank you for calling. I'll let him know." Vanessa poked at the phone, dropped it in the bag. "I guess that guy wants Mr. Sheridan—er, Burch—to come to his storage facility. He said somebody broke into the unit."

———

We got Burch into the shower, clothes and all. The hot water brought him around. As soon as he started swearing at me I left to get cleaned up. I put the new suit on—even better the second time—and met Burch and Eddie in the foyer. Eddie wore a light gray suit with a black turtleneck underneath that covered his mottled neck.

"I'm starting to remember what happened," Burch said. He was in his limo driver costume.

"Not a whole lot to remember."

"We're not done in there." He tilted his head toward the back of the house.

"I think one of us is."

"You see what you two assholes have done?" Eddie said. "We need one guy to go check on the thing from last night. But guess what? We're all going, because my head of security has a concussion, and I'm not staying here alone with him, and I sure as hell can't send him by himself. Congratulations. You're wasting my time and putting me at the scene of a felony. Ready? Let's fucking go."

———

Burch punched the location into the dashboard GPS and got in back with Eddie, his legs still a little unsteady.

I drove with the privacy panel up and ran through the worst-case scenarios for what waited at the storage unit. I was at number seventeen when I arrived at the open gate.

There was a small pickup parked inside. A skinny balding guy got out and approached my window. He wore faded jeans and a green T-shirt with a breast pocket bulging with the outlines of coins. The weight of it pulled his neckline down, but it didn't seem to bother him.

"Back here," Burch said.

The skinny guy changed vectors. "Mr. Sheridan?"

"What happened?"

I saw on the display panel that the back window was halfway open. I cracked mine.

"I didn't call the cops yet. I'm Mike, by the way, the site manager. I was doing my morning sweep and saw your unit had some damage to the door. I called you right away."

"Anybody been inside?"

"Well, I think somebody has, but it wasn't me. I gotta file a report, that's policy, but didn't know if you'd want to take a look first."

"I appreciate that. Any other units get broken into?"

"Just yours. Which is another reason I called. I figured it was something specific."

"Don't spend too much time thinking about it," Burch said.

"No, don't worry about that. But once I do the report, I can tell you what the owner's gonna say. He doesn't want any trouble for the other customers, you know?"

"We'll find another facility. Thanks."

"Like I said, his call, not mine. Go on back. I'll wait here in case you need anything."

———

I parked the same way Burch had the night before. He and I stood outside the storage unit and stared at the black hole in the steel door. The entire lock system had been cut out with a torch and placed on the ground.

"Tidy," Burch said.

Behind us, the limo window slid down a few inches. "Hurry," Eddie said. The window went back up.

Burch pulled the pistol out and checked the chamber. His hands had a light tremble. Maybe I'd hit him too hard.

"You okay?"

"Fuck off."

Maybe not.

I lifted the door and stepped aside. Burch led with the gun and cleared the space. The foul mattress set was still there, chuckling. I had a brief hope it had scared any intruders away, then Burch pointed at the freezer. I was ready to look at it this time, still didn't enjoy it.

The padlock was on the floor, also torched, and the lid was closed. We went over and Burch lifted it. The hot air swept in and mixed with the chilled, made a rolling cloud of mist that lapped over the edge of the box. Burch stuck his hand in and waved the mist out.

Empty.

"This your work?" Burch said.

"You know where I was all night."

"It's been established you have no shortage of acquaintances who could handle this sort of thing."

"It wasn't me."

"I don't believe you."

The mist shifted. Something flat was at the bottom of the freezer.

Burch saw it too. "Fetch."

I tried not to think about getting thrown into the bathtub and held underwater with the rusty mesh lid, Tezo and Parasite sitting on it and laughing. And that's all I could think of while I reached into the freezer and pulled out a brown envelope. I worked on breathing and opened it.

Inside was an unfolded sheet of regular paper. It was a photo of me and Burch carrying the dead body into the storage unit. The photo showed part of the limo and had been taken from the roof of the unit across the narrow aisle with some kind of night vision lens.

We stared at it in silence.

I turned the sheet over. Printed on the back:

We have two freezers ready for you.

Abandon Eddie.

Midnight.

CHAPTER 10

BURCH DROVE. BETWEEN THAT AND THE YAKUZA putting a midnight deadline on my pulse, I felt pretty confident I was going to die in a fantastic suit. It would be an epic mystery to Gil and the boys.

Eddie was on his phone talking about the Elite Combat deal, getting documents sent to him.

I stared out the window and tried to act like I didn't want to jump out of the limo every time it got below twenty miles per hour.

Eddie finished and dropped the phone on the seat. He looked like he was getting ready for horrible news. "Okay. What did you guys find?"

"Somebody broke in and emptied the freezer," I said.

"Was it the cops?"

"No."

He let out the air he'd been holding. "All right. Wait, how did they know he was there?"

"Nobody went through his pockets. Maybe he had a tracking

device on him."

Eddie scanned the interior. "You think he put anything like that in here?"

"All the killing he was trying to do, you see him stash anything under your seat?"

"No."

"Your ass hurt?"

"That's enough." Eddie spent a few seconds frowning. "Well, this is good, right? Saves us the trouble of getting rid of him."

"Good for you and Burch. My fingerprints are all over the place, the body, the sword."

"Oh yeah. If it makes you feel any better, I doubt they'll go to the cops. My guess is they'll use it to blackmail you into fighting Zombi."

"So the same thing you used it for."

"Different intent," Eddie said. "I want you to win."

"My hero."

He tried to bow sitting down. It came off looking like constipation. "So that was it? They just broke in and took their buddy?"

"That's it." The only part I didn't like about lying to Eddie was it had been Burch's idea.

Eddie stared at the side of my head. I thought he was scrutinizing me for honesty, but he must have been waiting to see if I'd catch him.

"Wait," I said. "How does the Yakuza know I might fight Zombi?"

"Busted. We announced it this morning."

"But that's only if the Elite deal doesn't happen. You buy them, Zombi fights a scrub in that promotion and I get somebody else in Warrior."

"Well, here's the thing." He glanced at the closed privacy panel between us and Burch. "Will you put your seat belt on first?"

"Why?"

"This sucks. I'm more scared of my security than the Yakuza. Just stay over there, okay?"

"Tell me." I got to the edge of my seat and leaned forward.

Eddie tried to slip back into a crease in the leather. "I need you to fight Zombi. Whether it's for Warrior or Elite."

"No. Elite is a huge step back."

"But a leap forward from where you were before."

"Yeah, that was before. And I wouldn't call it a leap."

"When I scouted you at the Porter fight for Burbank, one of the ring girls was six months pregnant."

"No, she was just tubby."

Eddie kept quiet and let me make the rest of his points for him.

"Gil will never go for it."

"I'll make it worth his pain. Yours too."

"Is this how you train to be an asshole? Max reps of making and breaking promises?"

"I'm just surviving. This is what needs to happen."

I scowled out the window and thought about the photo and note Burch had in the front seat. The Yakuza was giving me an out. Walk away from Eddie before midnight, and I'm off their radar. Stick around, I end up in a freezer, my blood frozen solid in my eyes, nose, throat.

If by some chance I happen to survive, I get to go back to fighting for a musty promotion against their secret weapon.

And here was Eddie, doing everything in his power to make me come across the limo and stomp his ears together, save them the trouble.

"Think about Gil," he said. "This is one step back so you can take three forward. He'll see that. We need to hold each other up."

Hold me up. Right. First an arm, then a leg, one piece at a time until I see the big picture and realize it's a spiderweb.

"Get me everything you can on Zombi."

———

We walked Eddie into his home office, down the hall past the security room, the far wall overlooking the pool. Vanessa was out there in a black bikini floating on an air mattress, one foot hanging off and dipping in and out of the water. Even a man walking to the electric chair would have noticed. We stared until it felt like we should put money in a slot to keep watching, then Burch opened the closet to make sure the Yakuza hadn't hired the boogeyman.

The walls were covered with faded battle flags and battered pieces of armor, dented shields, chipped swords. There was a small cannon pointed at the glass wall, which seemed irresponsible. Eddie's desktop was a map of North Africa under glass, lines and military icons sketched across it with red grease pencil. The date on the legend said it was from 1940.

"Which side do you pretend to be?" I asked him.

"Huh?" He was looking at a stack of papers churning out of a printer. He lugged it all to the desk and fell into his chair.

Burch said, "What else do you need, boss?"

"Tell Vanessa lunch."

We closed the office door and went to the kitchen. The view was the same through the glass wall.

Burch sighed. "Perks, eh? Almost worth the risk of life

and limb."

"I'll let her know about lunch." I wanted some privacy to call Gil. I needed to call Marcela back too, tell her what I could without making her worry. I didn't want to lie to her. I hadn't done it yet—and suspected it was linked to me still having an enclosed skull—but the truth would get her on a plane to Vegas. Usually my way and harm's way are the same one-way street, but this time I had a choice. I would lie to her to keep her safe and resolved to make up for it by turning my back while Vanessa got out of the pool. I moved toward the glass doors.

"Sit," Burch said and pointed at the slab table. "We have time. He'll be lost in those papers for hours, forget to take a leak, let alone eat. We need to talk about this." He dropped the brown envelope on the table and got two bottles of water from the fridge.

We sat across from each other. He slid a bottle over and pressed his water against his right temple, waiting for me to say something about it. I rubbed my bottle over my left knuckles.

"Fair enough," he said. "Who took this photo?"

"Great question. When we find out I'd like to ask him why he didn't just kill us and Eddie and be done with it. He had the drop."

Burch removed the photo, shook his head at it. "If the lads ever saw this, they'd take the piss 'til I'm dust and bones. In my defense, I was having too much fun watching you grimace with that blood bag slopping all over you."

"I was busy looking for a chance to kick your teeth in."

"Shame on us, Mr. Wallace. We're supposed to be professionals."

"That is my profession."

"One of them, eh? I'm having a hard time labeling you." He cracked his water and drank half the bottle. "What's this photo tell you?"

"It tells me you no longer have blackmail evidence framing me for a murder that I didn't commit. That evidence now belongs to an international crime syndicate, and I can stop them from using it and/or killing me by walking out the front door right now."

"Let's expand a bit, yeah? Try to think of other people."

I spun the photo, me and Burch eyeballing each other across the garbage-bagged corpse. "They have that same evidence on you too. I can drop you off at the airport."

"When that clock strikes midnight I'll be in Eddie's hip pocket. Where will you be?"

I stalled, spent some time studying the photo. "You know what this tells me? They don't give a shit about us. Live or die, whatever, but they'd rather not deal with the hassle. And they followed us the whole night but didn't just blast the limo, wipe us all out. The man they sent to kill Eddie made a ritual out of it. Eddie's death has significance to them."

Burch was a statue.

"This isn't about money, is it?"

———

Burch walked over, rapped on the glass wall, and waved Vanessa in.

I slid the photo into the envelope. "We're done talking about this?"

"What's left to talk about?"

"If this isn't about money, what's it about?"

"Keeping Eddie alive. Simple as that."

"Simple. Even when we show him the photo and the midnight deadline."

"Yeah, we're not doing that." He glanced at his watch, then at

Vanessa taking her time paddling to the pool's edge.

"Bad call." I tapped the envelope. "This'll scare him, and he needs to be scared right now. Keep him from doing something stupid."

"Mate, he was almost strangled and stabbed last night. If that don't temper the impetuous streak, naught will. We ain't showing him."

We slapped eyes across the kitchen. The pans hanging off the wall made soft gonging sounds, chanting us on to meet in the middle. I felt the table under my forearms. It would make a nice chopping block.

Outside Vanessa stepped onto the baking concrete, hustled toward the house on her tiptoes.

I let my shoulders relax. "For now. He decides to roll out for tacos at 11:45, it's going on the fridge."

Burch curled a lip at me. He looked confused, like he'd ordered gravity to release me into space, yet there I sat, yawning. "It's my call. You keep your mouth shut 'less I say otherwise."

"All this fucking secrecy. I have to lie to Marcela and Gil, we aren't telling Eddie about this, and you won't tell me what he pulled in the first place to bring it all down. What did Eddie do?"

Burch stared at me until Vanessa came through the glass doors, wrapping a sarong with orchids on it around her waist. "Holy crap, the pavement is a million degrees. What's up, boys? You playing nice in here?"

"The boss needs lunch."

"I'm hungry too." She opened the fridge. "Chicken salad with fruit?"

"Fine," Burch said, still giving me the ball bearings.

I was beyond staring down anybody for free, and Vanessa's

exposed tattoo was more interesting than Burch's flaring nostrils. It covered her back and looked half-finished, the vibrant colors at the top fading to hollow black outlines above her sarong. The red, purple, blue, and orange flowers started tiny at her neckline and grew down her spine and across her shoulder blades. Perched on those was a willowy white butterfly that looked like it could take flight at any moment.

She moved her arm and the scene shifted. I realized the flowers weren't growing out of a stem—the scaled green tendril behind them was a snake, its slitted yellow eye peering out from between the petals. It was watching the butterfly, and I couldn't tell if it wanted to keep the delicate thing safe or eat it.

Vanessa turned and caught me looking. She went pale and I thought she might vomit onto the food in her hands, then she clenched her jaw and glanced at Burch.

He shook his head.

I scooped up the photo and envelope and headed toward the hallway.

"Where you going?" Burch said.

"You two can stay in here and whisper to each other. I get to fight a guy named Zombi in two weeks, and I have thrown exactly one punch in preparation. Now, it happens to be one of my favorite punches ever, but still. Just the one. So I'm going into the gym. Wanna come?"

The kitchen was silent until Vanessa clanked some plates onto the counter and cleared her throat. "Is there any way you two will grow up before I serve this?"

I walked out. I don't like to disappoint women, but I'm used to it.

———

I went outside and past the pool to call Gil. I could feel the hot concrete through my shoes. The Jacuzzi rolled and bubbled. I tried to ignore the worm it put in my belly and gave it the finger.

The sun pressed an ember into the back of my neck until I got under a pergola covered with a dense vine that put shade over a long marble table and eight chairs. I sat facing the glass wall and couldn't see anything inside—just a reflection of the pool area and me sweating into my suit. Behind me the statues and landscaped walking paths rose high enough to block the walls and desert beyond.

Burch was on the other side of that glass somewhere, squinting at me and thinking British insults. I countered with American indifference, put my feet on the table and got my phone out.

"Tell me you're on your way here," Gil said.

"Sorry. What's the word on Zombi?"

"Cryptic."

I waited. "Okay, and? I know what it means. You don't have to demonstrate."

"Found some video of his judo competitions, typical Japanese stoicism, but this guy takes it to another level. His face never changes, whether he's bowing, tossing somebody over his head, or getting his elbow dislocated."

"Who did that to him?"

"Some Ukrainian in the World Judo Championship from a few years back. Guy's pulling like his kid is drowning; Zombi's arm goes the wrong way. They scramble. Zombi ends up using the broken arm to choke the guy out."

"Jesus."

"And that's without being able to strike. I got some grainy footage of his first MMA fight. It's from two years ago and his stand-up was shit, but he won. Fought a kickboxer, waded right through the guy's offense and put him to sleep."

"This is starting to sound bad."

"Well, the kickboxer's neck was longer than yours."

"The hell does that mean?"

"More neck, easier to choke."

I pulled my shoulders up to see if it made sense. "So what's the verdict?"

"From what I've seen, he's a bad matchup for you. Got a head like a cinder block and takes punishment for days looking for a window, then he pounces. Basically he's you, only with much, much better grappling and he doesn't bleed all over the joint."

"So if you throw in the towel now, will the ref see it?"

"Don't be a baby. There's a way through him. I just need more information. And that's the fucked-up part. I do a search for Japanese catch wrestlers and get video on everything from professional matches to teenagers jumping off garage roofs onto each other but hardly anything on Zombi."

"Huh. I told Eddie to get me everything he can. We'll see what he comes up with."

"And tell him and that Burch prick I'm training you in Eddie's bathroom if I have to. There's no way you're going against this guy without me."

"I know." I moved the phone away from my ear, just in case. "Oh, and we might be fighting him at an Elite Combat event instead of Warrior."

The line hissed. "Of fucking course. Listen to me. It doesn't matter where the cage is or whose name is on the canvas. What matters is the man across from you. Let me handle everything else."

"I appreciate that. Listen, what would you say if I walked away?"

"From what, Eddie and his drama? I'd say hip-hip and you know the rest."

"It would mean I'm done in Warrior, no matter what happens to him."

"That doesn't mean you're done fighting. Plenty of other promotions out there."

"Yeah. But this contract will put us over the hump. I don't go for it, I'll get eaten up wondering what if."

"Don't do any of this for me or the guys here. You never have to ask what if about us. You want to come home right now, do it. You decide to become a professional juggler, we'll wash your balls. That came out wrong."

"I hear you." The pool area was blurry. I wiped the sweat and other things out of my eyes. If Gil wasn't worried, neither was I.

About that, anyway. I caught movement in the reflection of the landscape behind me and watched one of the statues step out of the shrubbery and follow the path toward the pool. He was young and Japanese, and he carried a four-foot samurai sword.

"If I don't call you back in ten minutes, tell Marcela I love her."

———

I'd never fought a guy with a sword before, holding or facing. I don't count the little bulldog from Eddie's limo—he wasn't fighting me.

I picked up one of the chairs and walked along the table from the guy's right as he came off the path onto the concrete. The chair was much heavier than I'd expected, some kind of weighted base. I put in the work to make it look light.

He held the sword at a forty-five-degree angle toward the ground. Relaxed, just out for a stroll. He wore wraparound black sunglasses, black pants, and a white tank top. A full spectrum of fish and feudal Japanese scenery tattoos covered his arms and chest.

What do you say to make a guy like that stop in his tracks, rethink what he's doing, scamper off into the weeds?

"Hold up," I tried.

He didn't even glance at me. "You got our note. Why are you still here?" His English was unaccented. Locally grown or an early transplant. He wandered to the edge of the pool, stuck a hand in the water and slapped it against the back of his neck.

"Put the sword down."

"Or what, you'll chair me? That looks heavy."

I ran through it: throw the chair, watch it go two feet and bounce toward him. Maybe he jumps into the pool, cramps up, and drowns.

"It is heavy." I put the chair down. Took my jacket off and draped it over the back. The sun evaporated the sweat on my thin white shirt and started making more. Where the hell was Burch? "What are you doing here?"

He looked at the sword in his hand, the mirrored wall of Eddie's house. Turned to me with a little smile. "Selling Girl Scout cookies."

"Hey, I'm just trying to stall."

"I know. Doesn't matter. I'm still wondering why you're here. Our message wasn't clear enough?"

"It said midnight."

"Let the others wait. I want this now. And it's

midnight somewhere."

I didn't know if that was true. "Was that your buddy in the freezer?"

"My brother."

"As in gang brother or real brother?"

"Blood brother."

I still wasn't sure. "I can't let you kill Eddie."

"You don't really have a say in it. You should go. Now."

"What about the other ten guys in there?"

He smiled again. "You mean Burch? He thinks he's worth ten. He should stay. And the woman. We don't want to chase them, waste more time."

Vanessa's inflatable raft bumped against the pool's edge at his feet. He looked down at it and touched the tip of the sword against the vinyl. It went through like a torch through cobwebs. The raft sagged.

Burch was on their list too. Explained why he didn't consider leaving Eddie; it wouldn't change a thing for him. "Why do you want them dead?"

He watched water seep over the raft. "They didn't tell you? No surprise. You knew, you would have left already. Maybe killed them yourself on principle."

"My principles don't align with most."

"We know. We also know you understand dishonor. If I tell you why Eddie and Burch have to die, you'll know of my family's dishonor. Then I'll have to kill you too. Which is fine, but unnecessary. So go."

"You're so ashamed, why don't you kill yourself? What's it called, *seppuku*?"

He turned from the raft. I had a good idea how his eyes looked behind those sunglasses. "Watch what you say to me."

"Isn't somebody supposed to help, slice your head off after you disembowel yourself? I've never tried that, but I'll do my best."

"Would you leave if I told you we have people in Brazil, watching Marcela?"

The sweat on my back froze. "You don't."

"I'm sure your woman will understand why she has to suffer so you can try to protect these doomed men. These ghosts."

"My woman. That's enough to get you a broken arm, she hears you say it. Send your boys in. She's surrounded by the entire Arcoverde clan. It'll make for a nice family reunion."

Maybe we were both bluffing. The phone was heavy in my pocket, tugging me to call and warn her.

"Her family against the Dojin-gumi." He shook his head. "What's Portuguese for 'They're slaughtering us'?"

"They don't have a word for that. What's Doe Gin Goomi? It sounds spicy."

His knuckles turned white on the sword handle. "You're exceptionally stupid." He squared his shoulders to me.

I picked the chair up again, jacket and all.

"I am going to tell you why they have to die. And right after, I'm going to cut your fucking head off and take it with me. So I can always look at the expression on your face: regret for defending dishonorable men. Your last thought will be, 'My life was wasted.'" He slid his left foot forward, brought the sword up, and held it vertically behind his right shoulder.

I lifted the back of the chair frame level with my neck.

He said, "You're going to die because Eddie—"

The shot sounded like a cough. The black sunglasses split in half above the bridge of the guy's nose and flew away from his face. The skin on his forehead and around his eyes flapped out and snapped back like a fish's mouth. He dropped the sword.

Two more coughs as Burch strode out of the sculpted shrubs between the patio and the wall along the side of the property, a long, dull gray suppressor attached to his pistol. He wore a long-sleeve tan shirt and suit pants, dirt on the knees.

The guy was already dropping when the two bullets hit center mass, went through and past me into the backyard. His knees cracked against the concrete. He fell face-first into the pool, landing on Vanessa's limp raft. It wrapped around him and they both floated toward the middle of the pool with red ribbons spreading underneath.

Burch still had the pistol up, scanning the area. "He's alone, correct?"

I put the chair down. It had beaded drops of blood on it. So did the lapels of my new jacket.

"Woody."

"Fuck you."

That brought him around. "Say again?"

"That asshole was here for you too, not just Eddie."

"Looked to me like he wasn't discriminating. I believe that sword was headed for your spine, no?"

"It wasn't going to touch me."

He glanced at the chair, the sword. I don't think he did the same math as me. He kicked the sword into the pool. "Regardless, you're welcome. Goddamn ingrate. I need to sweep this area. Go inside and get the boss and Vanessa ready to move. We're not safe here anymore."

"I'm not doing anything until you tell me what he was about to."

"Having a chat, were you?"

"I think you heard most of it."

"Don't worry about it. Go inside and get them ready."

I didn't move.

Burch pointed the pistol at my left knee. "Go."

"I will remember this moment."

"Please do. Every time I give you an order."

I lifted my jacket off the chair and walked between the pool and Burch, who backed toward the path and kept the gun on me. I watched him in the house reflection. When I was close to the kitchen door he turned and drifted off the path into the landscape and disappeared.

I stepped into the coolness. Vanessa was by the table, staring past me with her hand over her mouth.

"There's blood on my jacket." I left it hanging on her shoulder. "Where's Eddie?"

"Burch put him in the panic room."

"Where?"

"It's, ah, it's off the master suite. That man is dead."

I headed for the stairs. "Keep those words handy. You'll need them again."

———

I chewed up the stairs and cut left, saw Eddie's double doors closed. Maybe they were unlocked, but I had a good thing going and put a foot between the knobs shaped like sword pommels. The doors split open, and something metal flew off, tumbled across the room, and hid under the bed. I got two steps into the room and froze.

Statues stood along every wall except the glass that overlooked the pool and garden. Twelve of them, geared up in everything from Spartan greaves and helmets to a Knight Templar with longsword and banner, starched in mid-ripple. The walls behind them were draped with dark fabric, making the room feel like a commander's tent. The soldiers were all posed at ease, and in the periphery they seemed to be nudging each other about what they were looking at, which was Eddie's barge of a bed.

A custom piece, built in place because no door in the house would have let it through. The headboard was white marble, carved into tiers of miniature benches with arches and sunshades made of wood and canvas at the top. It curved around the corners of the bed and blended in a smooth slope down to rounded nightstands on each side, bronze gauntleted hands rising out to hold torches with LED flames. It was a very accurate model of the Roman Colosseum, right down to the sand-colored pillows and bedspread with the Warrior logo embroidered in rusty blood.

"Eddie."

No answer. There was a closed door in the far corner. I booked a flight around the bed, opened the door to Eddie's bathroom. It was bigger than it had looked on the security camera. Eddie wasn't in the shower or on the toilet.

I stood in the doorway and wanted to smash something, but everything in the room was built to smash back. I settled for messing up Eddie's bedspread and must have tripped a sensor—a raucous crowd cheered me from hidden speakers, then faded.

"If you don't come out right now, I'm going to tell people about that."

Nothing.

Burch hadn't said anything about a panic room during the tour. Operational security, he must have figured. But he did say there was access from his room to Eddie's through a closet. I went to the corner where the glass wall met the wall shared with Burch's room. There was space to walk behind the statues. I knocked through the fabric—solid, solid, hollow—and pulled the cloth aside to reveal another door, plain wood stained a dark cherry. It was locked.

"Eddie, if I have to break this door down, I'll use the pieces to make your funeral pyre."

Silence.

I pushed the fabric away from the wall, hooked one side over a grim centurion and the other over a wild-eyed Zulu, stepped between them, and set my feet. Took a breath and tensed my core and stopped.

Something was off. I stared at the door for half a minute before I got it.

I'd never seen a panic room door made of wood before. They were all slabs of steel with recessed hinges and overlapped edges to keep crowbars out.

I took the fabric off the Zulu and kept knocking past the double doors with the shredded hardware and found solid wall until I got next to the headboard. It went from a sharp rap on drywall behind the fabric to sounding like I'd hit the side of a submarine. I draped the fabric over the headboard and studied the flat gray door. No visible hardware or access keypad.

"Eddie, I know you can hear me. Probably see me too."

His voice came through a speaker somewhere above me. "Why'd you mess up my bed? And where's Burch? He's not on any of the cameras."

"He said you can come out now, false alarm. I'll help you make your bed."

"I can see the dead body floating in the pool, asshole. And I've seen you upset before. I'm not coming out until you calm down and Burch says it's safe."

"I'm going to find out what you two did."

The statues leaned into the silence, waiting.

Eddie said, "If I find out you're digging even one grain of sand, I'll cut you out of Warrior for good. You and Gil can rot. If Burch finds out, he'll kill you."

"Damn right," Burch said. He stood in the doorway, the pistol and suppressor pointed at the floor. He stared at me and spoke to the panic room. "You can come out, boss; it's clear. But we need to move to the secondary location."

There was a clunk and a hiss, and the door eased open. It was six inches thick with steel cylinders that would extend into the jamb to make it all one piece. Impenetrable, sans artillery. Eddie still looked small in the small room, which had flat-screen monitors above a narrow table, a stack of bottled water, and a toilet. He held a chunky satellite phone and aimed the antenna at me. "Step back."

I moved to the foot of the bed. If Eddie and Burch huddled up, maybe I could clunk their heads together and pile the statues on top, set the whole mess on fire. I tugged the bedspread. The crowd cheered the notion.

"Stop that," Eddie said. He walked out of his vault, looked at Burch. "You're sure we have to relocate?"

"Afraid so. We move in five." Burch got out of the doorway and nodded for me to exit. "Get your clothes. Or don't. Take Vanessa out to the limo and wait for us."

"That guy outside said Marcela's name."

"A bluff."

"Doesn't matter. They know about her, so they know about Gil. His wife, Angie. The guys at the gym. I can't let anything happen to any of them. I'm leaving."

Burch and Eddie shared a look.

Eddie said, "You've had a hand in killing two of them. It doesn't matter where you go now. You're on the list, just like we are."

"Best to stay with us," Burch said, "so when they do come for you, all they find is you."

———

I stood in the living room and watched Burch drag the body out of the pool and go to work with the garbage bags and duct tape. The pool's filter and chemicals already had the blood broken down to a hint of pink here and there. Eddie and Vanessa were banging things around on the second floor, rolling luggage onto the open bridge at the top of the stairs. If they expected me to take it the rest of the way, they'd need some cobweb repellent.

My phone buzzed. Gil.

"It's been more than ten minutes. You still want me to call Marcela?"

"No. I'll do it."

"She's worried about you."

"If I talk to her, that will get worse."

"Thanks for practicing on me. See, you tell me to send your love to Marcela, then hang up. I gotta wonder what's happening. Conjure up all sorts of scenarios, and not one of them involves smiling."

"That's a rarity right now."

Gil said, "You need me to bring the cops in?"

Burch dragged the body under the pergola so he could work in the shade. He had to backtrack and pick up bits of skull.

"Nah, they wouldn't be interested."

"You might be surprised by what law enforcement finds interesting."

"I know their number. Don't worry about me. But I need a promise."

"Yes. Ah, wait. Give me a hint first."

"If I call and tell you to run, don't ask questions. Send everybody home, and you and Angie go somewhere I don't know about. Stay there until I get in touch."

"I won't make that promise. Don't you dare tell me to run. Time comes to make that call, tell me where you are. That's where I'm going. And I know what you're thinking: 'Then I won't make the call.' Fuck you. Call me. You got it?"

"Yeah."

"Woody."

"I got it."

Burch finished with the body—identical to the wrap job on the limo guy—and flopped it onto a rolling beverage cart he'd rolled from behind the outdoor bar. He pushed it toward the garage end of the house. I couldn't hear through the glass, but it looked like he was whistling. I tried to imagine pulling Gil into the scene and felt my guts twist.

That would not happen.

"My phone is with me," he said.

"Thanks. Talk to you soon."

I got Marcela's number up, took a breath, and called. Tried to convince myself it was to reassure her, but the selfishness scoffed at me. I needed to hear her voice.

"Woody, hello."

Woo-dee. I had to turn away from the glass wall and sit on the wooden ledge that framed the room. "Hey, how you doing?"

"Shut up with that. What's going on? Gil's worried sick over you."

"I just talked to him. He's fine."

"Oh, you talked to him. Did you *listen*?"

I felt better already. "Everything is fine."

"This is when I start to pray. Where are you?"

"I'm with Eddie."

"That one." She snapped out some Portuguese. It didn't sound like praying. "When his mouth opens it's a lie. Leave now. Go back to Gil."

"I'd like to."

"So? Are your legs not real? Are they painted on? Go."

"It's not that simple."

"It's always that simple." She talked rapid-fire to someone away from the phone. Incredulous needs no translator.

"Who's that?"

"Jairo says you're stupid to help Eddie after everything. He wants to smack some sense into you."

"Tell him no thank you."

After the shootout at Chops's, Jairo had vowed to pull Eddie's ribs out. One of the reasons Marcela and I had hustled him and his brothers onto a plane to Brazil.

If Marcela came to Vegas, I'd worry about her.

If Jairo came, I'd worry about everybody.

"What does he have you doing?"

I told her all of it, except the dead bodies. No need to indict either of us on an open line.

She said, "If I come up there to kick his face, would you stop me?"

"After a hundred or so. But please don't."

"I hate these people. They look at you and see a tool—a hammer or a wall."

"Are walls tools in Brazil?"

"After I finish with Eddie, I kick you for a while."

The line hummed until I said, "I miss you."

"Come see me."

"I will."

"Now."

"Soon."

"You sound like your head is down."

I lifted it, saw Burch staring at me from the foyer, covered in sweat and holding a fresh suit on a hanger. "I have to go. I'll call you."

"This hurts my stomach."

"I know. I'm sorry." I put the phone away.

Burch stared for a few more seconds, then walked into the kitchen. I heard him go through the doorway in there, probably on his way to the security room. The cameras had evidence of him shooting a man three times and preparing the body for disposal. He had some erasing to do.

I looked at the black cube table and wondered how much I'd give to have that button implanted.

CHAPTER 11

I RODE IN THE LIMO'S FRONT SEAT WITH BURCH. HE DIDN'T like it, but he couldn't leave me in the back with Eddie and Vanessa. I might convince her to hold Eddie while I checked his damaged throat from the inside. I offered to drive so Burch could ride in back, but he declined. Must have pictured me crashing the limo onto the runway at McCarran and diving out, hijacking a plane to Brazil, and never coming back.

I made a note to research British clairvoyance. "Where are we going?"

"Isolation doesn't seem to be working. Time to try the opposite." He got off 215 onto Flamingo Road, headed for the Strip.

"So now they get to kill bystanders too. This is a good plan."

"They made a play; we adapt. Sitting there until midnight would be suicide."

"Hey, I mentioned the midnight thing before you shot that guy. He didn't seem bothered by the breach of etiquette."

"I heard him."

"So you could have jumped out of the bushes sooner, distracted him while I gave him a chair massage."

"That's right," Burch said.

"You didn't have to shoot him. But if you heard all of what he said, my guess is you wanted to."

"Goes without saying. Everybody I've ever shot, I wanted to. Better now? Good. He was a probe, a scout. Looked to me like he got bored and started wandering around. No discipline. So the full assault, whatever that entails, hasn't started yet."

"Midnight."

"Or before, possibly after."

"Anytime, then."

"Now you're getting it."

We hit the overpass above 15 and dropped between Caesars Palace and the Bellagio, two sentinels welcoming us to Vegas proper. I made sure my wallet was still in my pocket.

"So the photo, the deadline, that was all bullshit."

"Wouldn't say that. I think the offer was good for you at one point. Not anymore."

"And it never was for you."

He gave a tight smile. "You heard the man before I gave him head vents. They want me almost as bad as Eddie. Probably included me in the note so you'd think I'm an idiot for staying, push you toward abandoning us."

Smart bastards.

Burch cut across the Strip and turned right on a narrow service road that ran behind the casinos. He wove through employee parking lots and loading areas, and I wasn't sure where we were until we crawled over a speed bump into the walled service lot behind the Golden Pantheon Casino, home of Warrior events. Eddie had part ownership of the hotel and casino looming above us, all columns and arches, scenery and statues worked into the facade. They were much bigger than Eddie's personal collection and wore formal Roman garb. They waved and beckoned and didn't hold any weapons that I could see.

It was a different access point than the one Jairo and I had blown through, both of us stinking like Tezo's pit, right before the Burbank fight. I could see where I'd dropped Eddie off that night. Marcela had been in the truck with me. I locked onto the scene, her looking out the window, then those little eyebrows going together when she saw my face was bleeding again.

Burch aimed the limo at a metal garage door and the scene slid away.

I let it go before it tore me right down the middle.

Burch hit a button on the dash panel. The metal door rolled up. He eased the limo into an empty underground parking garage that was big enough for a few stretch vehicles to turn around but small enough to feel exclusive.

He parked like an asshole. "You carry everything. I need my hands free."

———

The elevator had a numbered security keypad and two other buttons: Casino Floor and Penthouse.

Burch punched in a code and hit Penthouse. I stood closest to the doors, loaded with rolling luggage, laptop bags, my clothes and shoes in a plastic shopping bag, and a hard plastic case the size of a table that felt like it had floor magnets inside, pulling my arm out of its socket. Eddie and Vanessa were behind me and all the freight. If the doors opened and somebody sprayed me with a machine gun, the two of them might hear it.

I couldn't tell the elevator had moved, but the doors parted and we were in the penthouse suite of the casino hotel. Solid slabs of black marble pulled light into the walls and floor of the circular foyer, which had matching white curved sofas facing each other on the sides.

I lugged everything into a huge square room that looked like a villa courtyard. The floor was black marble tile with small white mosaics spaced evenly wall to wall, each one the shape of a different type of knot. White marble columns ran along the walls and supported a balcony that wrapped around the room. I could see the tops of doors up there. Above that the ceiling was domed glass. Despite the late afternoon sunlight pouring in, the room was almost cold.

Burch pointed at the elevator. "That's the only access point. We control the elevator from up here, so unless they have an air force we're safe."

I checked everyone's face: no incredulity. "I'm the only one? Why didn't you just come here to begin with?"

"My ass isn't the only thing on the line here," Eddie said. "I gotta save face too. I show up at my own hotel needing a room, people talk."

"If anyone asks," Burch said, "renovations are being done on his living room and master suite."

I looked at Eddie. "You should make that a reality. Your bedroom is fucked up."

"Stay here." Burch pulled his gun and walked through an arched opening in the far right corner. The soft soles on his shoes made no noise.

I set the hard plastic case down. It echoed.

Vanessa and I stood there looking around and Eddie poked at his phone until Vanessa said, "This is really nice."

"Be nicer if somebody else was paying to stay here," Eddie said.

"How pricey is it? Is that tacky?"

"A bit. It's eight grand a night. Burch called ahead, had the staff kick out a party of twelve. So not only are they not paying for this, they got comped for whatever rooms they're in now, plus dinner and who knows what else."

"Getting killed used to be free," I said.

Eddie went back to the phone.

Burch walked out of a matching archway on the left toward a set of wide marble stairs in the middle of the far wall. He climbed them diagonally to a landing, cut in front of a bronze fountain, and disappeared behind a thick column. A second later he popped out on the balcony, walked around opening doors and ducking in and out of rooms. Eventually he stopped and leaned on the thick marble railing. "All clear. Leave my case there. You can put everything else away."

I started dropping bags.

"Careful," Eddie said. "Jesus, here." He grabbed one of the rolling suitcases from me and handed it to Vanessa, then pointed at the archway on the left. "Through there, the master suite. You can't miss it."

Eddie headed for the one on the right, told me, "Bring everything else." He held his phone aloft. "I'm putting a meeting together for tonight. We're gonna lock in the deal with Lou, get you and Zombi in the cage for Elite."

I followed with the bags and cases and had to walk under Burch, who was on his phone.

"Dorian, I need an ETA on those suits. Our boy hasn't taken

the first one off yet. It's starting to smell like a bog."

I trailed Eddie through the archway, thinking that if things got any better I'd have to set my head on fire.

———

Eddie set up shop in the penthouse's full conference room—desk with dual monitors, a blocky copier/scanner/fax machine, and an oval table with eight high-backed chairs pushed under it. The table had some kind of electronics hub in the middle with a multiline phone and a projector pointed at a screen on the long wall. The windows opposite the door faced across the Strip.

The only piece of Roman-themed decor was a stone plaque above a table piled with hotel stationery:

Verba volant, scripta manent.

Spoken words fly away, written words remain.

Eddie was busy opening laptops and spreading papers on the conference table. I headed for the door.

"Have a seat," Eddie said.

"You signing my contract?"

"Will you relax with that? No, just keep me company."

"I'll send Vanessa in."

"She's getting dinner together. Sit down." He was hunched over, the top of his blue faux hawk pointing at me.

I glared at it on my way to the far end of the table, dropped into a chair, and watched him and his papers get closer. He'd pull from one pile and add to another or make a new one. I looked at the paint to see if it was more interesting. A push.

Eddie straightened up. "There." Whatever he saw in the paper chaos, it made him happy. He sat down, checked something on a laptop, grunted. He leaned back in the chair and spun around to look at me. "I had to hire a new marketing department because of you."

"No, that was because of Benjamin." Benjamin Walsh had been Warrior's head of marketing as well as twisted in with Tezo and Kendall. He hadn't done well when Jairo and I pulled him and Eddie into a locked room for answers.

"Regardless, I have to keep an eye on all this shit now because the new people don't know what the hell they're doing." He rubbed his throat through the turtleneck, glanced down and plucked at the front of it. "I look like my Stanford business econ professor."

And then I'm supposed to say, "Oh, you went to Stanford?"

Fuck him and fuck college.

"Tell me about Zombi," I said.

"I already told you. Catch wrestler, kind of a shoot fighter. Gold medal judoka, backed by the Yakuza. Probably chews bones for fun. What else?"

"You got any video?"

"What for?"

"There's this thing called a game plan. Some call it strategy, but that's a Stanford word."

"Please. Gil has you thinking you actually use a strategy? Is he watching the same fights as me?"

"He had a good seat for the Burbank fight. Seems like that worked."

"You know what you did to Burbank?"

"Kicked him in the face."

"That was the nail in the coffin. Before that, when you finally settled down and fought your way. What did you do?"

"I avoided the takedown best I could, stayed away from—"

"Stop. You're reciting Gil. This ain't a press conference. What did you do to Burbank? You fought like your fucking life depended on it. You tried to kill him."

I shifted, couldn't get comfortable. It wasn't the chair. "Kendall had Marcela."

"And that made you desperate. It didn't make you fight like you did. Like you *do*, like some wolf with a fresh moose carcass, and here comes the next alpha. Don't you know this?"

I stared out the windows.

Eddie said, "Don't tell me you're ashamed of it. It works. You take a guy like Burbank and fight him so hard he goes into survival mode, throws his game plan out of the building. I've kept tabs on him since your fight. He's slow, thinking too much. His trainers don't know what's wrong. I do, but I ain't telling. You broke him. That's what you do. You keep it up, I'll start calling you Social Security. The reason motherfuckers retire."

"Sorry."

"Bullshit you're sorry. You love it. Sitting here, maybe it scares you how much you love it. You can't look at it straight on. A lawful way to be what you are when what you are is outlawed. So you can tell your mom—if you have one—you're sorry and wear your citizen camouflage, but I know better. All this is just holding your breath, waiting to go again. In the cage, man. That's where you breathe."

I did a slow spin in the chair, checked out the ceiling.

Eddie said, "I took psychology at Stanford too."

"So if I go through your company breaking all your toys, you'll be happy?"

"Whoa. You knocked Burbank off his game for a couple months so far. Let's not crown you Jesus the Hun just yet. How many fighters you seen saying they can't be broken, they'll never give up, then they go out and get shattered? Nobody breaks until they do. All you are is a guy who hasn't met his hammer yet."

"You're wrong."

"Yeah? What fight?"

"It wasn't in a cage." I got up and walked out.

Eddie didn't say anything.

Stanford education.

———

Vanessa found me sitting in the foyer by the elevator and handed me a plate of grilled chicken over a bed of fresh greens and fruit, a thin dark glaze drizzled over all of it.

I made a silent preemptive apology to my suit and the white couch and dug in.

Vanessa hovered. "Burch is watching TV if you don't want to sit here by yourself."

"I'm fine. You should go."

Her eyebrows went up. She spun on one bare foot toward the fake courtyard.

"No, I mean the elevator. You should go somewhere safe."

"Oh. I was like, okay, *that* was rude."

"I'll tell Eddie and Burch I made you leave. Might save your job if Eddie makes it through this."

She sat on the couch across from me. "Burch told me I'm safest here with him. And you, I figure, but he didn't say that part." She pushed her palms into the couch, put one foot on top of the other, curled her toes.

I ate a piece of fruit that was new to me. It was good. "When you aren't with Burch, how often do guys with swords get shot and dumped into a pool?"

"None so far."

"Well then. My opinion, whatever it's worth, is he wants you around because you're one more person to put between him and them when they break through the door."

She eyed the elevator. "So let's go. Both of us."

"If Eddie had signed that contract, you'd already have a post-card from me. Someplace nice. Maybe a bomb shelter in Nebraska. Now I'm sitting here wondering if it's worth risking my neck to keep him alive just so he can own me."

"It's not. Being owned never is."

I gave her a closer look. "How did you and Eddie meet?"

Vanessa stood. "You need something to drink."

She got to the opening into the courtyard and slid to a stop to avoid a collision with Burch. Eddie was behind him, a laptop bag bulging with papers hanging off his shoulder.

"On your feet, soldier," Burch said. He had a new gun, a stubby black MP5 with an integral suppressor hanging from a rig across his chest. It looked pretty light; that hard plastic case must have plenty more to offer.

"What for?"

"I said so."

Eddie said, "We're meeting Lou."

Vanessa ducked around them and was gone.

I carried my plate to the elevator. "Why doesn't he come here?"

"Negotiations 101," Eddie said. "He wants neutral territory, even though the goddamn deal is done."

Burch nodded at my plate. "Leave it. Need your hands free."

The plate was still half full and my stomach was still

three-quarters empty. I started packing chicken into my mouth.

Burch yanked the plate out of my hand and spun it into the courtyard. The plate shattered. Chicken and greens and fruit and the delicious glaze scattered over the floor. Eddie pursed his lips and hustled his phone out so he could stare at it. Burch punched the elevator button and the doors opened. Eddie tiptoed on board.

Burch watched me chew. "All finished?"

"You ever fought in an elevator before? It's more fun than it sounds."

———

Burch split time watching me and the elevator doors on the way down.

"I was just teasing," I said. "Next time I hit you, I'm not gonna warn you first. So relax."

———

The meeting was at an RV dealership north of the city near a cluster of golf courses and suburbia, nearly an hour in the limo while Burch pulled fancy counter-pursuit maneuvers and Eddie jabbered on the phone to his people about what they had to do once the Elite deal was final.

We pulled through the stadium-lit front lot of RVs that looked like rolling yachts, past the showroom with its high glass walls, and through an open chain-link gate into the lot that surrounded a service garage. Just a few lights, enough to see the office entrance and airplane hangar doors.

The RVs were parked nose-out toward the building. Burch

idled the limo all the way to the back corner. I didn't see any other cars.

"Some cloak-and-dagger shit here, huh?" Eddie said.

I gave him a nod but wasn't impressed. I'd worked meets at the roaring base of the Hoover Dam, at the wrong end of a live firing range, and in a condemned, dripping mine shaft. The dark corner of a parking lot was for buying bootleg celebrity toothbrushes.

Burch curled the limo around and got it facing the gate, stopped, and lowered the privacy panel. "I don't like this one bit. Too many corners, not enough light."

"I'll call him," Eddie said. "Get him to come out to us."

"Don't like that either. We're fucked sitting here with the high roof on one side and the caravans on the other." His head swiveled around. "I need to clear Lou's first, but you can't stay here. We all move at once, yeah?"

"Whatever you say."

Nobody asked me.

Burch got out and shot a very white, focused UV flashlight beam under the last few RVs, took his time with the one at the end. He poked the beam through the giant windshields, the shadows and stillness inside them like a shipwreck exploration. He hopped onto the limo's trunk. I could see the beam dancing over the tops of the RVs, but the angle didn't look good, still plenty of blind spots. He jumped down and stuck the flashlight into a bracket on the side of his gun so the beam would light up whatever he aimed at.

He opened the back door, holding Eddie close to it until I got out, then stood in front of him and eyeballed over my shoulder, shuffled Eddie a step to the side and planted him there.

I glanced back. Anyone shooting from the service garage roof would have to nail me to get to Eddie. I damned my shoes for not having laces I could stop to tie a dozen times or so.

"Moving," Burch said. He tucked the gun into his shoulder and stalked toward the RV in the corner.

Eddie and I followed. When the beam wasn't on the RV windshields, they were black caves wide enough for five guys to stand side by side and count down to open season on us. I could feel the day's heat coming off them and the asphalt, a steady pressure that made the space feel too small. The primal instinct in me heard twigs snapping in a thick jungle, pebbles bouncing down from the cliffs above, something long slipping through the muck between my feet.

Burch sliced the flashlight into the alley between the last two RVs, pulled us into it. "Stack up."

"What?"

He put one hand on the door handle. "You're in first. Anything goes wrong, I'll cover us back to the limo."

"Is it supposed to be just Lou in there?"

"Supposed to be," Eddie said. "Hurry. This bag is heavy."

Burch opened the door and stepped away.

I put a foot on the steel grate step and felt the structure tip a bit under my weight. The door was thicker than I'd expected, actually looked like a real door instead of a flimsy piece of sheet metal. I smelled old cigar smoke, stale beer, and something else under it all, familiar but clouded. I stepped onto the thick carpet and saw the thing wasn't meant for families. It was a mobile private card room, with the cabinets and furniture pulled out to make room for a poker table in the back and a full bar along the wall across from the door. There was a closed curtain between the room and the front seats.

Lou sat at the poker table, another whiskey in front of him. He was looking at me with surprise on that hangdog face of his, just like last time, but now someone had pinned him to his chair with a samurai sword through his chest, the front of his shirt sagging with blood.

———

"Back to the limo," I said.

Burch held out a hand to stop me from coming down the steps. "What is it?"

I grabbed the straps across his chest and a handful of Eddie's turtleneck and shoved them toward the limo. "They're here. Go."

A shape moved on the roof of the RV next to Lou's. It was a man, crouched at the edge and bringing a long tube up to his face.

I pushed off the stairs and drove my shoulder into the side of the RV. It rocked, and I heard thumps and a clatter on the roof.

Burch aimed up there, came back down, dragged the beam across my face. It smacked into my eyes like a baseball bat. I clamped them shut and made a stupid face and tripped over the RV steps, almost went down and slammed backward against the RV door. I turned to my left and tried my eyes, watched a black shape slip out of Lou's wheel well and scamper toward me.

Something, maybe an arm, pressed across my chest and held me against the RV. Burch's flashlight beam pinned the Japanese guy in black clothes to the asphalt. He turned his head and raised a dagger to block the light. Burch shot him in the top of the head, the impact louder than the shots.

Burch moved away. "Watch our six."

"I can't see anything."

"Quiet down. Keep up."

Footsteps going away and whimpering, Burch stomping and Eddie getting pulled along. I staggered after them, my eyelids like hummingbird wings until something hit my shoulder. I elbowed it in the face and wrenched it off its neck, then felt the domed shape of a rearview mirror in my hands and dropped it. When I squinted one eye and closed the other I could see silhouettes, Burch shoving Eddie into the back of the limo and looking toward the gate.

"They closed it."

"Can you get through?"

"Stop shouting and get in."

I headed toward the voice and flinched at two coughing bursts, bullets slapping into metal and splashing through glass. "Who's shooting? Is that you?"

"Yeah, God bless these fools for not using guns. Fuckin' idiots, the lot."

"Who made that flashlight? The sun?"

I fell into the back of the limo and heard the door close. Eddie was somewhere in there, wheezing and swearing. I cupped my hands around my eyes and blinked at the carpet. The limo jumped forward and picked up speed.

"Fuck me," Eddie said. "Hold on."

I felt around and found Eddie's ankles.

"Ah! Let go." He tried to kick free.

The limo rushed forward, a lot of horsepower pulling a lot of weight. There was a slight tug in momentum when Burch went through the gate, and I rolled around on the floor until he corrected the fishtailing. The tires locked up, and I braced between the seats for the turn onto the road, then more speed in a straight line.

I crawled onto the rear bench seat. Oncoming headlights stabbed through the open privacy panel. I blocked them with a hand and spread out, held on while Burch drove around sparse traffic, fast but not dangerous. I hoped he was watching the rearview; I sure as hell wasn't going to look back and risk my head exploding.

"Was Lou in there?" Eddie said.

"Yeah. They killed him."

"Fuck. Well, there goes my deal."

"And Lou's dead."

He didn't say anything to that.

I blinked out the side window. My sight was returning, but the skin around my eyes felt numb.

"What the hell is this?" Eddie said.

The interior lights popped on. I yelled and tried to kick them. "Are these darts?"

I peeked through slits. There were three red blossoms sticking out of his laptop bag. He plucked one out and stared at the three-inch stainless needle.

"There's something on the tip." He held it out, looked up at me, and froze. "Shit. Hold still."

"What? Why?"

"Burch, we need some help."

I slapped at wall panels until I found one with a mirror and blinked at it until it made sense. One of the darts was threaded along my eyebrow, the red plume above the bridge of my nose and the needle point sticking out above the corner of my right eye. The shaft was buried. "I can't feel this side of my face."

"Burch," Eddie said.

The limo slowed, turned into a grocery store parking lot and slammed into the base of a light pole. Eddie fell back into his seat. I tipped forward out of mine, had to catch myself on the bench.

Eddie sprang up. "What the fuck?"

In the front seat, Burch leaned to his right and stayed there, two red plumes sticking out of his neck.

———

Burch was still breathing but the rhythm was off, lots of dramatic pauses and gasps. Eddie and I leaned through the privacy panel and watched him and the darts in his neck.

"Shit," Eddie said. "Is it safe to pull those out?"

I pulled them out.

"Whoa, man. What if he bleeds to death?"

Two beads of blood rose from the pinholes and shimmered in the dash lights.

"Stand back," I said.

Eddie looked at the cars rolling past. "Are they chasing us? How many were there?"

"I don't know but we have to move. Can you drive?"

"I think so, yeah." He tried to take the laptop bag off, flapped his hands around until he found one of the seat belts and tugged on it. He was in shock, his motor skills shot.

"Forget it." I jumped out and squinted at the traffic, didn't see any truckloads of assassins. The limo's front bumper was dented around the base of the light pole, but there wasn't any frame or body damage I could see. No crumple zones here; let the rest of the world cave in.

I shoved Burch over and got behind the wheel.

Eddie said, "You know the way to the hotel?"

"We can't go there."

"If we make it to the penthouse, we're—"

"Dead. Somebody's talking. Maybe Vanessa, maybe somebody on the staff. We can't trust it."

"It's not Vanessa. She didn't even know where we were going. Nobody did."

"But she knew we were leaving."

"Then what? They guessed we were headed for the RV lot, leapfrogged us, and set up an ambush?"

I avoided the fact that he had a point by backing the limo off the pole and rolling it toward an exit along a dim side street. I parked under a ficus tree, lights off, where we could watch for any followers flashing past. The limo was the only vehicle on the street and blended into the suburban scenery like a bullet on a cupcake.

Burch muttered something and started to spasm.

Eddie put a hand on him. "Is he dying right now?"

"Maybe. So they got to Lou. Did he sound strange when you planned the meet?"

"It was all texts. We gotta do something for Burch, man."

"Shit. I bet they tracked Lou after the first meet, maybe even grabbed him while that little guy was trying to choke you. Once we were headed for this one, they stuck him. We got Lou killed. We should have told him."

"Fuck that. He woulda run from the Elite deal."

"Yeah, this is better."

"Burch needs a hospital," Eddie said.

"We can roll him into the ER and leave him. Way things are going, my guess is he'll get stabbed before he wakes up."

"I can't let him die."

I watched the traffic go by. There were about a dozen people I could call to work on Burch and tuck us away, and I didn't trust any of them. Between their greed and the Yakuza's reach, we wouldn't last the night.

That left the people who trusted me.

The person.

Years of honesty, respect, and love between us, and I was going to repay all of that by bringing death to his door.

I hit the lights and pulled forward. My face was numb and I was glad; I'd never liked the feel of tears.

CHAPTER 12

G IL WALKED THROUGH THE GYM'S BACK DOOR A LITTLE past midnight, blinking the sleep out of his eyes, and looked around: Burch sprawled on the sectional couch, unconscious, the machine gun still strapped across his chest.

Eddie holding an ice pack on Burch's face to keep it from burning off.

Me standing in the door to the kitchen with a glass of milk and a dart sticking out of my forehead.

"Coffee," he said.

—

The Hole was the room at the rear of the gym where Gil's fighters hung out and sometimes slept during training camp. It kept us under his thumb and out of trouble—mostly—though every now and then he'd measure the doorways to see how many bricks he'd need to seal us in for good. The room had a big screen TV, game consoles, foldout cots, the black leather sectional deep enough it had an undertow, foosball, and a card table. One corner was walled off and had four showers and a small steam room.

Gil kept his face blank, nodded at Eddie, and walked toward me. Not the door at the other end of the wall I was holding up, the one to his office, where he dished out the prime ass chewings. This was good. He got close enough to put a knuckle against my sternum and drive me backward into the kitchen while he stared at my throat.

This was not good.

He closed the door behind him. I opened my mouth and he put a finger up.

I closed my mouth.

The coffeepot was loaded and ready for the morning. He hit a button and got it chugging, then leaned back against the counter and folded his arms. "What the hell is in your face?"

"A blow dart."

"Well, take it out. It bothers me."

"I can't. There's something on the tip of it. It's making my face numb. If I pull it out, I might end up like Burch in there."

Gil stepped close, frowned at it. "Hold on." He went into the hallway that ran the width of the building, separating the back area from the gym. I heard him rooting around in the bathroom and the utility closet, then he returned with cotton balls, a bottle of rubbing alcohol, and a pair of side cutters.

"Wait."

"Shut up and hold still." He wiped the upper half of my face with the alcohol.

The fumes burned my eyes, and scrunching them shut pulled on the dart. "Ah, man."

"Relax your face. I don't know what this is going to feel like, but it'll probably be weird."

I felt him tugging on the tip of the dart, wiping the toxic residue off. It was a distant sensation because of the numbness—no pain but it wasn't pleasant.

"Now don't move."

I still had my eyes shut. Between Burch's flashlight and Gil's first aid I'd qualify for a Seeing Eye dog. The dart pulled a bit, twisted, then there was a snap.

"All done." Gil pressed a towel into my hand. "That scar tissue finally did you a favor."

When I opened my eyes the dart was in two pieces on the counter. Just a needle with a red plume on the back end. I ran cold water on the towel, wiped my face and neck. The skin around my eyes felt heavy, like it was drooping off the bones. I could feel the pressure of the towel but not the texture.

"Okay, so now I get to hear the story about how you got shot in the face with a dart. Again?"

"Nope. This is a first for me."

"Goody."

I told him from the penthouse to when I'd called him on our way to the gym. By the time I finished he was killing his second cup of coffee, reaching to pour a third. "Dare I ask if anyone called the police?"

"About which part?"

"Any. All."

"Nobody called."

"So poor Lou's still sitting in that RV?"

"I'm sure they took the body. If not, some mechanic will find him in the morning."

He stared into the corner. "You know, I used to be a law-abiding citizen. Now, you tell me a story like this, the first thing I think about is how to make sure my ass is covered. Somebody ought to call the police, but I don't want them here asking a bunch of questions. Because that's bad for business. A guy's dead and I'm worried about appearances. What's that say about me?"

"It says you don't have anything to do with this, and I dragged you in anyway."

"I met Lou a few times. He was kind of an ass but harmless enough."

"I'm sorry."

"And I believe you. Doesn't change the fact we could all go to jail."

I thought about the photo in my jacket pocket of me carting another dead guy toward a freezer, wondered if that would get me a room on death row out at Ely State Prison. First chance I got I'd shred and burn it. No need to keep it around to convince Eddie things were serious. I think he was up to speed.

Gil said, "What happens now?"

"This is the only place I know is safe. If we can stay here until Burch gets back on his feet, I'll work on cutting you out of the loop."

"Do they know you're here?"

"Maybe. They seem to know where we are all the time, but I can guarantee you nobody followed us here. Nobody can see the limo from the street." I didn't tell him they knew about Marcela, must know about this place, and might have had it under surveillance before we showed up. Any justice in the world, the floor would have opened and let me drop to the circle of hell I'd earned.

Gil's halo didn't even flicker. "That Burch guy looks bad."

"He is. Needs somebody fast. Who's that old hippie Angie

brings in sometimes to cleanse the place?"

"You'll have to be more specific." Angie was Gil's wife. She ran yoga and Pilates classes in the gym, tried to get the fighters to stretch and breathe more.

"Wears a kimono, chants around with those smoking branches."

Gil pulled a face. "Christ, that guy. Denny. You think he can help?"

"He's got that pouch hanging off his belt. Every time he comes in he'll look at somebody, reach in, and hand them a tea bag or something. Tell them, 'Eat more lemons' or whatever."

"I don't know. If Burch was awake, what would he want?"

"He'd shoot himself in the foot, let the poison drain out, then grimace at the bullet hole until it closed."

"My kind of guy. I'll find Denny's number. We'll see what he can do." He topped off his mug. "Nice suit, by the way."

"It won't fit you."

"Yeah, I'm shaped like a human being. Well, kinda."

I went back into the Hole. "How's he doing?"

"Ragged," Eddie said. He still had the ice pack on Burch's head, though now it was a water pack. Burch was twitching and muttering. His shoes were off, and his toes were bunched into fists. "What are you doing?"

"Getting out of this suit, taking a shower, then I'm going to interrogate you."

"Interrogate?" He stared at the black TV screen, like it might remind him what the word meant.

"If there's any time left after that, I'm gonna sleep. So get ready to talk." I dug through my duffel bag, found some shorts and a cotton shirt that didn't smell too bad.

"What about him?"

I glanced at Burch. "Doesn't seem to be getting worse, and Gil's asking a guy to look at him."

Eddie took the sagging pack off and put it on the floor, patted Burch's cheek a few times. "Wake up."

"You wake him up, I'll knock him out. This is you and me time."

"Haven't I been through enough today? Let's talk tomorrow."

"Any second somebody could come through that door and fling a sword at me. If I die tonight, I'm gonna know why."

———

I got the water as hot as I could take, bumped it a notch hotter, and stood there until it felt good. I unfolded the photo and held it under the water. It was printed on regular paper, didn't take long to get heavy and start to come apart. I pulled it into pieces small enough to fall through the drain and ran the questions for Eddie: why the Yakuza wanted his money and blood, not necessarily in that order. Who the hell Burch was, how he was connected to all this, and the same for Vanessa.

If Eddie was still able to speak at that point, I'd ask him about Zombi and my fight contract. I wanted to ask about that first, but it seemed insensitive.

When I came out Eddie was still on the couch. He truly had nowhere else to go.

I searched for a place to hang my suit. There were a bunch of hooks and nails poking out of the wall outside the shower room for towels, shorts, jocks, wraps. Leaving it there would be like putting filet mignon in a Ziploc with dirty diapers. Gil had a narrow wardrobe in his office for his good gi and Angie's coat. I crossed to the door and it opened in my face.

Gil stood there with a man in a blue silk kimono with fish on it and cargo shorts, a leather pouch hanging off the belt. He was shorter than Gil, thin as a straw, and had gray hair jumping off his head. He leaned to his left to counterbalance the tall and wide tackle box in his right hand.

Gil said, "Woody, Denny's here. You guys have met."

"In this life?" Denny said.

I paused. "Pretty sure."

"Hm."

"Sorry if we woke you."

"With Saturn where it is? Who can sleep?"

"Right. Is that for me?" Gil plucked the suit out of my hand. "I'll hang this up; you're welcome. You kids have fun."

Denny stepped through the doorway, popped his hips, and wiggled his shoulders. "This space is heavy. You should burn some white sage in here. Do you have any white sage?"

I turned to Gil.

He grinned and closed the door.

"I'll look."

"Not right now. Stay with me. Is this our man?"

Eddie frowned over the back of the couch at Denny. "Who the fuck is this?"

"Wow. Fear lasers right into my mind. Breathe, my friend. Breathe." Denny walked around the end of the couch and saw Burch lying there. "Yes." He set the tackle box down and pulled one of Burch's socks off, tugged the big toe. "How long has he been like this?"

"An hour, maybe a little longer."

"So you don't like him?"

I shrugged. "He's all right."

"I'm asking why you didn't take him to a hospital."

"That's complicated."

"And it's a trick question." He sat on the table in front of the couch, brushed the machine gun aside, put a hand on Burch's chest, and looked up at the ceiling. "Hospitals are just big, shiny waiting rooms for the morgue. Gil said you can't go to the police or the western medical mafia. Whatever the reason, I say: duh. How did this happen?"

"He got shot in the neck with two poison darts."

"Yes." Denny rolled Burch's sleeve up to check his pulse or read his palm, then pointed at the bag of water on the floor. "What is that?"

"I had ice on his face," Eddie said.

"Why?"

"He was burning up. Still is."

Denny squinted at Burch. "Is this man British?"

Eddie's mouth hung open for a bit. "Yeah."

"Guys, come on. These are details I need to know. What kind of poison?"

"Don't know," I said. "I got some in my eyebrow, and it's making my face numb."

"Is that what happened to it?"

"Hey."

"I'm referring to your aura. It's clouded on that side of your face. I was going to ask later."

"We cleaned the dart that hit me, so it might not help. The ones we pulled out of him are out in the car somewhere."

"It's only a matter of life and death."

"Be right back."

I pushed through the steel door into the rear parking lot and stopped, listened. I heard a few cars rolling by on the street in front of the gym. Under that was the constant traffic of the roads farther out and the highway. The building had security lights mounted high on the corners that showed every detail of the facing sides of the vehicles and the Dumpsters and pushed long shadows away on the far sides. I waited for pieces of those shadows to break off and turn into men with swords and blowguns.

Nothing.

I opened the driver's door of the limo and killed the interior light so I wouldn't be onstage. I patted around the seat and floor, ready for the prick of a needle on my finger or the stab of a blade in my back. Finally my thumb brushed something fuzzy under the passenger seat. I pinched a few tufts of the dart and held it like a dead rat, closed the limo door, and made myself walk back to the gym, my ears twisted around for the slap of shoes on asphalt.

When I closed the gym door behind me, Denny looked me over. "Still that hot outside?"

I was drenched in sweat. The air-conditioning rolled over me, stretched everything tight. "Must be."

He winked. "Let's have a look."

I laid the dart on a white cloth folded across his palm.

He stared at the tip, smeared with dried blood and something else, then leaned in and sniffed it. "Sure."

"Sure what?" Eddie said.

Denny ignored him, opened the top of his tackle box, and took out some kind of leaf. He used it to wipe the tip of the dart and watched what happened to the leaf, then popped it into his mouth and chewed. "No. Really?"

Eddie ran a hand through his faux hawk, pulled in a breath, and glared at me.

"Okay," Denny said, still chewing. "Wow, this guy, all right." He swallowed and slapped his knees. "The good news is this isn't a lethal paste. Whoever made it will probably spend his next life as a dung beetle, but it's not meant to kill. Your face is numb?"

"It's wearing off but yeah."

"That's just the first phase so you're lucky. The next is unconsciousness, like we have now. Fever, nightmares, runny mucus. Here." Denny turned Burch's head to the side. Thin green liquid ran out of his nose onto the couch and pooled on the leather.

Eddie got off the couch.

"Yes," Denny said. "But the genius comes next, when he wakes up. Every nerve ending will be buzzing with high voltage. Stroke him with a feather, it'll feel like a baseball bat. Guys, this cocktail was designed for capture and torture."

Eddie was gray. "Can you help him?"

"Yes, which sounds like more good news, but it's not. He'll be a mess for a while. And by that I mean messy. Drainage."

"But he'll live."

Denny patted Burch's leg. "He might cross to the next plane a few times, but I'll keep him rooted here." He held the dart by the shaft and pointed it at me. "Now please take this to the nearest fireplace and—" He squinted at the red plume, then poked at it and pushed some of the tufts aside. "Slide that coaster to me, please."

I set one of the cork and wood discs next to him.

He eased the dart over and dropped it point-first into the cork, leaned above it, and stared. "Who shot these darts at you?"

"Some Japanese guys," I said.

"Yakuza?"

"Why do you ask that?" Eddie said.

Denny reached into his tackle box, came out with a thin paintbrush. He used the solid end to push tufts down and away from the center of the dart until there were just a few left standing. They were shiny and jet-black. "This is why. Are these men still after you?"

Eddie didn't say anything.

Denny turned to me.

"Yes."

He closed his eyes. "Please, please tell me you locked that door."

———

When Denny was done checking all the doors and peeking into closets, he sat on the table and felt the breath coming out of Burch's nose. His hand was shaking.

I said, "You gonna tell us why that dart means the boogeyman is around?"

"By the waves coming off him, I think your friend there already knows. His energy is jangling like a wind chime in a hurricane."

I looked at Eddie. He looked at the floor.

"He doesn't want to talk about it."

"I don't blame him," Denny said. "I need a cup of hot water. Hot, not warm."

"Start talking. I can hear you from the kitchen."

Denny glanced at Eddie. "Will that make you uncomfortable?"

"Fuck his comfort. He's lucky he isn't hanging upside down from the pull-up bar."

"I see. Actually, that might help him."

I headed for the kitchen. "The dart."

"Water first. In case you decide to leave."

——

I watched the microwave take ten minutes to count down from two.

The mug of water was steaming when I put it on the table next to Denny, who didn't even look at it. "Thank you."

Eddie was in the corner of the sectional staring at the dart growing out of the coaster. Burch's gun and chest rig were on the floor, and his shirt was open. His flesh was mottled with pink, and his ribs seemed to be collapsing. There was a small white bowl of smoldering herbs on the table near his head, giving off a smell somewhere between wet grass clippings and marijuana.

Denny removed a thin case from the tackle box, opened it, and slid out an acupuncture needle. He closed his eyes and stuck it just above Burch's collarbone. "Dojin-gumi."

Eddie sat back and pressed his palms against his eyes.

Denny looked at me. "That doesn't mean anything to you?"

"I thought you were chanting."

"Not that name. Ever."

"Wait. There was a guy, a Japanese guy, who said that to me."

"What was the context?" Denny said.

The tattooed man Burch shot into Eddie's pool. Something about Marcela's clan against the Dojin-gumi and how it would be a slaughter. I considered the best way to explain that. "He had a sword."

Denny put another needle into Burch's chest. "So a man with a sword mentions the Dojin-gumi to you, and you didn't think to look it up?"

"I figured it was another word for Yakuza."

Denny smiled. "That's like saying the *plague* is another word for *infection*. The Dojin-gumi is a syndicate within the Yakuza. They've been around since the nineteenth century."

"How do you know this?"

"Since you had one of their darts in your face, I'm wondering how you don't." He put a needle in Burch's cheek, sat back, and watched it. "Maybe you also didn't notice I'm wearing a kimono and practicing moxibustion." He pointed a needle at the bowl of herbs.

"I've been a little busy the past few days."

"Yes. Well, it's time to focus, my friend. When the Dojin-gumi joined the Yakuza, they were a family of executioners. And guess what? They still are."

I sank onto the couch near Burch's feet. "You're sure it's them."

"Yes, from the dart. The black plumes within the red is their signature."

"Makes it easy for the forensics team."

"See, you're thinking like a modern man. They are from another time, another code. They claim their kills with pride. I said before this toxin was made for capture and torture, and now that we know who made it, make no mistake: death will follow. It is their trade."

"Eddie."

He was still hiding behind his hands.

"Eddie, you knew all this?"

"Yes."

"Get up."

I closed the cage door behind us.

"I swear to God," Eddie said, "I'm so beat right now, you lay a finger on me I'll die. And I'll sue you from the grave."

"Calm down. This is a place of honesty, with yourself and the man across from you. If you lie in here, you only hurt yourself in the long run."

"Then what are those for?"

I tossed my sparring gloves onto the cage floor. "The short run."

Eddie moved as far away as he could, skirting around the gloves like they were a nest of cobras. He stopped directly across the cage from me and sat, looked down, and saw the old blood-stain beneath him. He scooted to the side until he was on relatively clean fabric.

I sat and leaned back against the fence. "What did you do?"

"Will you believe me if I tell you I don't even know for sure?"

I picked up one of the gloves.

"It's the truth. I mean, I know what I did, but I don't know exactly what happened after that. Me and Burch, we've been trying to figure that out. It's not like the Yakuza puts out a newsletter."

I pulled the glove on, opened and closed my fingers. The leather creaked. "You think they'd let me off the hook if I delivered you? I know for a fact you fit in a duffel bag."

"Okay, shit. About six months ago, a small MMA promotion out of Japan called Shinto started sniffing around for a Vegas debut. Little fish like that are always trying to jump into the big pond—my pond—and I always find a way to keep them out. I buy, I bankrupt, or I make sure the commission finds all the good reasons not to issue a license. So I do some digging, and Shinto is backed by the Yakuza. Well, no shit. They've kept all kinds of promotions and fighters in business over there, no big news. But coming over here, elbowing their way in without sitting down with me or anybody else, that's a problem. If I keep talking, will you take that glove off?"

"No. It's comfortable."

"I can smell it from here."

"That's a few years of blood and sweat. No tears, but you just got here."

"Christ." He took his suit coat off and looked for a healthy spot to set it. It stayed in his lap. "So I'm checking into ways to keep Shinto out of town. They won't sell, and the Yakuza coffers are basically bottomless. My guys at the commission know it's crooked, but they can't pin anything down. It's fucking grim. Now don't get me wrong—competition is good. Like Elite Combat and Lou, bless him. Keeps me sharp. But Shinto was a farce, just a bunch of thugs and sumo dropouts slapping each other around to amuse the Yakuza syndicates. I didn't want that garbage sharing the same air as my warriors, but it looked inevitable. Then I got a call from Burch."

"Did you know him already?"

"Shut up and I'll tell you."

I grabbed the other glove.

"Hey, I'm spilling it here," Eddie said. He watched me put the glove on. "All right, I'm sorry. Burch, who I'd never seen or heard of at that point, calls me and says he can help me keep Shinto and the Yakuza out of Vegas. Actually, I think he said, 'those tosser motherfuckers.' Tells me we have to meet face-to-face if I want to hear the details. Now, we get calls all the time from assholes saying they have dirt on so-and-so or they know how we can make millions doing whatever the fuck. But I was desperate. And Burch sounded serious. Professional. We set up a meet and he was legit.

Told me Vanessa comes from a billionaire family and she'd been kidnapped by the Yakuza. Her mother hired Burch to get her back; it led him to the syndicate running Shinto. The Dojin-gumi."

"Wait, kidnapped?"

"That's what the mother said. Her husband is Tim Brandenberg."

"Not the real estate guy from the billboards?"

"The same. And his teeth are that fucking white. Turns out he'd put Vanessa up in a game of *Oicho-Kabu* with the *oyabun* of the Dojin-gumi."

My face made him frown.

"It's a card game," he said. "This asshole Brandenberg was playing against the head of the syndicate, Omori, and bet his daughter."

"You're kidding."

"All caught up?"

I thought about the half-finished tattoo on Vanessa's back, the snake peeking out of the flowers. My stomach curdled, braced itself for worse.

"Jesus, you look like you're gonna puke. Wait'll you hear the details."

"Don't. I'll ask if I need them."

"Burch already got her back. What would you need them for?"

"Fuel. Tell me how this all helped you and Warrior."

"Burch didn't know where Vanessa was being kept, but he knew she was with Omori. He asked me to set up a meet with Omori, like a sting, so while I'm talking MMA deals Burch is kicking in doors looking for Vanessa. Said if he could snatch her, Omori would lose face and the Yakuza would take Shinto away from him."

"And it worked?"

"You see any billboards out there for Shinto?"

"Why is Vanessa still around?"

Eddie shrugged. "We tried to shoo her away, but she feels safe. And her father's moved on to gambling with Saudi princes. When she ends up on that table, she's gone for good."

"And Brandenberg's just letting this slide."

"Hell no. He and his wife want her back, but what're they gonna do? Hire somebody to rescue her from the last guy she hired? They're all ex-operators. Once they find out Burch is involved, they tell Brandenberg to fuck off. But he calls Burch all the time, even tries to get to me through the Warrior office, saying he has a great deal on some hotels going under. Bullshit. Goddamn, this wears me out." He pulled his knees up and rested his forehead on them.

I threw it all in a pile, shook it to see what settled at the bottom.

Yakuza, Dojin-gumi, Shinto, Warrior.

Omori, Brandenberg.

Burch, Vanessa, Eddie.

"So the Yakuza took Shinto away from Omori, but they wanted something for their trouble."

Eddie's head stayed down. "Smart guy."

"Then you stalled and promised, and when you couldn't do that anymore you gave them me against Burbank. The whole mess with Kendall."

"Yes."

"Which didn't work out so well. For them, anyway. And now they want to kill you. Us."

"No. When you beat Burbank, they said they'd get paid one way or another, and they need me alive for that. That's why they're sending Zombi."

"Ah, shit. That guy. So why are they trying to kill us?"

Eddie looked up. His eyes were flat, dead. Honest. "I don't

fucking know."

———

Eddie shuffled behind me into the kitchen. I got him a glass of water, and he held it with both hands, took small sips.

"We need to find out what happened," I said. "Why this went from cash to blood."

"I've called everybody I can think of. Same with Burch. Even the ones who know about the Shinto deal don't know why it turned into this." Eddie twirled a finger around. I found it a casual gesture for multiple murders and continuing attempts. Toss in a throat slash, something.

"What did the Yakuza say?"

"Uh, besides we're going to kill you? Not much."

"They said that?"

"Actions, brah. Somebody tries to choke and stab me, shoots poison torture darts at me, I get the message."

"But you haven't talked to them directly?"

"Hold on." He pulled his phone out. "Hello, Yakuza? Eddie. Hey, why you trying to kill me? I should go fuck myself? Okay, thanks." He gave me a look and tossed the phone onto the island, leaned over it. "Jesus, seventeen messages. I still got a company to run, you know."

I saw it in his face. A small animal dropped in the deep end, paddling like mad to find something to grab onto. Wearing out, starting to sink.

"Let's get some sleep."

He laughed but didn't smile. "Know what I used to say when somebody talked about sleep? 'I'll sleep when I'm dead.' Now that I've almost been killed a few times, sleep sounds pretty good."

———

I set up a cot for Eddie while he checked his messages, called Vanessa at the penthouse, made sure she was alive, and let her know we were generally likewise. He came out of the kitchen and tipped onto the cot before I could throw a pillow down.

"She okay?"

"Yeah." He spoke into the thin mattress. "Scared but safe. Told her I'd get her out of there tomorrow. Maybe she should stay. Who knows."

He was asleep by the time I'd walked to the couch to check on Burch and Denny. I heard Gil snoring in his office, probably crashed on the sofa in there. Denny sat crossed-legged on the coffee table with his eyes closed, chanting something barely above a whisper. If I had to guess, the language was monkish. He cracked an eye at me and kept chanting, tilted his head at Burch, and nodded. It seemed like a good sign, but everything about Burch denied that.

He was rolled onto his stomach with his face hanging off the edge of the couch so it could drain into a mop bucket. A thick cord of drool connected his bottom lip to the puddle at the bottom of the bucket, which was being filled by a steady stream of mucus from his nose. His back looked like a quivering slab of blue cheese. I thought about him rescuing Vanessa from whatever hell she'd been dragged into, and the only thing I hated worse than his ugly mug was the fact that I didn't want to smack it anymore.

Not much, anyway.

I flashed an okay sign at Denny with a question on my face.

He nodded and waved me toward the cots, the chant still going.

I dumped myself onto a cot and dreamt about Lou Gerrone standing next to a fountain shaped like Burch's head, bitching about the green water with a sword sticking out of his chest.

CHAPTER 13

G IL SAID, "YOU LOOK FAT."

I stopped jumping rope. "I've had a few days off."

He squinted at my torso and sipped from his giant coffee, his eyes hidden until he brought the cup down and was still squinting. "You're two forty at least."

"You let me finish this workout, I'll leave five pounds on the floor."

"I'm wondering if two weeks is enough time to replace it with muscle, bulk you up a bit so you're harder to toss around. Even that goosh you have now might help."

"You want me to put a shirt on?"

"Why?"

Eddie staggered out of the hallway at the rear of the gym, hair stuck to his forehead and clothes looking like used Kleenex.

Gil feigned terror.

Eddie frowned at us for standing up straight. "Can I have some of your coffee?"

"Help yourself."

Eddie shuffled out of sight.

"Coffee cannot help that man," Gil said. "I took a peek back there. Looks like Burch is still alive."

"Kinda. Denny left a note, said he had to get more supplies. And if Burch starts sleepwalking, we're supposed to strip him naked and lock him in the bathroom."

"You're shitting me."

"Read it yourself."

He glanced toward the front of the gym, the giant windows showing the parking lot and steady morning traffic. "So what should I expect today? Anybody stopping by to blow the place up? Drive-by? Darts and throwing stars when I go get the mail?"

"Man, I have no idea. There's no reason anybody should know where we are, but it's just a matter of time before they come looking for me here. It's weird, though. So far these guys haven't used guns. They're almost—I don't know—polite about killing."

"I don't think that's the right word."

"Honorable?"

"Better, but I'm not reassured. Is there anything we can do about it?"

"I talked to Eddie last night, found out everything he knows. I'm working on a way to get us all free and clear."

"How's that going?"

"So far I've decided to jump rope."

Gil drained the coffee. "Well, I'm gonna make a few calls, see about getting some judo guys and catch wrestlers in here to spar with you. We don't know dick about this Zombi guy yet, but we can start with the basics."

"Hey, about that. Eddie mentioned something about our game plans and the way I fight."

Gil got a look on his face like he was ready for the punch line.

"He said we're wasting time with strategies. All I do is go out there and fight like my life depends on it."

"He picked up on that, huh?"

"You agree with him?"

"Yeah, because it's true. But our strategies aren't a waste of time. They relax you before a fight, give you something to focus on."

I twirled the jump rope around on the mat, trying to make it into a noose.

"See," Gil said, "now you're thinking about the reasons behind it, the strings, which I didn't want. That fucker. Eddie isn't welcome to my coffee anymore."

"No, I think it'll help. My way gets wins but at what cost? I got more scar tissue than I do face."

"That is a problem. But don't shut it down; there's a balance somewhere between your instincts and whatever I come up with. We'll find it. Meantime, stick with your natural strategy of hitting the other guy so hard he forgets his."

The front door chimed and we both jumped.

I turned, expecting a horde, but it was just Roth and Terence rolling in for the morning workout.

Gil grinned. "You boys are just in time."

"For what?" Roth said. He saw me smiling too. "Aw, fuck me."

———

We did six-minute rounds with thirty seconds in between, Roth and Terence rotating in every other round to give me a fresh target. They're both smaller and faster than me, irritating when you're only going 75 percent to work on timing, slipping punches, and countering. They didn't like it when I hit them, so they worked extra hard to make sure I didn't.

Gil stood outside the cage with a notepad and mumbled about Zombi, every now and then nodding to himself and scribbling something down. "Guy is gonna attack or counter. We want him to attack. He counters, we fall into a trap."

Roth bobbed in and flicked a jab, sprang back, and worked his head around. I chased him with a looping hook that made me feel like a bear trying to catch salmon.

"Lucky we aren't grappling, son. I'd show you what's what." Roth had fought two weeks earlier and won via omoplata, a leg-over-the-shoulder submission he didn't know the name of and had pulled off by accident. Since then he hadn't shut up about his ground skills.

I slapped him with a leg kick and cuffed him with a straight right that knocked his headgear askew. He pawed it back and got the crazy Australian gleam, one eye pinched shut, and ran forward with fists pumping.

I covered, slipped and leaned and sidestepped. A few got through, just pats, then one landed with weight behind it. My neck cracked, and I felt some tension back there go. I sighed. "Thanks, man."

"Thanks?"

I dug a left hook into his ribs and he went sideways, a little scream popping out.

The ring timer buzzed.

"All right," Gil said, "gear off. Get some water. It's a beautiful day outside, great for getting tired."

Roth frowned.

"He's using it like a verb," I said. "Tired. The tire."

Dread fell across his face. "No. It's already a hundred fucking degrees out there."

"We can go in the shade," Gil said.

"We." Roth spat it out with his mouthpiece, stomped down the steps. He and Terence walked toward the back hall like they were headed for a onetime appearance on the gallows.

"It's like vegetables. The more you hate it, the better it is for you." Gil hooked my arm, walked with me to my water bottle. "I got a few catch wrestlers coming in today or tomorrow. And I found some bootleg DVDs with some of Zombi's fights. We gotta be careful, though—those fights could be fixed or just exhibitions."

"What about guys he's fought?"

"Dead ends. Anybody out of Japan, I say the name Zombi, I get a dial tone. Figure your friends with the darts told everybody to shut the hell up. I'll call around to the guys he went against in the Olympics if I have to, but that was judo. Might help. Might not. Shit. I'll call 'em."

I nodded and gulped water, tried not to think about how this was all supposed to keep me relaxed, focused on tactics instead of fighting. The recipe instead of the meal. It wasn't working so far; since waking up and having some time to think about it, I'd tried to picture how the man across from me would look, act, move. He was just a black shape, a ghost. I put faces and poses on him and they just fell off, made a nice soft pile for me to land on when he finally came to life.

"I will guarantee you this," Gil said. "No matter what Zombi brings into the cage, you'll be stronger than him and your gas tank will be bigger. That's the fight right there, anyway. Where it's won or lost. Mostly."

"Okay." I watched him nod to himself and realized he needed

the game plan as much as I did. It gave him control over something up until the cage closed and the bell rang. He was staring at a ghost too, but he couldn't give it a smack. At least I had that.

"See you out back. Five minutes."

"Hey, there might be guys out there watching. You know, the killers."

"Nice try. Anybody shows up to kill you, drop the tire on him." He muttered into the hallway and turned left toward his office.

Maybe it was the gym, this altar of suffering we all knelt before, or the ridiculous amount of testosterone ground into every surface of the place, but it seemed normal to joke about death threats.

Impending doom? Yeah, we did that workout yesterday.

But I was worried about Gil. He and I had arrived at this point from opposite directions—me dropping down from a couple days of adrenaline and paranoia, unfamiliar faces and places, Burch and his mouth. Gil had to ramp way up out of his comfort zone, personally and professionally, his sanctuary turned into our safe house.

If he latched onto strength and conditioning as his anchor, drilled it too hard, I'd limp into the fight with no reserves and a fried central nervous system. He knew better. Least he did when we knew who the hell we were fighting and could develop a strategy.

Fucking Eddie and his pep talk.

Summoned by the curse, Eddie stuck his head in. His hair looked a little better. "Burch is awake."

———

I followed Eddie into the Hole. He had his papers and laptops spread over the card table, covering a playground with manure. I glanced at the screens—multiple chat windows scrolling and blinking, stock charts, a database. Combined, it looked like the instruction manual for going cross-eyed and having a seizure.

Eddie dropped into a chair and pointed toward the couch, then leaned into a screen and attacked the keyboard.

Burch was sitting on the couch with a mug of steaming water held near his chin, the water trembling a bit. His eyes were bloodshot, sucked back into his head, his skin like damp wax. Denny sat on the table with his hands hovering above Burch's knees, whispering to him.

"Morning, Burch," I said. "You look like dog shit."

Denny frowned. "Please, no negativity."

"You look like living dog shit."

Denny closed his eyes, waved at the air around Burch's head.

"Will he be okay for a few minutes if you go get some tea or something?"

"He's stable," Denny said. "What are you going to do?"

"Just talk. Thanks for keeping him alive, really."

Denny nodded. "You can't touch him. Like we talked about, his nerves are wide open right now. One finger will feel like a gunshot."

"How come he can touch the mug?"

"*He's* touching *it*, not the other way around."

I suspected nonsense.

Denny looked at Burch. "Remember: breathe in, hold, release. Feel it in your genitalia." He picked up the drainage bucket and carried it to the kitchen, the weight or smell of it making him lean away.

I took his place on the table. "How you feeling?"

Burch sipped his hot water, those bloodshot eyes waiting for a question worth answering.

"I talked to Eddie last night. Found out about Vanessa, her father. The Dojin-gumi, all that. If you know why they want to kill us, you need to tell me."

Burch cleared his throat. Sounded like concrete sliding down a metal chute. "You think I'm keeping secrets after this?"

"So who do we need to talk to?"

"We tried that route. Silence."

"Told you," Eddie said without turning around.

Burch shuddered. A drop of water fell out of the mug and landed on his chest. He gasped and made a face like someone had jabbed him with a red-hot poker, glared down at the drop as it rolled between his ribs.

Without thinking I wiped it off.

Burch's eyes rolled back in his head and he went rigid, spittle frothing out between his teeth.

"Shit, sorry. Ah, breathe. Genitals."

Eddie peeled away from the laptops. "What'd you do?"

"Nothing. We're good here."

Burch spasmed and blood fell out of his nose. More water slopped onto his chest. He rocked forward, then stuttered back.

"Goddamn it. Denny."

Denny ran in with his kimono flapping behind him. "Did you touch him? I told you not to touch him."

"Water fell. I wiped it off and—"

"You need to get that cup away from him."

"Can I touch him?"

"Try not to. Try, try, try."

Burch had the mug clamped in both hands under his chin. I

hooked two fingers from one hand over the rim and got two from the other underneath, tried to pull it away. No good.

Water fell. Burch started to hiss.

"Well," Denny said and slapped Burch's stomach with both hands.

Eddie's gasp was loud enough to cover mine.

Blood sprayed out of Burch's nose and he went limp, passed out from the shock.

Denny caught the mug as it fell and handed it to me. "You can go now."

I carried the mug and a good helping of shame toward the kitchen.

Shaking his head, Eddie turned back to the screens.

I dumped the water in the sink and watched it fall down the drain. A black hole, plenty of room down there for me and Gil and the rest of the gym. Eddie, Vanessa, Burch. Or Burch's body, if I kept trying to help.

One by one or in a big thrashing clump, we'd get pulled down.

I left the kitchen, leaned on the table next to Eddie. "Any good news?"

He didn't look away from the screens. "Oh yeah. I just approved the concessions contract for the next Warrior event. Now we're gonna have hot dogs as well as hamburgers. Pretty fucking exciting when you're fighting for your life and guys are passing out from water drops, right?"

"Yeah, thrilling." I walked back into the kitchen, scratching my stomach to keep Eddie from seeing his phone in my hand.

I ducked into the gym, found my phone near the cage and scrolled through Eddie's call list. A bunch of names I didn't recognize with the same phone number and different extensions—had to be drones at Warrior's corporate office.

I checked times, got to Saturday night after the meeting with Lou, the one at the restaurant when he hadn't been dead. A few numbers around then with no names attached. I punched one into my phone, listened to it ring while I checked the hallway: clear.

"Thank you for calling Elite Combat Sports. If you know your party's extension—"

I killed it and tried the next number. I could hear someone banging around in the kitchen, willed whoever it was to stay there.

"Law Offices of Argo and Taylor, how may I help you?"

Who and who? "I'm trying to reach the management team for Zombi."

A pause, the woman on the other end either confused or stalling. "I'm sorry?"

"Zombi, he's a fighter. I need to talk to whoever's in charge of him."

Another delay. Then: "Who's calling, please?"

"Woody."

"Woody?"

"Aaron Wallace. I'm the guy he's fighting a week from Saturday."

"We don't handle attempts at promotion through this office. Please have your management—"

"Can you keep a secret? You tell whoever runs Zombi I'm on the phone, and I want to talk about taking a dive."

CHAPTER 14

ROTH AND TERENCE SQUATTED AGAINST THE FENCE IN the parking lot behind the gym under a ragged tree that drooped over from the property next door. The single oasis of shade was sliding toward their shoes and would soon be gone for the day.

"Question," Roth said.

I squinted in the heat blasting up from the asphalt, checked the lot and fence line for Japanese guys trying to look casual, twirling their blowguns. "Go ahead."

"Is that Banzai Eddie sitting at our card table?"

"Yes."

Eddie had his phone back, slipped under a pile of papers on my way past while he was cranked around watching Denny feed leaves to Burch.

Roth said, "Probably makes that his limousine."

"Correct."

He and Terence mumbled to each other, conspiring.

"Ask him," Roth said.

Terence looked at me. "Is he here to scout our gym? Us?"

"Act like he is. Maybe that's what it'll turn into."

Roth got a sour face. "The hell kind of answer is that? And who's the asshole in there chanting with Denny, taking up the whole couch?"

"Don't worry about it."

"Oh. Hear that, Terence? Woodrow says don't worry about it. It's just our careers, livelihoods, and such."

"I ain't worried."

"Nor I," Roth said. "Just curious about why the president of Warrior and some guy who looks half-dead are hanging out at our gym."

They'd earned the right to know everything that happened inside those walls. At the same time, they didn't deserve the trouble that came with this. "Eddie's putting a fight together for me, a Japanese guy named Zombi. Ever heard of him?"

"Awesome fucking name, but no, we haven't, have we, Terence?"

"Nope."

"And I doubt very much that Eddie makes house calls for the men he pays to fight. I imagine those men go to Eddie."

"You do, huh?" I nodded, squinted some more. "Let's get the tire out."

Roth gave a low whistle. "This must be very serious if you'd rather play with Gil's tire than talk about current affairs."

I couldn't look at them, sitting there hoping this could be their shot at catching Eddie's eye, needing it to be, when I was already in and rising and I'd just talked to a man about throwing it all away. "It is serious."

Roth was silent until Terence nudged him. "How can we help?"

Jesus, these guys. These brothers of mine. I blinked a few times.

"If you can, just act like everything's normal."

Gil opened the gym door and saw us huddling around the shade. "Assholes. Where's the tire? Where's the sled?"

"Fuck me. The sled too?" Roth stood and clapped me on the shoulder. "You wanted normal. Misery awaits."

———

I don't know how long the workout lasted.

It started with me and Terence taking turns flipping the four-hundred-pound tractor tire, then jumping on, off, while Roth dragged the steel sled with three hundred or so pounds of steel and concrete piled on across the parking lot and back.

When Roth touched the fence he sprinted over and tagged me, took my place on the tire while I ran to the sled and started pulling. When I got back I tagged Terence, both of us already forcing the jagged asphalt air in and out.

At the beginning I focused on how the tire carried over to take-down defense, stuffing the shot and lifting, opening my hips and popping the guy back. Then the jump—exploding into a counter, feeling the burn in my lungs and legs and fighting through it, dropping into my stance and sidestepping to keep my feet from getting crushed by the next flip.

The sled was a grind, weathering a clinch or driving the other guy back, constant tension, working, working.

After a while I stopped thinking and just worked.

Flip. Jump. Step.

Breathe.

Flip. Yell. Jump. Move.

Tag. Run. Pull.

Pull. Dig. If you stop you have to start all over again.

Sweat in my eyes, burning, boiling in the sun, and heat blasting up from the ground. Squeeze them hard enough to wring it out, spots skittering across the blacktop.

Chase them.

Touch. Sprint. Tag somebody, just a hand sticking out.

Flip. Jump. Scream.

I couldn't think about anything and it was beautiful.

———

I left the showers feeling good, comfortable. The kind of tired I was used to and liked, instead of Eddie's brand. He was still at the card table, his laptop screens pinging and flashing.

Burch was sleeping on the couch with his legs straight, arms tight against his sides, his chest making small dips and rises. No sign of blood or spasms. Denny wasn't around.

"You have to go get Vanessa," Eddie said.

"And take her where?"

"Here."

Someone in the showers—Roth by the violence of it—blew a snot rocket.

Eddie jumped. "Jesus."

The other nostril went, louder than the first.

"Vanessa knows she's coming here?"

"She just doesn't want to be alone."

"Anybody trying to get into the penthouse?"

"Not yet. But she says they're watching it."

"How does she know?"

"Just do it. And Dorian called. Your suits are ready."

I thought about the one hanging in Gil's office, my first: I won't forget you. What we had. "Do I need them?"

"They're paid for. You don't want them?"

"Just don't know when I'll wear them."

From the shower, Roth hawked something that landed with mass.

"Probably not around here."

Eddie leaned back and scrubbed his face. "I'm taking care of what I can online, but there are places I have to show my face. That means you do too."

I looked at Burch twitching on the couch. "How soon?"

"I'm pushing things out. I'll let you know."

"You guys are okay here?"

"What's okay anymore?"

No answer for that. I headed for the back door.

"Hey, Woody?" Eddie still had his eyes covered. "Don't bring them back with you."

———

I found Dorian's place with Eddie's shitty map drawn on the back of some spreadsheet.

Dorian opened the door, looked me up and down, shook his head at my sneakers, jeans, T-shirt. "This is offensive. Where's my baby?" He glanced over my shoulder at my truck idling in the covered parking area. "Never mind. Don't wear any of my suits while you're driving that around."

He pulled six garment bags off a rod inside the door, handed them to me like he was throwing fine china into a landfill.

"Thanks."

"How's Eddie doing? Looked a little ragged the other day."

"He's okay. Busy."

Dorian nodded. "None of my business what you're dealing with, but take care of him. Even if he is an asshole."

"If?"

I carried the suits to the truck, didn't want to fold them over in the passenger seat, and they'd have to move for Vanessa anyway. I laid them flat in the truck bed and gently set the spare tire on top to keep them from blowing away. Got in and started to pull around when I saw Dorian still watching from the doorway, peeking through his fingers at my defilement.

My window was already down, no AC in the truck. "Sorry."

He pushed me away with both hands.

I turned out of the lot and had to stop right away, a line of cars waiting at the light ahead. Almost five on a Monday, business traffic mashing into the tourists, clogging everything up.

Vanessa knew I was coming but not what time. I checked my own map, a much better sketch on a paper towel. When I got to the light I turned left, away from the Strip and the Golden Pantheon, toward the Law Offices of Argo and Taylor.

———

The building was tucked between a four-story parking ramp and a mirrored cube of office suites, those modern structures looking like they'd elbowed in on the Victorian mansion with its thick lawn and wraparound porch draped in ferns.

Problem was, this part of Vegas had been desert ten years ago. Somebody had spent a lot of new money to look like old money.

I was parked on a side street, pulled up just enough to see the place around the corner of a cafe. Through the ferns I could see couches and chairs arranged on the porch, cushions with a green and white floral pattern that looked like they hadn't touched human skin since the movers dropped them in place. The sign on one of the porch pillars was small: Argo and Taylor, Attorneys at Law.

What did I expect it to say?

Yakuza, Las Vegas Franchise

No Solicitors (Excluding Souls)

I stared at the windows, most of them as big as doors, draped to keep me and the Vegas sun out. I pictured Argo in there somewhere, just a blank face floating above a suit, talking on his phone.

"He wants to throw the fight with Zombi."

Omori, Brandenberg, or a messenger flunky saying, "In return for what?"

"He didn't say. Wants to meet with me. I told him I'd be in touch."

"Do it. See what he has."

"Yes, sir."

I stared at my phone, willing it to ring.

Waited an hour, carried my phone into the cafe, and got the biggest black coffee they had, strong enough to make my ears twitch.

No call. The sun started to disappear. People would worry soon, ask me where the hell I'd been. Couldn't tell them the truth and lying takes a lot of work. I rolled past the mansion, the tall windows leering down at me, small me in my small truck.

I'd offered to trade the one thing I had of tangible value. Set it on the table and wiped the smudges off. Everything I'd worked for.

Their response so far: We'll call.

Maybe.

———

The code scrawled next to Eddie's map got me into the private lot under the Golden Pantheon, no cars or people waiting inside or trying to dash under the steel door as it dropped behind me.

I called Vanessa from the phone next to the elevator, watched the lights in the panel drop. The doors slid apart, and the first thing I noticed was she probably hadn't slept since we'd left for the meeting with Lou. She sat on the pile of luggage in a wrinkled sundress, hair falling out of a ponytail, eyes and the skin around them looking stung.

The second thing was what she carried.

"Is that a bazooka?"

She glanced down at the long tube, capped at both ends, the dull black surface swallowing the fluorescent lights. "I don't know. Eddie told me to bring it."

"For him or Burch?"

"Can we just go?"

I took the luggage and the tube—much lighter than expected—and dropped them in the back of the truck around my suits. Carefully. Wanted to peek inside the tube, but if it was Burch's, the damn thing was probably booby-trapped. I left it alone and got the truck up near the steel door and stopped. "You think they're watching this place."

"Feels like it, yes. But I always feel that way."

I saw the small flowers blooming on the back of her neck. Hidden farther down, the snake, watching. Owning.

"Eddie told me what he and Burch did for you. Not everything, just how they got you out."

"Hm. They tell you how I got there in the first place?"

"Yes. I'm sorry about that."

Vanessa picked at the dress on her thigh. "At least they put the tattoo on my back, so sometimes I can forget about it. For a while. But my father—that's always there. Whether I think about it or not. You know?"

"Yeah. You know what helps?"

"What?"

"Punching people in the face."

She tried not to smile. "I'll have to try that someday."

I opened my door, got out. "You know how to drive, right?"

———

The steel door slid up and the truck rolled out into the service lot, idled toward the street access then cut right, stopped so the driver's side of the truck made a sharp angle with the eight-foot concrete wall.

I was staring at the passenger side from the service hallway of the Golden Pantheon Arena, one eye pressed to a crack in the same door I'd carried Eddie through in a duffel bag after the Burbank fight. One of my favorite door memories.

I had a light sweat going from the last five minutes—to the elevator, out on the casino floor, bullshitting the security guys who recognized me, finally finding this door and calling Vanessa. She sat out there in the truck with the tinted windows up, engine running.

Waiting.

I watched the street outside the lot and wondered what Burch would think about me talking her into the bait bucket. Looking in her eyes, the fear running deep in them like veins in granite, and telling her I would keep her safe. Then putting her out there on the hook to wriggle.

Hell, I felt like a scumbag. Burch would be right to want to shoot me.

"Can I help you?"

I turned and saw a stocky guy in a maroon blazer with a walkie-talkie in his hand. "I'm just waiting for a ride."

"Do you work here?"

"Kinda." I checked the street again. Cars rolled and people walked past the lot entrance. No sign of what I wanted.

The security guy snapped his fingers and pointed at me. "You're Woodshed."

"Busted."

"Hey, man, great fight. I lost two hundred on you, but still. You need a cab?" He held the walkie-talkie up. The ID badge on his chest said Nestor.

"Thanks but I'm good. Just don't want to hang around out there. Groupies."

"No shit?" He peeked through the crack, trying to glimpse all the naked women out there clamoring for me. He checked over his shoulder, leaned in. "You need a room, let me know."

"My guy."

"When's your next fight?"

I checked the street again. The hazard lights on my truck started flashing, Vanessa's cue that she'd had enough. "Not sure. Soon, I hope."

"No doubt. And my money's on you. Man, that kick."

I started to push the door open. "My shin hurt for a week

after. Can't imagine how his face felt. Looks like my ride's here. Nice meeting you."

"Same here. Go get 'em."

I opened the door and spotted the Japanese guy crossing the street toward the lot entrance. I let the door close to a sliver.

Nestor walked away, didn't look back.

I watched the Japanese guy check left, right, behind for traffic or witnesses. I couldn't tell where he'd come from or if he was alone. He wore black pants, a blue dress shirt, and black sunglasses. Carried a loosely folded map. The only difference between him and the guy Burch had shot into Eddie's pool was a lack of bullet holes.

Brothers, maybe twins.

Great.

He sped up across the sidewalk and cut the corner around the wall, stepped to the driver's window. I heard tapping. The truck rocked to the passenger side. I pictured Vanessa falling across the cab to get away from the guy's face. Maybe a face she knew.

I crouched and moved toward the tailgate as the guy opened the map and flapped it around. "Can you help me find something?"

I got to the tailgate, stayed low around to the driver's side.

"Anybody in there?" He cupped his right hand next to his face and peered inside. "Oh. Hello, Vanessa."

I stepped past the rear wheel and uncoiled out of the crouch, drove my right elbow into the spot where his jaw met his ear. His feet left the ground. His sunglasses snapped off his head, flew over my shoulder. He drifted through the air toward the wall with his toes pointed and I had a moment of satisfaction before he came back to life, planted a hand on the wall, and kicked me in the chest.

I turned to avoid the full impact, glanced at the truck window, and tried to show a reassuring face to Vanessa. We're fine out here, all part of the plan.

I moved in and he kicked me again, a solid shot with his heel to my pelvis.

Still fine, but that hurt like a motherfucker. I considered the black tube in the truck bed, wondered if he'd stand still long enough for me to extract whatever was inside so I could destroy him with it.

Nope.

He shot out of the corner with his right hand and tried to spear rigid fingers into my throat. I slapped his arm to the right and drove in, got my head next to his shoulder, and wrapped my right arm around his neck. Clasped hands behind him and squeezed like I wanted to pop his head off. That would have been fine, but I'd settle for cutting off the blood flow to his brain.

He went slack, started to twitch, then the truck door slammed into both of us and I had to drop him to keep from leaving most of my face on the concrete wall. I looked back at Vanessa sitting sideways on the driver's seat, her feet still in the air from kicking the door open.

"He has a knife," she said.

The twitching wasn't him passing out. He'd been digging the eight-inch dagger out of his belt so he could stick it in my kidney, watch me bleed out. I almost deserved it, going for submissions in a street fight. He was a bit loopy, staring at my knees while he slashed the blade around in front of his face. Probably practiced it every day. I stomped his knee against the pavement. While he was grimacing about that I kicked him in the side of the head, a tight little arc, not too much hip.

He sagged to the side and went out but didn't drop the knife. These guys and their blades.

I nodded at Vanessa. "Nice work. Thanks."

She looked like she might vomit.

"Come on out. Get some fresh air." And away from the truck and my suits, just in case. "Can you do what we talked about?"

"Yes." Vanessa got out and put a hand on the truck, took a few steps toward the tailgate.

"You all right?"

"I know him. Shuko."

"Wanna give him a couple smacks?"

"No."

"I'll hold him down."

She shook her head and retched.

"Let's go. He stays here."

"No. I'm okay." Vanessa let go of the truck, took another shaky step, then spread her sundress away from her legs, twisted side to side like she was enjoying the evening breeze.

It blocked the view while I closed the truck door and ground my heel around in the guy's forearm until his hand popped open. The blade fell out and I sent it skittering along the wall.

"Ready to move him."

She turned her head enough for me to see tears falling from her jawline. "Sure."

I took a moment to accept my Asshole of the Year award, then opened the truck door again, the guy's feet showing underneath, and grabbed his ankles so I could drag him through and somehow get him into the passenger footwell. There were half a dozen places around the city I could stash him until I got Burch off the couch. No way was I taking this guy to the gym.

I had a good grip when Nestor said, "Woody, you okay?"

I stood. "Yeah, why?"

He charged through the doorway to the service hall, carrying his walkie-talkie. "Cameras, bro. They saw some guy hassling you and your lady, but the truck is blocking them."

I moved to the tailgate next to Vanessa. "Yeah, this guy comes up, looked like he was gonna jack us."

"I'll get the police."

"No, I think we're okay. He's a little messed up."

Nestor leaned around me for a look. "Shit yeah, he is."

"Might need a hospital. Hey, I can drop him off."

"You?"

"I feel kinda bad."

"No, I gotta check him out, get the police and EMTs here. Protocol."

"He had a knife," Vanessa said.

I winced.

Nestor's eyes got big. "A weapon? Where is it?"

I nodded across the truck. "Think it ended up over there somewhere."

Nestor walked around the tailgate, his head pulled in like the knife was waiting to jump out and scare him.

I scuffed at the pavement, kicked a domino that knocked over the next one, raced along the thread back to Gil's gym, the guys, Burch and Eddie. The cops would follow it, bringing a slew of inconvenient questions with them.

Vanessa leaned against me. Maybe the other way around.

Nestor came back. "I don't see it right away, but I'll get some more guys out here. Fuck, where'd he go?"

I turned.

Nobody there.

———

We left Nestor in the service lot after he threw his hands up, said, "Sorry. Not much I can do without the perp here. And hey, don't sweat it—I won't tell Mr. Takanori about this."

I watched the mirrors for anybody following and the skyline for plumes of smoke, the gym besieged and burned while I was away. Nothing either way. Good news, if confusing.

Shit. I needed to talk to Burch.

Vanessa rode with her feet on the seat and her face on her knees. I wanted to pat her on the back but figured she might flinch sideways right through the window.

In just about any situation there are two phrases that let the other person know exactly where you stand.

One is: "Fuck you."

I tried the other: "I'm sorry."

She didn't say anything, but I heard the first phrase all the way back to the gym.

CHAPTER 15

BURCH WAS AWAKE, SITTING UP AND SHIVERING WITH A blanket wrapped around him. He dropped his scowl long enough to smile at Vanessa, then went right back to it.

She pursed her lips, wouldn't look at me. "Did you hit him again?"

"Not yet. Showers are in there, hot enough to burn just about anything off. Kitchen through that door if you're hungry. If you see an Australian named Roth, come get me."

She carried her bag into the showers. The water kicked on.

I laid my new suits on the foosball table, walked over to Eddie's mess, and showed him the black tube.

"Good, she remembered." He put his hands out: gimme gimme.

"Whatever this is, do we need to keep it away from children?"

He plucked the tube away from me. Popped one end off and pulled out a handful of what looked like plastic explosive. Then a thick roll of vinyl. He went to the grayish, scuffed wall behind the table and unrolled the shiny black banner with the Warrior logo all over it, used the handful of poster putty to secure it.

He sat down, checked the laptop's camera feed to make sure his backdrop took up the whole frame. Then he put on a headset with a microphone and hit a few laptop keys. "You guys see me okay? All right, let's go."

I leaned in to see who he was talking to and caught a glimpse of a beer logo before Eddie kicked me away without moving his torso.

I left him arguing with the screen, sat on the table in front of Burch. "You look better."

He huddled in the blanket and glared. "Than what? Convulsing into a coma because some idiot slopped hot water on me?"

"You remember that?"

"I remember all of it. Another awful beauty of the poison, according to Denny."

"Where is he?"

"Out helping crippled orphans walk and grow parents. Bloody miracle worker, that one. Saved my life."

"You up for talking tactics?"

"With you? Put me back in a coma."

"We ran into one of them."

He stopped shivering. "You and Vanessa?"

"Yeah. Shuko."

"Did anything happen to her?"

"She's fine. A little shaken up. She's tough."

"You have no idea."

I told him what happened, got all the way to Vanessa driving out of the garage alone before he swore and tried to choke me. I pushed his hand back under the blanket. "Stop that."

He shook while I told him the rest, but he wasn't cold anymore.

"Now listen. I thought they might have somebody watching

and he'd expose himself if the truck sat there long enough. I see where he is, then I go around and blindside him. I never thought he'd walk over and knock on the window."

"And what if ten of them had knocked on the window with an Escalade?"

"For one, broad daylight behind a Vegas casino. They have to know anything that overt brings cops pronto. I had a tussle with one guy and security was on top of it."

"Security," he said, like I'd called piss beer.

"Main reason I thought it would be one guy is because that's what they send. The first time, one man through the moonroof. I bet it was one guy who took that photo of us. Then your friend by the pool. Now this clown."

"A clown you let get away, pissed off with a headache. We'll see him again."

"They've sent a single man each time, except for once."

"The RV lot."

"Then it was how many? I counted six."

Burch nodded. "I slotted a few, saw more."

"So what was the difference? Night, secluded location they chose or got from Lou before they killed him. One way in and out. What else?"

"That's the recipe for an ambush. Don't need anything else."

"There's something."

He didn't disagree. We stared at each other, no answers flashing.

The door to Gil's office opened. He leaned through, spotted me. "Hey, you're back. Wanna wrassle?"

I thought it would be nice to get more training in, clear my head and let the missing pieces fall into place while I was looking away.

Then I met the Snarl brothers, standing in the cage in denim shorts and tank tops, thick hairy arms crossed over barrel chests, and the only thought I had was: survive.

"This is Vince," Gil said, pointing to the older one, I assumed. He was about five and a half feet tall, bald, built like a bricklayer. "And this is Robbie."

Robbie was exactly like Vince, only his name was Robbie.

I shook their hands, which were much too big, and tried to match the grips. They didn't seem to notice.

Gil said, "They run a catch wrestling school out of their garage, were nice enough to come down and help us out."

"Great. Thanks, guys. How'd you get that name?"

"Our pop's name was Vince," Vince said, with enough New Jersey in it I could smell the ocean. "How much you know about catch wrestling?"

"Pretend he knows nothing," Gil said. I appreciated the straight face.

"Well," Vince said, cuffing Robbie in the side of the head hard enough to tip him sideways, "couple centuries ago all these immigrants came over with their different fighting styles."

Robbie squared up to him. They stalked around the cage, trying to grab each other's hands and wrists.

"Tough guys hooked up with travelling shows, carnivals and whatnot, challenging any local to a match. Winner got cash and bragging rights."

Robbie dropped to a knee, shot in, and tried to grab Vince's foot. Vince sprawled, shoved him away with a forearm to the face.

Vince smiled. "So these guys, they're fighting hard-as-nails hillbillies. They gotta know all sorts of tricky shit. And they can't be taking all day with a match, you know? They gotta get it over with quick, save their energy, and take on the next comer, hopefully get his money too."

Vince got hold of Robbie's hands and they collapsed into a clinch, forearms draped over ducked heads, until Vince spun and dropped in a blur, reached between his feet, and clamped onto Robbie's left ankle, sat back and they both went down in a tangle. Vince curled around Robbie's foot, working for something. Robbie latched his arms around Vince's face, muffling him.

"Course, it was usually the nastiest guy in town who stepped up. His rep's on the line, and he'll be damned he's gonna let this carnie whup him. They'd eye gouge, fishhook, bite, you name it. But you'd never hear a catch wrestler complain. He'd just think: all right, motherfucker, if that's how you want it."

Vince scrambled to the side and got Robbie's left knee in his left armpit, both of them facing me and Gil. Robbie was still going for the choke until Vince switched, dug his left elbow under Robbie's shinbone. Something bad happened inside Robbie and he rocked backward, couldn't sit up anymore. He slapped Vince on the shoulder. Vince ended that torture and went for another type, cranking Robbie's ankle around while Robbie kicked him in the spine.

Vince said, "The end result was a brutal, efficient fighting style that maimed people. Broke bones, ripped tendons, ended lives. This here is the sport version, much nicer."

Robbie grabbed Vince's nose and yanked it sideways.

Through the plug, Vince said, "It's about control. Catching any hold you can and making your opponent as uncomfortable as possible, as quickly as possible."

I nudged Gil. "I'm uncomfortable from over here."

"This is spectacular."

Robbie finally got Vince's head around. He tucked it under his arm and grapevined his legs through Vince's, pulled an arm up, and stretched him until I heard skin creak. Vince tapped his brother on the face. Robbie let go and they both sat there, not even out of breath.

"Okay, you and Robbie. Let's see what you got."

Gil held up his little HD video camera. "You mind? For training."

"Hey, your gym."

I eyeballed Gil. "Training?"

He was giddy with professionalism. "Potty, if nothing else. I'm almost certain you're going to shit your pants."

I did not. It was worse.

———

Another new noise came out of me from somewhere, and I tapped. Again.

Robbie and I were starting from our knees, getting me used to the hand fighting and transitions to the clinch. No striking yet, which was good for both of us—for him because I couldn't punch him, for me because that would just make him mad.

Vince walked around us, reaching in to tug my elbow up or down, move a hip into place. "The terminology's different from MMA, jiu jitsu and all that, but you'll see a lot of the same stuff. Robbie, give him a Saturday Night Ride."

"Wait," I said.

Robbie hooked his hands behind my head and yanked, shot

his legs around my waist, and landed on his back.

"You call that full guard. Same shit."

I spoke into Robbie's sternum. "Feels a little different."

"That's catch wrestling," Vince said. "He's using his whole body against your whole body. He's controlling you from his back, which a lot of grapplers can do, but what's he gonna do next?"

I shifted my weight, got hold of his forearms, and pulled my head out. Felt for the tension, the spring he had coiled and ready to snap. Was he trying for a kimura? A sweep? "I have no idea."

"Damn right. You don't know what's in danger because everything is. He ain't going for a hold. Why should he? That's a waste of his energy, and you're gonna give him something soon enough."

"I don't want to."

"Too bad, friend. And this Zombi guy, Gil said he's got judo too?"

"Rumor has it."

"See, that's gonna give you more trouble. Keep going."

Robbie started to pull my head back down. I pushed his arms away, tried to pin them to his chest and break out of his guard.

Vince said, "This guy knows judo. He can come in all nice and gentle for a friendly hip toss or something, then bang, he's into lock flow. Next thing you know he's handing your arm back to you."

Robbie snaked his right arm around my left, pulled my hand underneath him, and popped my elbow straight. I tapped three times, once each for the simultaneous locks he put on my wrist, elbow, and shoulder.

"Jesus," Gil said. "Do that again."

———

Two hours of it, Vince narrating and stepping in every now and then to make sure I felt what he was talking about, then handing me back to Robbie so I could tap out.

Gil had given up on the video. Now he had his nose an inch away from my foot so he could note the exact angle Robbie was using to saw my Achilles tendon back and forth. "Yes," he said.

I tried to kick him in the face, but Robbie wouldn't let me. Then he let go and we scrambled, ended up on our knees hand fighting again. Robbie took a deep breath, shook his right arm out like it was giving him trouble, let it drop to his chest.

Don't mind if I do.

I pounced onto his right side and hooked my arm over his, wanting to gnaw it, got my hand through his armpit and against his chest, and started to pivot into a whizzer to drive his face into the canvas.

He reached around my back and grabbed my hip, shot his left hand across to my right knee and dropped to his left, rolled, tossed me over, and knelt on my ribs with my shoulder cranked.

Vince tsked. "He sugar footed ya, and you fell for it like a bum chasing a Lotto ticket down the street. You're fighting a catch wrestler. This is what you gotta remember: what you think he's doing, he ain't. What you think he's giving up, he ain't. What you think is safe, brother, it ain't."

"That's a lot to remember."

"Well, here's the good news for you. You been gettin' your ass kicked, but we've just been wrestling so far. You fight the Zombi guy, you get to strike too. Robbie, you wanna glove up?"

"Whatever."

Vince socked a fist into his palm. "Right. Couple more things I want you to see, then let's take a little break, come back, and do some sparring. Gil, that work for you?"

"Just be careful. We can't have anybody getting cut."

All three of them looked at the lumps over my eyes, the white lines slicing through my eyebrows, like they were storm clouds over a picnic.

Vince said, "Woody, so far you been getting caught, but not with anything too uncomfortable."

"Stop lying."

"Let's get you into something nasty, see if you can get out. Lay down."

I put my back on the canvas. Robbie knelt next to me and hooked his left arm behind my right knee, got it in the crook, and pulled it toward my face. He wrapped his right arm behind my head, clamped his hands together, and squeezed.

Vince squatted. "Ready? Break out."

I tried to straighten my leg; all that did was pull my head farther forward. My throat was pinched shut and my diaphragm had nowhere to go. My left arm was trapped under Robbie; my right flailed around and tried to connect with his head, show that I could punch my way out.

Nothing there.

I relaxed to see if he'd tire and give me a gap, but he compressed everything, leaned into it, and out of nowhere I was in that bathtub filling with water, no air or room to move, a steel mesh pressing into my face.

The room started to go dark from the freezer lid closing over me.

I panicked.

Kicked out to shatter the end of the tub and let the water spill, rolled right, then left to slosh it over the lip for another half inch of air. My hand went toward the ceiling to keep the lid from closing. I thrashed.

Robbie squeezed harder.

Black.

———

Through the water somebody said, "Woody, you okay?"

I blinked, saw Gil leaning above me. "What?"

"Lie still."

I tried to sit up. He held me down with one hand. The Snarl brothers were across the cage, talking low and not looking in my direction.

I smacked my lips and tasted copper. "What happened?"

"You went out. From the exertion, I think. Looked like your eyes were gonna pop out."

"Shit. Sorry."

"Don't apologize. But you know better. You don't blow your wad like that. Take yourself out of the fight. What's up?"

I heard water sucking into my ears and a freezer lid thumping shut. "That was a really tight hold."

"It was bad. You've been in worse."

I sat up. The trapped feeling was fading, losing weight, getting winched high above my head to come back down and smash me again. "I don't know then."

Gil rubbed my neck. "I think we're done for today."

"No. I'm not ending in that. On that."

He waited until I looked him in the eye. Whatever he saw made him say, "Just take it easy for a while."

I walked to Vince and Robbie on slow legs. "Sorry, guys."

"Please," Vince said, "I been put to sleep so many times this asshole here calls me NyQuil, put a buncha sheep on the garage ceiling so I can count 'em on my way out."

"Helluva grip," I told Robbie.

"Ambidextrous," he said, jerking both hands up and down.

I took my time down the steps. Got some water and checked my phone, something to banish the cold clamp of the tub, at least for now. No calls from Marcela. Just seeing her number would have cheered me up. Nothing from the Law Offices of Argo and Taylor. Maybe they were pissed about me slapping their soldier around, taking his sharp toy away from him. Looking back on that made me feel a little better for about a second.

I'd hoped putting the dive on the table, even without talking to anyone important yet, would get them to hold off on killing everybody. Trying to, anyway.

The guy in the service lot had dashed that, unless he'd gone rogue like his twin by the pool.

Best to leave the offer out there, just in case, but I wanted to call and pull the whole unofficial, nobody-seems-to-care-any-way deal.

Not because of pride or second thoughts.

The way things were looking, if Zombi had the skill set of the Snarl brothers plus Olympic-caliber judo, even a drizzle of striking, I wouldn't have to throw the fight.

I'd lose fair and square.

———

Punching Robbie in the face cheered me up some, not a lot. I could breathe and move. Small victories.

We started at half-speed, Vince telling me, "Just do your thing. We'll see how it looks."

Robbie had a small head and he moved it well, kept his hands up. I pawed at it, kept him honest with some slapping leg kicks.

"Careful with those," Vince said. "He catches one, you're on your ass."

Gil took notes. Robbie snapped some jabs at me.

"You got good slipping," Vince said, weaving around us like a referee. "Not a lot of wasted movement. I like it."

Robbie jabbed again and shot, went for my right leg. I sprawled and shoved him into the canvas, thought for a second about going down with him to see if my elbows fit in his ears, but stayed up and backed away.

Vince clapped. "Smart boy, you stay away from the ground with this guy. But, hey, he gets you tied up on the feet in a clinch, he can crank your arm just as easy."

"Let's see that," Gil said, then, "What?" when I glared at him.

Robbie and I got in a clinch, a bit awkward with the height difference, and I tried to spin him and get his back against the cage.

"See how solid his base is?" Vince said. "He's balanced; he ain't going nowhere."

I kneed Robbie in the ribs. He took the opportunity to hook my raised leg with his and pull it out while he drove forward, making me fall back against the cage. I was trying to get my feet under me when he wrapped his left arm over my right, pinned my forearm against the outside of his shoulder like I was hitchhiking. He clasped his hands in front of his chest, then cranked my elbow forward and my wrist back.

Something clunked in my shoulder and I tapped.

"Gotta watch out for that one," Vince said.

They showed me a couple dozen more I needed to watch out for, my shoulders, elbows, wrists, knees, ankles, and neck agreeing: let's not make a habit out of those, thanks.

Then we got into how to avoid them, what to do if I couldn't, how to padlock my joints so they wouldn't get shredded. I spent most of the time making sure I could still breathe and spread out. I didn't look at the claw-foot bathtubs and freezers gaping in the corners.

After ninety minutes of that, I sat against the fence and closed my eyes.

Gil hunkered down next to me. "You good?"

"Just a lot to process."

"This is the crash course, so don't think you gotta remember it all. Vince and Robbie are here every day until the fight. Got some guys they can bring, closer to your size. We'll figure it out."

All these friends working hard, sacrificing to get me ready for a fight I didn't think I could win, might even lose on purpose.

Hurt worse than anything all day.

———

I stuck my head in the back. Vanessa was curled up next to Burch, holding a mug near his face. They were watching something with a laugh track, the volume at a whisper. They glanced at me, mumbled to each other, and didn't look again.

Eddie was video chatting with somebody in front of his backdrop, telling them, "Sorry. I'm booked up until the fights. Whatever we need to handle, let's do it now." He moved his hand off camera, slid an empty glass toward me.

I gave it the sour face, snatched it off the table, and put some ice water in it. Set it back on the table so Eddie could lift it without looking, take a sip, and go on chatting.

I took a shower and tiptoed into the kitchen to find some food.

The rest of the week was more of the same.

Vanessa helped Burch recover while Eddie handled his business.

Nobody tried to murder us, unless you count the Snarl brothers bringing their manglers over to keep me miserable.

I called Marcela every day and talked about things that didn't matter to one of the only people who did. She knew I wasn't telling her everything but didn't push it, ended every call with, "I love you. Do you need me to come?"

"No," I lied.

Train. Eat. Sleep.

Argo and Taylor didn't call.

CHAPTER 16

SATURDAY AFTERNOON, ONE WEEK FROM THE ZOMBI fight, Eddie came into the kitchen dressed for battle. Full suit, blue silk tie that matched his molded faux hawk. "We're leaving in fifteen."

"This is a bad idea."

He shrugged. "People are already wondering what the fuck is going on with me. If I skip the press conference, shareholders are going to walk."

"It's on the billboards. The Yakuza has your itinerary today. They'll be waiting."

"That's why you'll be glued to my side."

"Great. I'll use my other arm to hold Burch up."

"He says he's fine."

"Looks like shit."

Another shrug. "He's British. Nice suit."

It was a new one, deep brown with a pale green shirt and a green tie with subtle squares. "I said thanks already."

"Brah, ease up. It's almost showtime. You feel it?"

"Yeah. Feels like crosshairs on my forehead."

"We get to see Zombi today, the myth, the legend."

"If he shows. Don't be surprised they keep him away, just blow the building up once we're inside."

"Hey, don't let that happen, okay?"

———

The conference room was packed with rows of folding chairs facing a long table, everything draped with Warrior logos. Burch had me and Eddie and Gil in a corner behind the backdrop, ringed by six burly security guys in maroon blazers until the thing started. He'd told the team leader, "This isn't a racial thing, but no Asians get close to Mr. Takanori."

"Chicks too?"

"Not even babies."

Burch was pale and sweating but seemed alert, almost relieved after the tense drive over, holding himself up with the steering wheel while he tried to look in every direction until we dropped into the private garage.

Now he had a line of men and women wearing expensive clothes and Warrior credentials waiting to talk to Eddie, each one getting a thorough pat-down from a blazer, then Burch, before they could step to Eddie and say, "Where the hell have you been?"

The hum from the other side of the backdrop got louder.

Gil slipped out of the group and leaned around the corner for a look at the dais, turned back, and waved me over. "Zombi's out there."

"Should I look?"

"Why not?"

"I don't want him to see me peeking out at him. Or shit, have somebody take a picture of it."

"Just look. Christ."

I stepped past the corner, hands in my pockets, scanned the faces in the seats. Some of them disappeared behind a camera. My suit soaked up flashes. I looked to my left at the dais, the empty chairs with water bottles and name cards in front of them, the podium and microphone in the middle, all the way to the other end at the guy who had to be Zombi, wearing a suit and sitting with a red-haired woman.

She was listening to a guy from Warrior, nodding, then leaning toward Zombi and talking. Interpreting. He said something to her, sipped his water, then turned and saw me.

All the noise fell away. The room closed into a tunnel, just me and him, rails running between our eyes. This man wanted to slap food out of my hand. Drag me out of my home and burn it down. Shame me, exile me from my tribe.

Back at ya, buddy.

But more than that, he and his crew wanted to invade, infest, conquer. Eddie had tried to build a wall; now it was time to sharpen the spears.

Zombi was bigger than I'd expected. Wide shoulders and a solid neck. Large, angular jaw with plenty of room for my fists. Lumps of putty for ears from all the grinding and a head of black stubble. His face was right there but it showed me nothing. The original stoics looked like slapsticks compared to this statue.

He stood up.

Turned his whole body toward me.

Bowed.

Cameras chattered, paused, waited.

I took my hands out of my pockets and bowed in return.

Just before he turned away he studied what he had to deal with. His mouth pulled to the side, a twitch, allowing one reaction to slip through the facade:

Unimpressed.

———

The press conference was a bunch of monotone noise interrupted by softball questions. The main event for next Saturday's card was between two lightweights for the belt at one hundred fifty-five pounds, training partners until the challenger decided he'd be a better champ and broke from the team.

Eddie spent most of his time at the podium with the champ sitting to his left, challenger to his right, the two of them sniping across the microphone until Eddie told them both to shut up and wait their turn.

I was at the opposite end of the table from Zombi, had to look past all the other fighters and Eddie to check on him. Burch prowled the perimeter of the room and drilled his bloodshot eyes at anybody reaching into a jacket. His skin looked gray and slippery under the fluorescents. People stepped out of his way even without knowing he had a machine gun strapped under his coat.

Zombi didn't seem to care about Burch, just another shape moving in front of him. He sat there with no expression, staring out into the crowd of fifty or so reporters and staffers.

I scanned the faces and clothes out there for his handlers, waited for someone to give me the slicing finger across the throat or a cocked finger and thumb.

Nothing.

The clothes didn't help a bit. Everybody dresses like a gangster in Vegas.

Eddie finally got to the bottom of the card, me and Zombi, and called Zombi to the microphone. I had to admire Eddie—no sign that this fighter was the embodiment of his ruin.

Zombi sent his interpreter to the podium so she could spout some canned shit about being honored to fight for Warrior and American fans, he'd do his best, let's all be friends. Didn't take any questions or say anything about box freezers or snake tattoos on sex slaves. Points for PR savvy.

When Eddie called me up I said some canned shit about being honored to fight for Warrior, ready to prove the Burbank fight was just the beginning. Any questions?

"Where'd you get that suit?"

I sat down and Eddie wrapped up, made sure the two light-weights exited in opposite directions. I looked around for Gil and saw a fiftyish guy in a suit making his way toward me. No press credentials or anything else to identify him. He looked soft, gold-rimmed glasses and a little roll of skin spilling over his collar and tie.

"Mr. Wallace."

"Yeah."

He leaned in too close, put his hand out.

I waited.

He seemed amused, gave a slow blink and nod to reassure me. "You want to shake my hand."

"Not so far."

He let the hand drop, apparently my loss. "I'm Howard Argo. You and I need to talk."

———

Argo seemed to know where he was going. I followed him down the hall into a conference room with the tables pushed against a wall, chairs spread out, and one run of lights making the space look bigger than it was.

He moved some chairs around, dropped into one, and put his elbow on the back of another. "Have a seat."

I sat across from him. He looked confused by my suit.

"So what's all this about? The phone calls."

"Throwing the fight."

Argo leaned in, whispered, "I didn't want to be the first to say it."

"I don't want to say it at all. But here we are."

"I have to ask: Why?"

"Why?"

He raised his eyebrows.

I sensed lawyering. Leaned in, whispered, "I didn't want to be the first one to say it, but you're trying to kill us."

"Interesting."

"Try my side."

"You're serious right now. You're talking literally kill. Not figurative, like you guys do."

"Yes."

"And you're under the impression my clients are somehow involved."

"The Yakuza. Involved to the extent of being entirely responsible."

"First," Argo said, "let's not call names. It's petty. I represent legitimate businessmen. What their associates do is none of my concern."

"You should be concerned right now."

"Name-calling and threats. I must say, on top of offering to throw your fight, we're disappointed in you."

"My manners slip when swords come out."

"Swords?"

"Short and long."

"Interesting."

"I'm tired of being interesting to you. Let's get this done."

"We just want a fair fight. My clients would like to create a partnership with Mr. Takanori, and backing a successful, clean fighter is their best course."

"Bullshit."

"I'm afraid not."

"Then why are they trying to kill us?"

"See, that's what's interesting. You think you're up against the entire organization."

"Yakuza."

"If that were the case, the opportunity for us to talk would have long since passed."

"Maybe."

"Jesus, you're like a bumpkin in the mountains, stockpiling shotguns in case the government comes to take your rifles. Hear that? No. It's a drone. Boom. Do you see now? It isn't us."

"What the hell are you saying?"

Argo spread his hands. "It isn't us."

"Then who is it?"

He sat back and studied me for a while. "You might want to bring Mr. Takanori in for this part."

———

I pried Eddie away from his staff, walked him and Burch into the room with Argo, who stood up and put his hand out.

Eddie shoved his hands in his pockets. "Burch, be ready to kill this motherfucker."

"Done."

"Please, let's be grown-ups." Argo glanced at Burch. "Besides, you look like you'd have a hard time swatting a mosquito."

"Lucky me I'd just have to squish a leech."

"You gentlemen have a nice day."

I put Argo in his chair. His sternum was very soft.

"That's assault," he wheezed.

"Damn. I was going for battery. Start talking."

He straightened up, blinked a few times. "You guys. So tough, huh? I'd laugh, but I have a cracked rib."

"Jesus," Eddie said. "As much as I'm enjoying this, all the times I wanted to smack you across the table, can you pull it together?" He dragged a chair over and we both sat facing Argo.

Burch stood behind him, which made Argo turn sideways in his seat.

"Don't think you're impressing me here. I've walked away from desert negotiations between Italian families. So, you know."

"Who's trying to kill me?" Eddie said.

Argo winced. "As I was telling Mr. Wallace here, my clients want a partnership with you. You know that. Why would they want you dead?" He winked at me. "Now, he and I have been discussing one possible scenario, but we think it's moot at this point. Don't we?"

"What scenario?" Eddie said.

Argo, controlling the room again, looked at me with a smile I wanted to kick across the room.

I said, "Throwing the fight."

"*What?*"

"I let Zombi win in exchange for the Yakuza letting us all live."

Eddie covered his ears. "No, I can't hear any more. Even a whisper of a fix gets out, we're done."

"I'm curious as to what they'd do, though," Argo said, "if I brought that offer to them. It might have worked. But you all have to know how ridiculous it is, thinking you've been up against the entire organization. I mean, really? To think you'd survive this long?"

"Move on," Burch said.

"No, I want to make sure no one in this room is delusional. It's a requirement of mine. Who have you been fighting?" He checked each one of us.

"Omori and the Dojin-gumi," I said.

"Right. One family. That's it."

Eddie said, "It still makes no sense."

"Which part?"

"The Yakuza doesn't want me dead, but the Dojin-gumi is a Yakuza family."

"Is it?"

Eddie looked at Burch, me. Blank faces all around. "What does that mean?"

"I should be charging you for this. This kind of disclosure, what's it worth?"

"Walking without a limp seems fair," I said.

Burch nodded.

Argo checked his watch. "Okay. Let Uncle Howie enlighten you for a bit at the request of my clients. They want the Zombi fight to happen. They want you all focused and ready. Otherwise, I'd wish you good luck and let you go back to hiding with your used-up whore in that cave you call a gym."

Burch's jaw clenched. I heard his knuckles crunch.

Argo said, "The Dojin-gumi was expelled from the organization after Mr. Wallace's fight with Junior Burbank. But you can't take all the credit, son. It was that plus Omori letting the Brandenberg girl get snatched by Eddie and Mr. Burch here. Guy lost so much face he'd need Mount Rushmore to get him back to zero. So the family was out. Omori went old school, committed *seppuku*. Slashed his own bowels out and had his eldest son finish the job, took his head off with one swipe."

"Goddamn," Eddie said.

"The sons swore a blood oath to kill all of you. That's who you're up against."

"How many sons?" Burch said.

"Three. Three whole men, and you thought you were against an army."

I said, "That's wrong. The night they killed Lou there were six. At least."

"First, I have no knowledge of anyone being murdered. Let's get that on the record. Second, you must be mistaken. This family is born and bred to kill people, so I imagine they can be over-whelming, confuse you."

"I wasn't confused," Burch said. "Woody's right. I put at least two down when we found Lou, on top of the two brothers already cold and stiff. Your numbers are wrong."

Argo shrugged.

"Mercenaries," Burch said.

"Not possible," said Argo. "This family does not work with outsiders. They're insular to a fault, one of the reasons there are only three of 'em left. But listen, I haven't even told you the best part yet."

Eddie said, "Is it something about the Yakuza killing this shitty family? That would be pretty good."

"Afraid not."

"They're allowing this clan to come after me?"

Argo looked at the ceiling. "How to put this. I spoke before about how silly you were to think the entire organization is trying to kill you yet failed. Ridiculous. Well, they are trying to kill the Dojin-gumi. And they cannot."

"Shit," Eddie said.

"Indeed. The sons are taunting them, letting them know, hey, this is what we're going to do and you can't stop us. It's been frustrating."

"Son," Burch said.

"Sorry?"

"You said sons. If there were three, they're down to one."

"Again, I have no knowledge of any deaths, but that's the part I was getting to. Now, I only get the information my clients want to share, so I don't know the details, but apparently the eldest son had a confrontation with Mr. Wallace outside the casino."

Shuko, the window knocker. "He and I had a talk."

"Whatever you talked about, he's unhappy. According to my clients, he feels you've all had your chance to die honorable deaths. He's going to wait, make sure everyone sees you suffer. This whole week you've been in your little bunker, and no one has been trying to kill you. Great, huh?"

We didn't say anything.

Argo said, "I think Mr. Wallace can answer this best. Is it better to think you're going to be killed every day? Or to know when it's coming, like a scheduled fight? It's probably different for your death, though. I mean, how do you train to die?"

"He's coming for us during the Zombi fight," I said.

Argo winked. "For some reason he seems fixated on putting you on ice—no, in a freezer. What's that about? Is that some kind of fighting term?"

I heard the lid thump shut and felt my arms and legs clamped against me. Wondered how quickly a person can go insane.

Argo looked at Eddie. "Last chance. My clients are going to get a piece of Warrior whether you're alive to see it or not. Let's work something out. Maybe they can try a little harder to stop this crazy bastard."

Eddie didn't move, didn't talk.

Argo stood. "Enjoy the next week, gentlemen. Look for me at the fights. I'll be in the front row, wearing the blood-proof poncho."

CHAPTER 17

EDDIE TOOK HIS TIME PACKING EVERYTHING—THE laptops, papers, Warrior backdrop rolled up and back in the tube. Burch was slumped on the couch, exhausted.

I stood in the doorway to the kitchen and told myself I didn't need to lean against the frame to feel something solid.

Vanessa slid past me with a warm cloth for Burch. When she knelt next to him, he caught her hand. "Omori's dead."

She froze, water dripping on the couch. "How?"

"Offed himself, too much shame. Coward."

She stared at the blank wall, saw something there none of us could imagine. Her knuckles turned white around the steaming cloth. Water ran onto Burch's shoulder. He didn't seem to notice, kept his eyes on Vanessa.

"Good." She touched the cloth to Burch's forehead.

Eddie kept his voice soft, told her, "They're cut off from the Yakuza. It's just the Dojin-gumi coming for us."

"Just. Where are we going?"

"Home. Too much to do and I'm going nuts in here."

Burch said, "We can't base any actions on what Argo says. He could be working for the Dojin-gumi."

"They all know we're here," Eddie said, "so what's it matter?"

"This could be a ploy to get you out for a public killing."

Vanessa put her hand over her mouth.

Eddie said, "Burch, you're still in fantasy land. Anytime he wants, this Shuko guy can come through the door and drag me into the street, chop my head off."

"That's incorrect," Burch said.

"Vanessa, what's the deal on him?"

Burch sat up. "What's the matter with you? Don't ask her to talk about it."

"He's a demon," Vanessa said, her voice dead. She eased Burch back down. "A demon."

Eddie leaned close. "Woody, you saw him. What do you think?"

"I think I won't get the chance to blindside him again. I should have stomped him out for good, ended this."

"You didn't know he was the last one."

"Is he? Burch, you see Argo's face when I mentioned Lou getting killed?"

"Enough. We'll talk about this later."

"It's okay," Vanessa said. "This needs to end, the sooner the better."

Burch let out a breath. "I didn't see his face. I was behind him."

"Guy had no idea what I was talking about."

"Well, he has no knowledge of any deaths. He said so. Twice."

"Yeah, bullshit. That was deniability for the two sons you put away. We start talking about the swarm of guys who killed Lou and ambushed us, he gets all fussy about how that's impossible, not with this family."

"The blow darts were Dojin-gumi."

Eddie looked between us. "So Argo's lying or he's ignorant. Doesn't matter. But your faces tell me there's something else."

I said, "This last son. Shuko. He's getting help from somebody."

———

The limo was packed, idling in the front lot. I stood with Gil and Eddie at the front of the gym, where I'd first seen Burch come through the door. Give me that moment again, I'd lay bricks, dig a moat, light a ring of fire. By the look on Gil's face, he'd buy the matches.

Eddie saw the look, put his hand out anyway. "Sorry we took up your back room and stepped on your dick all week. But business had to get done, you know?"

"Any of that business involve our contract?"

"Ah, that. I'm afraid all negotiations are on hold pending the outcome of this weekend."

"The outcome," I said. "Meaning whether you're alive or not?"

"We," Eddie said.

"You should wear snakeskin suits. Save everybody the hassle of guessing."

He shrugged. "Game face. Your full contract isn't signed yet, but we're locked in for the Zombi fight. It's the one thing I'm sure of right now—you will be fighting him on Saturday. So please fucking reassure me: You got this?"

Fighting a man I didn't know how to beat and waiting for a man no one could kill.

Zombi, the tip of the Yakuza spear, ready to drive into the heart of Warrior and bleed it dry.

Shuko, maybe crawling out from under the cage to hamstring me, cut me down before anyone can stop him.

Lying to Eddie was easy. "I got this."

"We," Gil said.

I almost believed him.

———

Train. Eat. Sleep.

Try to sleep, anyway.

Sunday night I dreamt I was fighting Zombi in Tezo's pit, Tezo standing above us with chunks of his swollen head shot away.

"Well?" he said. Blood and cold water poured out of his skull into the pit.

Shuko was hiding in the filth along one wall, half-buried in a puddle of piss and hair. He stayed very still, just his eyes whirling. I didn't look directly at him—that was his cue to emerge.

I stared across the pit at Zombi, standing there in his press conference suit with a gold medal hanging from a snake around his neck.

He bowed.

I bowed, saw I was standing in the claw-foot bathtub, half-full of stagnant water and trash.

"My poor feet."

I straightened up so I wouldn't have to see them down in there. In my peripheral vision I watched Shuko slip something out of the puddle and slide it onto his face. It was Gil's face, the edges straight and raw from Shuko's blade. It was much thicker than I'd expected, maybe just swollen from the puddle.

"You can't get me," I said.

Gil laughed. "What do you call this?"

———

Monday morning I slopped into the cage with Gil and the Snarl brothers and one of the guys they'd been bringing in, a wiry pole of beef jerky named Ronald.

"Technique and conditioning the rest of the week," Gil said. "We can't risk you getting cut."

This was good. Get lost in the movements, the kind of discomfort I could get comfortable in.

Vince said, "No problem. We can dig into the real shitty stuff, the dirt, case this Zombi cat pulls any of it."

I froze, mouthguard half in. "What the hell have we been doing so far?"

"Huh?"

"Don't worry about him," Gil said. "Show me some nasty."

———

Ninety percent of what they did to me would get Zombi disqualified in an MMA fight. The other ten was legal but might make the ref vomit.

I almost hoped Zombi would try some of it. I'd never wanted to win that way, but considering I'd been ready to toss the fight a few days earlier, I wasn't feeling picky.

After a break Gil set up a circuit for me and the catch wrestlers, a bastard workout he called Dante's Inferno. He put a barbell loaded with three hundred fifteen pounds in the middle of the mats and had us spread out and jog around the edges.

"Lunges," he called.

We lunged, one knee dropping to kiss the mats, hands up and chins down. Drive up; open the hips.

Gil said, "Dead lifts, Woody, eight reps. Everybody else, burpees."

I sprinted to the barbell, gripped it shoulder-width, and set my feet. Ripped it off the floor and let it hang from my arms like they were cables. Set it down and pulled again, again.

Vince and Robbie and Ronald stopped circling and banged out burpees, dropping to touch their chests and thighs to the mats, then springing to their feet, jumping and clapping overhead.

"Eight," I yelled.

"Shadowbox backward."

We circled again, shuffling backward. Slipping, bobbing, weaving, jab-cross-hook. I saw Zombi stalking after me, stepping into the punches. I felt the impact, watched him react to it.

Hard as I tried, I couldn't get him to blink.

Gil said, "Vince, dead lifts, eight reps. Rest of you, tuck jumps."

Vince took a few deep breaths over the bar, then got to work. We stood in place and jumped as high as we could, pulled our knees to our chests at the top of the jump. Vince put the bar down after four reps and shook his arms out. Around the mats the jumps were getting slower, turning into hops.

"Eight," Vince said.

"Push-ups."

I didn't bother counting.

"Ronald, dead lifts, eight reps. Peanut gallery, bear crawl."

We circled on all fours, hands and feet, scampering after the heels ahead and fighting for air, cores locked down for stability.

"Eight." Ronald's face was an alarming shade of red. He tilted his way into the circle and tried to join the bear crawl, ended up with some kind of camel/crab hybrid.

Gil called Robbie to the bar while the rest of us planked out, rigid on toes and elbows, dropping sweat and curses onto the mats.

"Eight," Robbie said.

"Shake it out." Gil pulled weight off the bar, got it to two twenty-five. After one minute of rest, he said, "Shadowbox forward. Go."

Zombi retreated from me, shot for my legs. I kneed him in the face and rocked him with an uppercut. He just stared back.

"Woody, hang cleans, eight reps."

I pulled the barbell up and let it hang, the weight feeling much lighter compared to the dead lifts. That didn't last long. I bent at the waist, let the bar drop to mid-thigh, then shot my hips forward. Shrugged the barbell up and pulled, got it chest-high and threw my elbows underneath, racked the bar across the front of my shoulders.

Reversed the process, yanked it up again. My forearms screamed.

"Eight." I couldn't open my grip to let the bar go. Had to put a foot on it and shove myself away.

Everyone ran through the hang cleans while the circle suffered. Squat jumps, shrimping, frog hops. If a guy failed on a barbell rep Gil sent him back to the circle—for safety, not as punishment—but nobody wanted it to come up.

Another minute break, then Gil stripped more weight off and called for power snatches, taking the barbell from floor to overhead in one explosive movement. The hundred thirty-five pounds felt like a truck axle.

We spiraled down the circles of hell. Split squat jumps,

backward sprawls, more burpees.

"Eight," Robbie said. It sounded thick, pushed through a gag reflex.

Guys dropped to the floor like strings had been cut. I closed my eyes, rocked side to side on my back, and fought for air, the burn in my lungs scoffing at the lactic acid in my legs.

As I cooled off I knew another layer of armor had been forged, body and mind.

Another level of pain I could go to, settle in, and survive.

No, thrive.

I felt great.

Opened my eyes and saw Zombi standing over me, no expression or damage from the shadow fighting. Shuko's shadow stood next to him, leaning on a sword.

"You done with him?" Shuko said.

Zombi nodded, bowed, and turned away.

———

The week slipped by, hours broken down to either work or rest. During work I felt like a beast; at rest I felt it was all just preparing me for the slaughter.

Burch checked in each night, his voice stronger but still hollowed out. The calls were all the same: "Everybody still alive?"

"Yes," I told him.

"Same here. Any unfriendlies hanging about?"

"No."

"Right. Cheers."

Click.

Eddie didn't send an interview crew like he had for the

Burbank fight. He wanted Zombi—and possibly me—to come and go as quietly as possible. I didn't know if we'd even be on pay-per-view, maybe slipped in before the prelims when the stands were still being swept.

Shuko was either keeping his word about Saturday or lulling us. Three times I made it all the way to my truck, keys in the ignition, ready to drive to Argo's office and find a ceiling fan to put his face in until he told me where to find Shuko. At least find out if Argo was lying about not working with the Dojin-gumi. Each time I gripped the steering wheel, thinking, *Then what?*

My house was already full of trouble. No need to go begging for more. Eddie was right; the only thing I knew for sure was who I was fighting Saturday night.

Thursday I pulled Vince aside. "If you were me, how would you go at Zombi?"

He crossed his arms and tugged his lower lip. "In sparring, what's the hardest you've hit me?"

"Fifty percent, maybe less."

"Okay, fuck off. I can't chew anything tougher than deli meat."

"Sorry."

"Your natural style is all straight lines. Right at him, right through him. Problem with that is the more you throw at him, the more opportunities he has to catch something. Combine it with his judo, your straight lines got a good chance of getting tossed and bent. That's option one."

"I gotta tell you, option one sounds pretty terrible."

He put a hand up. "I apologize. I should have said the worst one first. Two, you take his style and go beyond it. Not just imitation, I'm talking mimicry. You become him and therefore know what he'll do next, beat him to it."

"I only see one flaw."

"Your catch wrestling sucks. There's no way you can pull it off."

"So it's not really an option."

"Well, nobody wants to feel cornered. I figured you'd take option one anyway, no matter what two was."

Just like Eddie and Gil said. When my strategy is survival, the other guy has to come along or die.

"Cheer up," Vince said. "You're so worried about all the things he might catch you're forgetting the good news. If you catch him—once—with one of those wrecking balls you got hanging off your arms, he's spending a few days in the hospital. Guaranteed."

CHAPTER 18

THE WEIGH-INS ON FRIDAY STARTED EARLY WITH A FAN expo at the Golden Pantheon Arena, sponsor tables manned by Warrior fighters and lines of fans hopping up and down to get a photo.

"Choke me."

"Can you punch me in the face?"

"Like you did to Corman, the knee to the ear."

Everybody smiling, nobody's teeth covered in blood. It was pretty nice. I stood in a corner with Gil and felt mildly racist for putting hard eyes on all the Japanese guys walking around.

"You're scaring people," Gil said.

I rolled my shoulders out and stopped squinting. Put on a nice face and looked over the crowd in time to see a man cutting a path toward us. Baseball cap, slight build, head down. I spotted the lower half of his face. Asian for sure, possibly Japanese.

I handed my bottle of water to Gil.

The baseball cap was twenty feet away.

Ten.

It tilted up.

Thirteen-year-old kid, maybe fifteen. He pushed an event poster and a Sharpie into my hands. To occupy them?

"You charge, bro?" SoCal accent.

I checked him over.

He checked me back, glanced at Gil. "Uh, for your autograph?"

It didn't feel like a trap. "No."

"Not yet," Gil said.

I hovered the Sharpie over a blank spot on the poster while I thought of something to write.

"Just your name, man. I don't need any affirmations."

I signed it.

"Thanks. Wait, what's this say?"

"Aaron Wallace."

He considered it. "Can you—?"

I slashed *Woodshed* over my name, spun the poster back to him.

When he was gone Gil said, "You gotta relax. That kid thought you were gonna elbow him in the neck."

"Nah."

"Have we been here long enough?"

"Lady from Warrior said two hours. What's it been?"

Gil checked his watch. "Twenty minutes."

"Jesus. Let's get out of here."

We hugged the wall to an exit, which dumped us into the part of the arena they had curtained off for the weigh-ins. Security had the doors roped but recognized me or the fighter credentials around my neck. The production crew was running around tilting lights and checking sound.

Davie Benton spotted us and headed over. He did color commentary for Warrior broadcasts and hosted the weigh-ins. His red hair looked a foot high and his muttonchops were dyed black, possibly to mourn themselves.

"Gil, Woody, welcome back. What gives, man? You pull the biggest upset of the year, and Eddie has you fighting some no-name at the bottom of the card?"

"Thank you," Gil said.

"Right on. Just seems like bad business. You got some heat going. He should be jumping you in line for a title shot."

"Quite a few guys been working their way up to that. I don't want to cut anybody out."

"My man, rather knock 'em out, right? People are talking though. A fight between you and the Coroner? Don't blink."

The heavyweight champ was a slab of granite from Eastern Europe who'd served as a mortician in the Soviet Army. Gil and I had talked about the matchup and decided by the time I got a title shot—if it ever happened—the Coroner could be vanquished, even retired. It wasn't worth the anxiety yet.

I asked Davie, "Heard anything about Zombi?"

"Not much. He's a bit of an enigma—that's what I'm gonna say on air, *enigma*—but it came down from Eddie this guy won't be around long, so don't hype him too much. Question is, why is he here at all?"

"You ask Eddie that?"

"When would I? Guy's been a fucking ghost lately. We had a meeting last week about something big, I mean, big, an overseas event. He shows up on a computer screen, video chatting from some place looked like a bomb shelter. Cheap-ass Warrior banner behind him, acoustics all fucked up."

"He around now?" I said.

"Somewhere. Look for the gang of hotel security. But don't

plan on talking to him. He's got some British asshole giving every-body the pointy finger. 'Fack off, mate.'"

Hard to pretend I didn't know that was a dead-on Burch.

Then the real thing walked through the door leading a crowd of blazered security, a blue faux hawk in the middle somewhere.

Burch pointed at me. "You. Over here."

Davie said, "See what I mean?"

———

Burch still looked rough. Waxy with dark circles under his eyes, which were too shiny and sucked back into his head. He secured Eddie in his nest of casino security below the stage and left him talking to a sweaty guy wearing a headset.

We walked to the far end of the stage. Nobody close but Burch still pulled me in. He smelled like he was rotting. "Bran-denberg's here."

"Vanessa's father?"

"He's searching for her. Got some men with him who look like cops, but I'm not sure."

"Yakuza?"

"Not Japanese. Besides, the whole mess with his daughter led to Omori's suicide. I doubt they're on good terms."

"Is she here?"

"Come on. I put her someplace safe. Don't ask me where. Listen, if they take me, you have to cover Eddie. Glued to his side, yeah?"

Babysitting Eddie the night before a fight. I tried to keep my face from souring. "All right."

"We're staying in the penthouse here until after the fights.

Roads are too risky."

"Don't let them take you."

"I don't fight cops. That's a whole new load of trouble."

"Kick Brandenberg's ass out of the casino. Him and his crew, whatever they are."

"He's already on the unwelcome list. We don't know how he got in, but fucking management doesn't want to make a scene unless it's necessary. Trust me, it already is. The men around Eddie are prepared. If Brandenberg gets close, they take him down. I'll drag him out myself, take the long way. Face on the carpet, stairs, the whole bit."

Noise from the other side of the room made us look. Fans were streaming in from the expo floor, hustling for the front rows, separated from the stage by a narrow lane. Well within blowgun range. Could probably poke a guy with a sword, you give it a good stretch.

"Enough people here to qualify for a public humiliation."

"He'll wait," Burch said. "Not to say he isn't here now, though, so smile."

We grinned and checked the crowd. I scanned for Brandenberg too, the tan face that loomed from billboards promising great deals on time-shares, commercial property, burial plots. "Don't know if I'd recognize Shuko. He had sunglasses on. Happened pretty fast."

"I'll know him."

"How close did you get?"

"Not as close as you," Burch said. "Still can't believe he let you creep up on him like that. Won't happen again, so don't plan on it."

"Face-to-face, I'll still put him down."

Burch let that sit for a while. He kept smiling and scanning.

"When I went into the building to grab Vanessa, I had a man with me. Hired him to keep the exit clear and drive. He had a shotgun and a .45. I went in and cleared the rooms. It was a Yakuza brothel, where they kept sex slaves. Shuko had his own floor, because none of the gang members wanted to hear what went on and they sure as hell wouldn't touch any of the slaves he'd claimed."

"The snake tattoo."

"Stage one. Stage two he shaves their heads. Stage three he slices open the skin over their clavicles and tucks it behind the bone, lets it heal so the bone stays exposed. He likes handles."

"Jesus."

"Yeah. Couldn't believe what I was seeing. I moved down the hallway, kicked in a door, and saw what he likes to do next." Burch's jaw muscles boiled under the skin. "It's the only woman I've knowingly killed, and I'm glad I did. I still hear her beg for it."

"This motherfucker needs to go."

"Agreed. But don't for a second think you can handle him."

"My experience, guys who like to hurt women don't like to fight men."

"Half of the slaves on Shuko's floor *were* men."

Some guy with press credentials and a camera that looked like it could shoot down a plane skidded to a stop. "Hey, Woodshed, give us a smile."

I gave him a face.

He looked at his screen, raised his eyebrows. "Hm." Hurried away.

I turned and Burch was gone.

Gil caught my eye, pointed backstage, and headed that way.

I followed, remembering what it felt like to choke Shuko unconscious. I replayed it, kept him off his feet, and squeezed harder and tighter until things started to crack and collapse.

A flash went off.

The same photographer, clicking away. "There's that smile."

———

We occupied a corner backstage while Davie got the crowd rolling. Talked to some fighters and trainers we knew. I tried to act like the fight with Zombi was the most important thing in my life. Must have done a piss-poor job; Gil ended up sealing me off behind him, telling guys, "He's really focused right now."

When they called me onstage I glared at the ring girls, the crowd, the scale.

"Somebody has his game face on," Davie said, then apologized when I turned it on him.

I drilled into the faces in the seats, praying to find Shuko raising his fucking blowgun or sword or just sitting there with a smug look I'd peel off and shove down his throat.

Be here. You wanted public. Let's show these people what you're made of. Start with cracking your ribs open.

I didn't notice Zombi was onstage until Davie pulled me over for the stare down. Eddie was between us, gray and tired, Burch behind him with half the security team trying to look like they were always onstage, perfectly normal.

"Anything to say?" Eddie asked.

Zombi's interpreter was behind him. She murmured in his ear. His expression didn't change, chiseled out of sandstone.

Eddie said, "Fine, let's do it."

We put our fists up, leaned in, and stared.

Zombi looked into me.

I looked through him, still hoping for a sign of Shuko. Big mistake.

CHAPTER 19

G IL DIDN'T KNOW EXACTLY WHAT WAS GOING ON, BUT he knew what to do. Backstage he put a hand on my arm, checked my eyes. "Okay. Let's get you out of here."

We were ten feet from the door to the service hallway when a thick guy in a brown suit stepped in front of it and clasped his hands over his belt buckle.

"Coming through," Gil said.

The guy gave him a bored face, set his feet.

I wasn't in the mood. "Move or be moved."

"Mr. Wallace." Brandenberg came in on my right, trailing another side of beef. The two thugs could have been brothers, but no mother would do that to the world. White teeth flashed, and a tan hand cut toward me. "I'm Tim Brandenberg."

I stared at the hand, a graham cracker hanging there waiting to be crushed.

He let it drop. "I understand you've been doing some extra-curricular work with Mr. Takanori and Mr. Burch."

"Go fuck yourself."

"Whoa. Sorry, I don't speak caveman. Before you go completely primal, you should meet Detectives Karp and Eugene. They're big fans."

"Buncha queers humping each other in Speedos," the one blocking the door said.

Brandenberg smiled. "I lied. Detective Eugene hates it, more of a boxing fan. Where the fuck is my daughter?"

"We're leaving," Gil said. He pulled my arm.

Karp swung around in front of us and adjusted his suit coat so we'd see the badge and heavy revolver tucked underneath, the wooden grip scuffed and dented.

The backstage crowd flowed around our little pressure tank, everybody wrapped up in their own fights.

Gil asked me, "What is this?"

"It's mine. Walk out. I'll handle it."

"He stays," Brandenberg said. "You're too stupid to help yourself. Maybe he'll chime in. Where is Vanessa?"

"Why? You lose her to some crackhead playing Go Fish?"

White flashed again through tight lips and he snapped a hand across his body, showing me the back of it. A heavy, wicked ring caught the light.

I pushed my face toward it. "Please. You get a free one. After that, I keep any teeth I catch."

"Careful, Woody," Gil said. "Guys, I train plenty of cops at the gym. Maybe I'll ask about you two, see what they have to say."

"Same thing I'm telling you now," Karp said. "Shut your fuckin' yap."

Gil shifted his weight, a subtle relaxation that rooted him to the floor. Only reason I noticed, I'd seen it hundreds of times right before I got tossed through the air.

"Last chance," Brandenberg told me.

"You're right."

"Look. I understand your frustration. You're in the midst of all these significant moments—Eddie's business problems, my family issues, your great big fight—and you are not a significant man. Let me help you, take some of this pressure off. Tell me where she is."

"Happy and safe. Because she'll never see your face again."

Brandenberg sighed. Nodded.

I spread my feet and got ready for the bum-rush, felt Gil dip into a slight crouch next to me.

Detectives Karp and Eugene didn't close in.

Eugene reached under his coat and brought out a pair of nicked-up stainless steel handcuffs. He leaned in close so only I could hear: "Aaron Wallace, you are under arrest for the kidnapping of Vanessa Brandenberg and the murder of Louis Gerrone."

———

They didn't make a show out of reading me my rights, but enough people saw and got the word going until the room was all wide eyes and open mouths.

Gil tried talking sense to them the whole time. They ignored him until he said to me, "I'll meet you at the station with a lawyer."

Karp pulled everything out of my pockets and put it in his. "Get a good one. Maybe you can get bail under a million."

I couldn't meet Gil's eyes and didn't want to see any of the other faces. If I looked at the cops or Brandenberg I'd start kicking, tripping, stomping, so I kept my mouth shut and didn't look at anybody.

"Hey." Eddie's shout cut the whispers off. "What the fuck is going on here?"

"Stay back," Eugene said, his hand on the butt of his pistol.

Eddie and Burch and the security guards made a half-circle around us and the exit. Some of the security moved people away.

Eddie looked at Brandenberg. "What is this?"

"What happens when you don't cooperate."

Burch's suit coat was open, his hands loose at his sides. He stared at Eugene with flat eyes.

Eddie said, "You serious? You come in my place and embarrass me with your trained dogs?"

"Not everything is about you, Eddie."

"How about I get some real cops in here?"

"I'm sure they'd like to talk to you about a few things, just like these detectives are going to talk to Mr. Wallace. Or you could tell me where Vanessa is."

Burch glanced at me.

I shook my head, as if he was asking.

"No?" Brandenberg shrugged. "All right. Let's go."

———

Brandenberg got into a silver Town Car without saying anything or looking back. It floated away while Karp and Eugene folded me into an unmarked sedan, the upholstery cracked and stained. It smelled the same as every other cop car: industrial disinfectant draped over a stadium of body odor.

They got to the Strip and turned left.

My pulse perked up. Las Vegas Metro was north of the Strip, not south. "Police station is the other way."

Karp drove on. "Now he talks."

"That's the new station," Eugene said. "We're still operating out of the old one. Don't mind it, though. We like to do things the old way."

"The way that works," Karp said.

———

Karp rolled through the parking lot past a few dusty squad cars, backed into a spot with empty slots all around and no lights above. Nobody said anything while they walked me, hands cuffed behind, to a solid metal door set in a cinder-block wall, rust growing down from the steel handle.

Eugene pulled a wind chime of keys out and found a thick one. He only needed his thumb and forefinger to flick the dead bolt open. Walking through I could smell fresh oil.

The hallway was dim and stale, a piece of paper stuck on the yellow brick wall with brown masking tape, letting everybody know about the family cookout on Saturday. I was only four years late.

At an intersection past a few banks of dead fluorescents a sign was hanging from the ceiling. It showed an arrow pointing left, Holding, and right, Booking.

I turned right.

"Wrong." Karp yanked me forward through the intersection past a row of blank gray doors. "I ran your sheet. You been a good boy, stayed out of trouble 'til now. You don't really want your picture took and fingers rolled, do you?"

I walked and stared down the hallway at nothing. The building was silent around us.

"This'll do." Eugene opened a door. The room was square and

yellow and cold, a single bulb on the wall behind a metal cage. Four wooden chairs around a chipped green table. Eugene kicked one. "Park it."

Karp put me in front of the chair and shoved it against the back of my knees. I dropped into it, didn't show the jolt of pain from the wood digging into my arms.

Eugene closed the door.

This was bad. No record of my arrest, no one saw me enter the building or get hauled into this room. Used to be if cops wanted to have a private chat they'd take you for a drive in the desert or arrange a chance meeting in the bowels of a casino next to the laundry tanks that thumped and hissed and moaned and sounded a lot like somebody getting worked over.

These two having the balls to do it right in the police station— even an abandoned one—was an admirable level of brutality.

Karp stayed behind me.

Eugene sat across and put his feet on the table. "Anytime you're ready." He waited, then said to Karp, "He's giving me the dead eyes."

Karp smacked me across the back of the head with something, either his forearm or a log.

"He blinked," Eugene said. "Least we know he's still alive."

"Using up all my good air in here."

"You see the scars on his face? The light in here, they pop right out." Eugene spent a while looking at them, puckering his lips and nodding. "You're a tough guy, huh? Like to throw down."

The Zombi fight was about twenty-four hours away. Felt about as close as the other side of the moon.

"You ever been shot, tough guy? When we strip you down, we gonna find any bullet holes?"

Something clicked behind me, the sound of a folding knife locking in the open position. Fingers tugged my collar away from my spine.

"Can't call yourself a tough guy, you never been shot. We don't find any, I'll give you one for free. You can even pick the spot."

The blade poked through the fabric, purred down an inch, and stopped.

"Where's Mr. Brandenberg's daughter?" Eugene said.

Two choices: play dumb, which I was, or let them think I knew something. If they believed I didn't know, there was a good chance I'd go from this room to the bottom of a construction site, cozy under a few feet of concrete. If they thought I had something to give up, they were ready to rip it out of me. "I want a lawyer."

It wasn't any easier than the last time I'd said it. I don't like lawyers and hate asking anyone to fight for me. But it would stall these two mutts. They were legally bound to stop questioning me until a lawyer was present.

Eugene said, "I want steak and eggs for breakfast. Guess which one's coming true?"

Karp spit on the back of my head. "There's your lawyer."

I was almost sure they weren't going to give me a lawyer.

Eugene said, "If you don't want to tell us about Mr. Brandenberg's daughter, we can talk about how you murdered Lou Gerrone."

It hadn't been on the news. "He's dead?"

"Don't even. Anytime we want, his body shows up. Where you want it? Your truck? No, the gym. Hang him from the ceiling like a punching bag. Take you and all your hump buddies down."

Karp leaned into my ear. "You tell us where the daughter is, maybe Lou's body goes away."

"Maybe," Eugene said. "But hey, maybe you'll like it in prison. They love to fight in there. With less clothes on so there you go."

They were sealing me in. I needed time to think. Space to breathe. Most of all, I needed to get out of this tomb. "Put me back in the car. I'll take you to her."

"Well, that was easy. Karpy, how are we on gas?"

"Plenty."

"This is just super. I thought we'd be here all night, have to keep you through the fight tomorrow. But here's the thing: we know this guy Shuko. You heard of him?"

I kept my teeth together.

"You don't have to answer. Your face tells me yes. Shuko wants you dead, and he sees you riding around with us he'll get your blood all over our car. The paperwork on that shit is ridiculous. So we'll put you in the trunk."

The trunk.

"About the size of a freezer," Karp said.

Sweat fell into my eyes. I don't remember getting hot.

Eugene said, "You change your mind? Sounded pretty good to me. Drive here and there, let you out to look around. Plenty of opportunities for you to jump us and scurry away. Right, Karpy?"

"He woulda taken me completely unawares."

Eugene pulled his key ring out again, jangled it. "Wanna go for a ride? Huh? Do ya?" He wrapped the keys in his fist, looked between it and my face a few times, shook his head. "How about this—we stay here, and if the next words out of your mouth don't tell me where Vanessa is, Karpy gives you another mouth on the back of your head? We'll see if that one has anything good to say."

The blade pressed against the back of my skull. I waited for the heat of the slice, the tug of skin parting before the sting, then the pain. As soon as it happened they'd both pause to get my reaction.

In that pause I would go to work. Stand up, shove the table into Eugene, and get space between me and the blade. Crush his nose with my forehead.

Turn and kick Karp in the balls hard enough to catch a glimpse of them in his open mouth. Let him slash my leg if he has to, long as it isn't near the femoral.

Lead with a roundhouse kick back to Eugene. Chop it into his face if it's exposed, break his arm if he tries to block. If he's reaching for his gun, drive the kick into his humerus, kill that arm, pull back, and stomp him in the face.

I stared at Eugene and waited for the blade to move.

Karp pushed hot breath onto the back of my head.

Eugene blinked. Something happened to his face—I wouldn't call it fear, not entirely—there was wisdom mixed in. Instinct. He shifted sideways and eased his gun over the table to point it at my chest.

I heard Karp shuffle to the side, out of the line of fire, but the knife stayed against my skin.

"Keep going, Karpy."

The blade slid off and left an itch behind. Karp moved to my left away from the door. Eugene had a double-action revolver. The hammer was down—it would take a good pull on the trigger to raise and drop it. Maybe I could do something in that time.

Like get shot.

"Stand up," Eugene said.

"What for?"

"Stand the fuck up."

I did, wanted to curl around my stomach and chest to hide them from that black tunnel of a barrel.

"Back against the wall."

I moved until my hands touched cinder block.

Eugene opened the door and stepped into the hallway. "Come on."

I looked at Karp, who changed his confused frown into a stern frown and kicked me toward the door. "Go on."

Eugene walked backward and kept the gun on me to the hallway intersection. He flicked the gun to my right, down the hall toward Holding. I turned that way and stopped at a locked steel door with a mesh window.

Eugene stuck a key into a box on the wall and twisted. The door buzzed and I pushed through. It was bright on the other side, all the fluorescent tubes humming.

The left wall was holding cells, ten-by-ten yellow cinder block with the front wall and a sliding door made of dull gray bars. Metal bench along the back wall, cut short for the stainless steel toilet in one corner.

The right wall was solid cinder block so you could sit on the bench and stare out at nothing. The first holding cell was open.

"Shoes off," Eugene said.

I checked my options, ran out after one. Kicked my shoes off and left them near the wall.

Karp reached to pull my belt off, didn't find one. "Huh. Thought you were some kinda black belt. Inside."

I entered the cell and heard it close behind me. When I turned Eugene's gun was holstered.

"Know what I'm thinking, Karpy?"

"Not really."

"If Shuko wants this guy so bad, what's he gonna do he finds out we had him and didn't say anything?"

"Brandenberg—"

"I know but he ain't here with this beast. We are. And Shuko's gonna get Vanessa anyway. Why not let him do all the work finding out where she is?"

"What about the other thing?"

"I got it covered. Let's go call Shuko. I wanna see what happens when you get these two animals in the same cage."

———

There was a round patch of lighter paint at the top of the wall across from the cell next to an exposed piece of conduit dropping out of the ceiling, a few capped wires forking out of the end.

I thanked whoever had come through and taken the video camera down. I didn't want Karp and Eugene watching me the whole time, and I didn't want anybody watching while I flopped around on the floor and got one leg through the handcuffs, then the other. I gripped one of the bars above my head and stretched my shoulders, heard the pops, and let some of the blood flow out of my hands.

Gil was probably calling every cop he knew, maybe stalking around the Metro Police station looking for me. He'd find a lot of blank faces. I didn't even know if Karp and Eugene were on duty. I hadn't heard or seen a radio since they picked me up.

One thing I did know: Brandenberg and his dirty cops were working with the Dojin-gumi. Possibly just long enough to give Vanessa back to Shuko, make things right so he wouldn't drag them up to his private floor for tattoos and torture.

Or maybe Eugene and Karp were bluffing. Getting me to sweat and stew, tenderize myself thinking about Shuko and his freezer.

It was working.

I sat down on the bench and tried to keep still. Knees kept bouncing, hands opening, closing.

Eddie and Burch knew these guys. Maybe they'd know where to find me. Then they could stand outside the abandoned station and pound on the front door and be ignored.

Until Shuko rolled in.

Shit. If Eddie and Burch showed up, Shuko would have all three of us sealed inside an empty building. Not the public executions he wanted, but no way he'd turn down a gift-wrapped body count.

I tried to pull the handcuffs off.

Not a chance.

Peeked into the toilet. Maybe the blue water would make things slippery enough.

It was dry, shut off, dust in the bowl.

I paced the cell and thought about freezers and bathtubs and the woman Burch had mercy killed. Tried to think about anything else. The walls moved when I wasn't looking, went from ten-by-ten to a phone booth. I stopped, took a deep breath, pictured Marcela, and felt dirty for even bringing her image into this.

Back to pacing, hearing the tattoo needle bounce off bone, and waiting.

Two hours later the waiting was over.

———

The door clicked like a gun switching off safe.

Karp pushed through and held it open for Eugene, twirling his keys around a finger. He glanced at his watch. "It is now officially Saturday. You want to fight tonight? Hell, see the sun again? Tell me where Mr. Brandenberg's daughter is. When we find her I'll come back here and cut you loose."

"Then what?"

"Life goes on. For most of us."

Karp still had the door open, peering down the hall where I couldn't see. He was sweating. "My advice, pack your shit, get out of town, and don't look back. Eddie's a walking corpse. So's Burch. Don't factor them into your decision."

They waited.

Eugene shrugged. "Okay." He pinched a key and let the rest fall away, stuck it in the cell lock, froze there, and pointed at me. "Don't you move."

The cell door slid open. Shuko walked out of the hallway and into the cell and sat next to me.

Eugene locked us in. "You boys play nice now."

They walked out, Karp smiling as the hallway door eased shut.

I stared straight ahead and listened to Shuko breathing next to me. He was much larger than I remembered from the parking lot. Six two and thick, probably two fifty. Colorful neck tattoos sprouting above his black T-shirt. Smelled like stale smoke and greasy food.

I turned to him. "Remember me?"

He tried to show me how dead his eyes could look. Pretty dead, not bad.

"You don't because I've never seen you before. Who are you?"

"Shuko, motherfucker."

"Bullshit. I met Shuko. Those clowns just don't know it. At least you're Japanese so they got that right. They paying you for this?"

He smiled. He was on something.

"They letting you walk on a bust for coming in here, throwing me around?"

He stood up, rolled his neck and fists. Scars laced over his knuckles and forearms, trails left behind by knives, glass, teeth. "Where's the girl?"

"What girl? You don't even know."

"Vanna."

"Jesus. This is offensive."

He stepped back, gave me a good look at his black steel-toed boots. "Tell me where the bitch is, bitch."

"Take it easy. What are you getting out of this?"

"I get to fuck you up."

"You should renegotiate. Hey, you know any catch wrestling?"

He smiled. "I get to fuck you up, then I get to fuck her. Karpy said so. Shh, don't tell her daddy."

I sat still. "What do you do?"

"Huh?"

"Your job."

"Man, stand up."

"Because this is what I do. Get locked in cages and fight my way out."

He frowned, some alarm going off in the fog of drugs and dementia. He shook it off and took a step toward me.

"Don't do it."

He reached out and everything slowed down. Among the scars I could see calluses on his palms and fingers, recognized them as barbell-made. A weightlifter in addition to the brawling.

So what.

I shot my hands out and got the handcuff chain between his right thumb and forefinger, pushed off the bench, and drove into him. His thumb bent back and he went with it, hissing and trying to belt me with a left hook. I took it on the shoulder and kicked him in the balls.

He dropped to a knee and shoved me away with his right arm, then locked the elbow. I still had the chain against his thumb, plowed my hands forward. His thumb snapped at the joint and flopped back against his forearm. I kept the chain going and slammed it into his upper lip, got it under his nose, and kept pushing until his skull thumped into the cell bars.

I wedged it in tight, got my fingertips around the bars on either side of his head, and pinned it there while I drove knees into his diaphragm, worked my way up, and compressed his rib cage in a few places.

Blood sprayed out of his nose with each impact. I don't know what was crawling around in it, but I didn't want it on me. I stepped back and let his head slip out of the bars. He tipped forward, folding over his cracked ribs, and on the way down I stomped my left heel below his ear, sending him flopping across the floor against the wall where he didn't move.

I checked his pockets for a phone, no luck, then wiped any blood I could find on his jeans and sat on the bench to wait.

———

Twenty minutes later the door opened and Eugene walked in with his hands over his eyes. Karp followed with his ears covered, a grin splitting his face.

"I see no evil," Eugene said.

Karp giggled. "I hear no evil." He looked into the cell and stopped.

I said, "Both you idiots oughta cover your mouths too. I happen to have two fists, so whenever you're ready."

Eugene dropped his hands and stared at the guy heaped against the wall. "Fuck."

"You should get him to a hospital."

"I should take him out back and shoot him. Fucking worthless."

Karp said, "That's not Shuko."

"No kidding?"

"Just so you know, you didn't beat him."

"Not twice. Not yet."

Eugene showed me his back, leaned in toward Karp. He wasn't close enough to the bars for me to grab him, even if I could squeeze both arms through. After some choppy hand gestures and raspy whispering they agreed on something. Eugene turned around with his revolver pointed at me.

I fought the urge to dive and huddle behind the guy on the floor.

· "Come off the bench, turn around and kneel right here at the bars."

"No."

"I'm gonna take your handcuffs off."

"You're gonna shoot me and you don't want a hole in the wall."

Karp's face proved me right.

I asked, "Down through the top of the head? Or tucked behind the collarbone into the chest cavity?"

"Just get over here."

I was breathing fast, loud. Couldn't help it. "Get Brandenberg on the phone."

"That ship's sailed. Seems you don't know where she is, and there ain't no way you're walking out of here."

"Take me to Shuko. We'll work it out."

"Buddy, you don't know what you're asking for. Trust me, the bullet's much better."

I put my hands in front of my face, like it was already on the way. "Don't be insane. How many people saw you arrest me? Gil and Eddie and Burch are looking for me right now."

"Our report says you walked out of here a free man two hours ago. What happened to you after that is anyone's guess. They ask me, the Yakuza caught up to you. Now come on, one loud bang, then it's over. Never pay taxes again."

I thought about Marcela. What was the last thing I said to her?

"You want the shotgun?" Karp asked.

Eugene squinted behind the revolver. "Nah, I'll put a hole in the wall—I don't give a fuck—but my aim's not that great. He might linger."

My heart thumped, tried to escape my chest so it could attack him.

Karp must have heard it too. He cocked his head and looked down the hallway. "Wait."

The room was silent except for the guy breathing on the floor.

I heard it again: *thump, thump, thump.*

"The fuck is that?" Eugene said.

"Somebody's at the side door."

Eugene stared at me, finally let the gun drop, put it in the holster. "Time for one last confession. Make it count."

They walked out.

———

My little taste of waiting on death row stretched out, every second taking about five minutes to pass.

I couldn't hear anything through the door, decided to fill the silence by yanking off one of the steel-toe boots and banging it against the bars. Accompanied that with some hollering. The guy on the floor stirred and moaned. Our combined lyrics were pitiful and would have made a great country song.

This was not how I'd ever imagined fighting for my life. I clanged the bars and ran back through the night from when Karp and Eugene arrested me, replayed all the moments I could have—should have—acted.

Easy to do afterward. Tell me at the beginning I'd end up getting shot through the bars of a locked cell, then watch me chainsaw my way out of the casino the second I saw Brandenberg and his lumps.

The guy on the floor sat up.

"Yell," I shouted at him.

He looked at his thumb dangling against his forearm and yelled.

In the racket I heard something, maybe the door click. I froze with the boot cocked behind my shoulder. "Shut up."

He dialed it down to a whimper.

The door opened. Eugene walked in, then Karp. They both looked sorry for me, embarrassed by how I was going out.

No.

They were just embarrassed. Howard Argo, the Yakuza lawyer, walked in behind them. He jerked to a halt. "Jesus, don't throw that boot at me."

"Tell me you're here to get me out."

"What have I said from the beginning? We just want a fair fight." He glanced at Eugene and spread his hands out to encompass me, the cell, the building. "This is not very fair, gentlemen. What'd you do? Send some muscle in there to lean on him? How's that working out?"

We all looked at the guy on the floor.

"I need an ambulance," he said.

Eugene put his hands in his pockets. "All we want is Mr. Brandenberg's daughter, then he's free to go."

"He's free to go now," Argo said. "Open the cell immediately or just hand me your guns and badges. That's how fast I'll have a lawsuit open and shut on you."

Eugene's jaw flexed but he got his keys out.

Argo kept going. "As for Brandenberg, it's his fault for siding with the Dojin-gumi. That's a sinking ship, and he's riding it all the way down. So are you two, you don't wise up."

Karp was pale in the fluorescents. "You know what Shuko would do, we try to cut loose now?"

"Yes, I do. My sympathies to your families."

Eugene opened the cell door. I stepped out and held the handcuffs up. He popped them off, put them in his coat pocket.

I looked him in the eye. "Ready?"

"Go ahead."

I hit him with a left elbow in the right eye socket, tried to connect with as much real estate as possible. Give him an impressive bruise he'd have to explain for the next month. If something fractured, no sleep lost. He cupped his face and fell against the wall, slid to the floor.

"Shit," Karp said.

"Yeah." I held my hand out so he could drop my wallet, phone, and keys into it. I put them away.

He squeezed his right eye shut and pulled that shoulder up. I smacked a right elbow into his left eye, sent him staggering against the bars. He sucked in a lot of air.

I put my shoes on. "My advice? Pack your shit, leave town, and don't look back. You ever see me again, hide."

Argo followed me through the door.

———

Argo steered his maroon Escalade with two fingers, relaxed in the flow of cabs and Strip workers on their way to or from a shift. The interior was a complex aroma of leather and superiority. The clock on the dash showed twenty after three.

I kept checking the rearview for lights and sirens.

"Don't bother," Argo said. "Even those morons know when to back off. I'm not going to ask you what they said or did, because frankly I don't care and it's not my business. I don't mean that in a polite way. It's literally not the business I'm in. Understand?"

I let silence answer him.

"Good. You don't owe me for this, but you should thank Eddie. They looked all over for you. Finally he called me. Soon as I heard who arrested you, I knew where to look. But that's all done. Forget it. All I need to know is, are you able to fight tonight?"

"Yes."

"It's very important to my clients that this fight appears legitimate."

"Ask Zombi how it appeared. After he wakes up."

Argo laughed. "Immature bravado aside, this is the first transaction in a long business relationship. Let's get off to a good start."

"You still gonna wear your poncho for when Shuko jumps out and executes everybody?"

"I'm told there are people trying to prevent that, and we're all hoping for the best. But my clients are prepared to work with Warrior under any circumstances."

"Whether Eddie is alive or not."

"I believe that falls under any circumstances."

"Are you recording this?"

"No. Why?"

"So you just can't help talking like a goddamn lawyer."

"You fight; I talk. Either way, the training shows."

The rest of the ride was quiet. When Argo pulled into the gym's parking lot, Gil burst out of the front door and had mine open before the Escalade stopped.

"Jesus, are you all right?" He was halfway in the vehicle, pressing fingers and palms against my face, neck, shoulders, ribs. Turning my head to look at him. "Are you?"

"I'm fine."

He pulled me out and pointed at Argo. "You're a lawyer."

"True."

"Get the paperwork started. We're suing those two mother-fucking cops, Brandenberg, the Las Vegas Police Department, the whole fucking city."

"It's Gil, right? Gil, I'm going to advise you against that. The fees alone will bankrupt you, and no one will ever set foot in a courtroom. Trust me on this. But here's my card in case you—"

I slammed the door.

The Escalade idled for a few seconds, then sped away.

Gil's face was a new shade of red. He walked in a few circles, came around to me, the veins on his forehead flexing. "What did they do?"

"Just asked some questions. They wanted to know where

Vanessa is."

"We don't know where she is."

"That's what I told them."

"Motherfuckers." He checked the street, lowered his voice. "What did they say about Lou?"

"They can pin his death on me anytime they want."

"You believe them?"

"Yeah, but I don't think it's up to them. I hope it isn't."

"Christ, listen to us. Like a couple of mob guys. Enough of that shit. What do you need?"

"Sleep. Wake me up a half hour before we have to leave."

"Look at me. How many times have I said going into a fight, relax, focus on the technique, not the man?"

"I got it. You don't have to say it again."

"I won't. I want you to look Zombi in the eye and see everything he represents, all this bullshit, and smash him. Fucking smash this guy."

———

I took a hot shower, got the smell of Argo, Karp, and Eugene and their kill box out of my nose. Fell onto a cot and brought Marcela up on my phone. Almost 4 a.m. here, 8 in Brazil.

"Crazy boy, you have a fight tonight. What are you doing awake?"

"I wanted to hear your voice."

"Aw, I should be nicer then. How are you feeling? You sound tired."

"I am. Lots of nonsense leading up to the fight."

"Last time wasn't exciting enough for you?"

"Please. Don't remind me."

"You don't want to remember any of it?"

"Well, once it was just you and me, that part I replay every day."

She laughed, a miracle tonic, and I was right back in the truck with her, Marcela taking her shirt off, pulling mine over my head and laughing. Hindsight, I should have locked the doors and driven us both out of the city. Any direction, just away.

I closed my eyes and listened to her breathe.

"Go to sleep," she said. "Fight hard. Don't bleed so much."

"I'll try."

CHAPTER 20

W E WERE THE THIRD FIGHT ON THE CARD, EDDIE trying to slip Zombi in before the seats were full. The cameras would roll, but we'd only run on pay-per-view if they needed filler.

The prep room wasn't crowded: just me, Gil, the Snarl brothers, and our gear spread out. I was on the mats with Vince going over important details like balance and footwork and not getting my head twisted off.

Robbie kept his back against the door. Reporters from websites, maybe even an AP guy or two, were thumping on it and asking about the arrest. They wanted details, not answers. The blood in the cage wasn't going to be enough. Gil turned the iPod dock up and pushed their voices back through the door, a finger in the dike.

I put Zombi's face on Vince and watched the dead features come in for a single-leg. I stuffed it, patted the air with an upper-cut-hook combo, and finished with a head kick, pulled my knee in and let it carry me around.

"Good," Vince said.

The Zombi face knew better.

We flowed in and out of locks, slipping and sawing, cranking just enough to feel the hook. Gil brought the mitts out, and I tore into them, jab-cross-kick, the impacts booming in the small room.

Robbie had his ear to the door. "That shut 'em up."

"Easy," Gil said. "Don't burn out."

I hit them harder, trying to get Zombi to blink. Wince.

Nothing.

"More head movement," Gil said. "He's not a striker, but no reason to hang your face out there so he can open you up. Or latch on and wring you out."

Vince and Robbie had showed us how Zombi could wrap around my head and grind his forearm bones against the scar tissue around my eyes, splitting me open. They'd been as gentle as possible, still almost got the blood flowing.

Gil stepped back. "Relax. Shake it out."

I rolled my neck, shoulders, hands, walked in a circle, and told myself the instinct would kick in. Soon as the bell rang I'd switch into survival mode. Savagery. Then Zombi wouldn't be in a fight—he'd be facing life or death.

Try not to blink then, buddy.

Forget Shuko and Brandenberg. Forget the Yakuza and the fact that Zombi was the tip of their spear thrust into Warrior.

He was just a man.

Smash him.

I expanded a bubble around myself, let the pressure build against it. Nothing inside but fists, feet, knees, elbows. I'd let it explode the first time I touched Zombi.

"Hold up," Robbie said. He slashed across his throat.

Gil cut the music. The reporters outside had shut up, but somebody else was talking. Telling people to move, step back, cheers.

Shit.

The door opened and Eddie stepped in, Burch beyond him facing the small group of press. Eddie was crisp in a shark-gray suit, but something was off—he seemed bulky.

One of the reporters said something about Warrior fighters being criminals.

Eddie gave me a flat look, turned around, and told the group, "You're all pursuing a nonissue. Check the police records. You'll see none of my fighters were arrested last night. There was some confusion. They had the wrong guy. Any other questions, ask the cops. If I hear anybody bothering my fighters with this, you're banned from the premises."

"You can't do that," one of them said.

"Security."

Maroon blazers hustled the guy away.

Eddie paused. "Only one of you was a complete idiot. That's a good ratio; keep it up. And don't be here when I come out."

Burch followed him into the room and shut the door. Eyeballed Vince and Robbie. "Private chat, lads."

Vince checked with Gil, who nodded. "Thanks, guys. Give us a few."

Eddie pulled a roll of bills, held a twenty out. "Grab some food. On me."

"Ought to get us a hot dog," Vince said.

"This ain't a customer survey."

Vince snatched the money and followed Robbie out the door.

Eddie took a deep breath. "Woody, man. This is huge. I need

you to focus."

"I was."

"Don't worry about Shuko," Burch said.

"I wasn't."

"Event security is scouring the gates, the crowd, the hallways. I'd let the Queen Mum sit front row."

"Shit," Eddie said, "right next to Brandenberg, out there tapping his watch every time I look at him. Argo's sitting with a bunch of Japanese assholes. I guarantee you they got tattoos under those suits."

My precious bubble was long gone. "Vanessa is safe?"

"Don't worry about that," Eddie said.

"Tell me she's safe and I won't."

Burch nodded. "She is."

"What's the drill if Shuko rolls in?"

"Concentrate on your fight, mate."

"Give me a goddamn answer."

Eddie slapped his chest, made a dull thud. "I'm armored up. So's Burch. We'd give you one, but the ref might take points away. They'll stop bullets, but we aren't sure about swords or arrows. Can't hurt."

"What about darts?"

"Fuck."

"You spot Shuko," Burch said, "let me know, then get down. I'll be one seat behind Eddie."

Somebody rapped on the door.

Burch opened it enough for Hollywood the cutman to peek in. "Gotta wrap this boy up and let the doc check him."

"Thank Christ," Gil said.

Burch said, "One minute." Closed the door.

Eddie grabbed my shoulders. "You have to win. You *will* win. I know you can handle this."

That made one of us.

———

I walked in to music I didn't hear, past hands and faces I didn't see, scanning it all for the flash of a blade. The cameras didn't help, and jet-engine decibels made sure I wouldn't hear anybody coming up on me.

I fought the urge to look over my shoulder. Gil and Vince and Robbie were back there, along with six security guards. If Shuko pounced I'd maybe hear the screams before he got to me.

I was caught up in it, breathing too fast and fighting to get the bubble back, didn't see the blowgun come out of the crowd until it was an inch from my face.

I grabbed, twisted, yanked it out of Shuko's hands, and crumpled it. Turned to crush his head and saw a kid with eyes bigger than his face.

He started to cry, pointing at the rolled-up poster I'd destroyed.

Some guy put an arm around the kid's shoulders. "Nice job, asshole."

I handed him the poster. "Sorry."

Gil moved me along, stayed close so he could yell at me. "You get a paper cut?"

"Man, I'm all fucked up."

"Nope."

"I'm not ready."

"Of course you are."

"I need to relax."

"Calmest I've ever seen you is in the cage."

We got to the bottom of the steps. Everybody waiting there to check me out before I could ascend. I looked at their faces, made sure nobody was Japanese or screaming for my decapitation.

I tried a deep breath, hit the shallow bottom too soon. "This isn't gonna work."

Gil pointed through the black fence.

Zombi.

"Your work is waiting for you."

———

My work stood across the cage and stared at me with no expression while one of his cornermen leaned over the cage and talked in his ear. My work looked solid, strong, square from shoulders to hips, a block of muscle.

My job was to shatter it.

From the moment Eddie dangled the fight at me in the back of his limo, all I'd wanted was to get in the cage and do my job.

Now it was time, Jim Lincoln belting out the details for people still wandering around finding their seats, and I felt my suit of armor cinching tight. It was old. Dented and stained from twenty-eight professional fights, countless very unprofessional ones. It was comfortable.

I was not.

Zombi looked like a pool of deep, dark water. I felt an undertow sliding under my feet, tugging me off-balance. I fought it, burning fuel just to stand still.

You're not ready for this.

I'm ready for anything.

He's better than you.

Lots of guys are. Some are stacked up in my win column.

His mission is to beat you.

He's not willing to do what it takes to beat me.

When are you going to calm the fuck down and stop listening to me?

The referee stepped forward. His name was Brubaker and he was dressed like a mortician. "Fighter, are you ready?"

Zombi nodded.

"Fighter, are you ready?"

When?

I stomped the mat.

"Fight!"

Right now.

———

The crowd may have cheered. Everything outside the cage fell away, dim and distant. I moved to the middle of the cage and met Zombi there.

We did not touch gloves.

"He's gonna feel you out," Gil shouted.

Zombi dove toward my legs, tried to scoop an ankle and drag me down. I sprang and danced away, keeping my distance while he stayed on one knee and watched me.

"Never mind," Gil said.

Zombi stood and walked forward, hands up near his shoulders with the palms facing me. Wide stance on his toes, light and quick, economical. He wasn't worried about me shooting in to take him down. Maybe wanted me to.

I cracked a left kick into the inside of his left thigh.

There, how you like that?

From his expression, he thought it was somewhere between pinkeye and peanut butter cups.

I kicked him again in the same spot, rolled my hip over, and felt a solid impact.

"Careful," Vince said through the fence, "don't let him catch those."

Zombi stuck his left leg forward, dangling that meat out there.

Interpreter my ass.

I lifted my foot for another kick, shot it back, and lunged at him with a Superman punch that grazed his forehead.

If he blinked, I missed it.

"Good," Gil said, "make him worry about something else."

I liked the idea of making him worry, knitting that smooth brow with concern. I bounced on my toes and flicked a right jab in front of a left hook into his stomach. Moved my feet, head, connected with a solid jab. He countered with a hook that started at the concession stands. By the time it went past my face its hot dog was half gone. Not a natural striker, this guy.

I bounced some more, switched leads a few times and threw a right jab, a lazy piece of shit, and paid for it.

Zombi turned inside the punch and came around with a wild spinning backfist that went past my head, but his forearm smashed into my ear. I lost my balance and looked at the mat to make sure it was still down there. Zombi piled me against the cage and hooked his left arm over my head, got that forearm around my neck in a guillotine.

"Wrist!" Vince said from somewhere.

I grabbed Zombi's left wrist with my right hand and tried to pull it away from my throat. It was welded in place.

"Get some space," Gil yelled.

Air was hissing in and out of my mouth, and a buzz in my ear got louder. The blood trapped in my head flooded into my face.

Fights can be won or lost in the gym, the prep room, the stare down. Sometimes the decision is made the first time you lock up with a guy, swap strength, and see what you're dealing with.

Toss him around or shrug him off, you think, *All mine.*

He thinks, *Uh-oh.*

I pried on Zombi's arm as hard as I could.

Uh-fucking-oh.

Turned my chin toward his ribs so he couldn't cut off both arteries, hooked my left arm over his right shoulder, and pulled. That took another millimeter of pressure off my throat and made Zombi hold me up.

He seemed okay with that, started to back up so he could drag me face-first onto the mat and probably gator roll me or spin to take my back if he didn't just bear down and pop my head off. I worked my legs around, got my left knee behind his right, and pushed my weight over it.

When he started to fold I took a chance, let go of his wrist and dropped my right hand to catch his left knee and pick him up. In the fraction of a second it took to lift and slam him, Zombi squeezed hard enough to crack something in my throat. I planted him, my body perpendicular to Zombi's and my knees against the right side of his rib cage. Sank some weight down and made sure I could still breathe. No good. My trachea was too busy fighting the back of my tongue. I tried for wheezing, got something close. When I swallowed there was a massive rebellion—ended up spitting a glob onto the canvas near Brubaker's feet and saw blood in it.

Zombi abandoned the choke and put his left forearm against my face to push me away. The stretch on my throat felt like it was getting flossed with barbed wire. I held on, stupid, determined to stay there just because he didn't want me to.

"Get up," Gil said. An angelic voice of reason.

I shoved off Zombi and got to my feet, registered a cheer from the growing crowd; nobody wants to watch three rounds of lay-and-pray.

Zombi rolled to a knee, his face a stone mask. He studied me for a moment.

What did he see? Weakness?

He stood and walked forward. Hands raised, eyes dead. I pulled air in, flicked a jab, and whipped a left kick into his ribs, going for that juicy liver. The bastard was waiting for it—probably scouted the Burbank fight. He turned away and caught it against his belly, stepped in and snaked his left leg around my right, snagged me with an inside trip. My back scraped along the cage. I flailed, trying to stay up.

"Don't grab the fence," Brubaker said.

I quit fighting it, let Zombi take me down. Soon as my back hit the mat I exploded for a reverse, rolled and tried to keep his momentum going over so I could end up on top, but the cage was there. He bounced off it and landed in my half guard, his left leg trapped between mine.

Gil and Vince were inches away, leaning on the apron.

"Easy," Gil said. "Breathe."

He could have made it easier and tried, "Levitate."

Zombi wedged me into the cage and sank his weight down. He was a lead blanket dipped in quicksand. He put an elbow into my diaphragm and a forearm across my throat, driving the air out and keeping it there. Black spots grew and burst halfway between us. I looked into his shark eyes and saw nothing. If I could have talked, I'd have thanked him. He was making me fight for my life.

For survival.

I winked and elbowed him in the face.

Again, left elbow slicing across his temple. He eased off my diaphragm to raise his right arm to block. I elbowed that, thumped him sideways into the cage.

He tried to pull back, put some punches in my face to keep me busy. I clamped my right hand behind his neck and kept him close. He leaned into my throat and I ignored it. Changed the angle of attack, tucked my wrist next to my ear, and brought an elbow straight down on his face again and again.

Eyebrow, nose, mouth.

Blood fell on me. He was cut.

Blink now, motherfucker.

He shook his head, sending a drape of blood onto the canvas. I shoved my right palm under his chin and pushed him away. He latched onto it and started to spin to my right for an armbar, but the fence was too close, no room.

His weight shifted. I shoved him into the cage and pulled my feet back, got them under me. Stood up. He rose with his bloody face hidden behind forearms.

I pummeled all of it. Hooks, uppercuts, power.

Zombi covered and weathered and sprayed blood.

Brubaker hovered, watching.

I kneed Zombi in the stomach, tried to get those arms down. Again. He caught the second one, hooked an arm under it, and shot forward. I hopped backward and battered him with right elbows, slicing him once more over the left ear.

We traveled across the cage. I hit the fence again, and he dropped to scoop me up for another takedown when the bell rang.

He let go. Straightened up and looked me in the eye, no expression behind a veil of blood.

———

"Looking good." Gil knelt in front of my stool, holding my mouthguard and a water bottle.

Hollywood wiped me down to see if any of the blood was mine. It wasn't.

Gil dumped some water on me. "Good pace, good explosions, fantastic elbows, I want more. More punches too but watch the kicks. When he turns to the side like he did to catch a kick, switch stances and attack the lead leg."

"Be ready for him to shoot on that," Vince said. "Soon as you switch, bring a knee up, see if his face is there to meet it. At least make him think about it."

"Okay." It was a ragged whisper, ended with a click.

Gil whistled. "That guillotine was tight, huh? You're fine. You can breathe? Good. Knock this asshole out, we'll go get ice cream and talk like the Godfather. Elbows." He stuck the mouthguard in, patted my cheek, and followed Vince and Hollywood out.

All positive, nothing about how strong and balanced Zombi was, how I got smacked by the backfist and let him get an arm around my neck while we were both still fresh and dry, no sweat to help me slip out.

Brubaker walked to the middle of the cage.

"Woody," Gil said.

I looked at him through the cage.

"Who the fuck does this guy think he is? You're smashing him."

I smiled, was turning away when I saw a red tuft sprouting from the pad along the top rail of the cage. The blow dart had missed me by about a foot.

Shuko was here.

———

"Fight!"

I moved forward and scoured the apron for any sign of Shuko, searched the front rows for Eddie and Burch to let them know. Didn't see Zombi shooting in until he had both legs wrapped up.

I sprawled, pushed my hips into him and threw my feet back, planted some elbows in his shoulder blades. He drove me against the cage to bring my feet in, dropped to a knee, and yanked at my legs.

All I could think about was Shuko spitting a dart into me through the fence or rising from across the cage. Nothing I could do while he took aim and put one in my chest so the toxins could get right to work.

I panicked. Thrashed and beat Zombi's head and pummeled his back with double hammerfists, some kind of howl coming out of me. He dropped lower. I fell over him and grabbed his left ankle, stood and tore that leg out from under him, tried to touch his heel to his kidney.

He let go. I shoved him, sprinted away from the cage, and kept moving, sidestepping around the perimeter to be a moving target. For Shuko, anyway. Zombi just stood there and waited for me to dance into his web.

I heard Vince: "The fuck's he doing?"

Didn't hear Gil's answer, if he had one.

I yelled, "Shuko." The whisper flew six inches and died. My throat checked out, left a note it would be back in a few days. Maybe.

I came around to Zombi. He was leaking again, blood framing his face from cuts over his right eye and left ear. He raised his hands. I smacked him with a jab and kept moving, left him standing there with a tiny wrinkle between his eyes. Felt a slight boost for causing a look of utter confusion.

"Engage fighter," Brubaker said. "Engage or I take a point."

The ref. A train of thought steamed past: *Can't tell Burch tell everybody cause panic ruin Warrior piss off Eddie fuck it.* I made the time-out sign, ran to the dart, and pointed at it.

"Stop, time!" Brubaker hustled over. "What's the problem?" He pulled at the padding for rips or foreign substances, then brushed over the red plume and plucked the dart out.

I gripped his arm. "Don't touch the steel."

"What? Speak up." He pinched the dart between a finger and thumb, peered at it, and carried it to the gate.

The fight would be a no contest; I didn't know what that meant for Eddie and the Yakuza, but it didn't matter. The crowd would boo and forget about it as soon as the next fight kicked in.

Brubaker showed Hollywood the dart. Beyond them I saw Burch standing at his second-row seat. Eddie was beside him, eyes wide. Burch plowed over Eddie's shoulder and jerked him to his feet. I searched for any sign of Shuko and lost Burch and Eddie when they ducked into the aisle that led to the prep rooms.

Gil checked to see what Brubaker had, turned to me, and tapped his neck where Burch had been stuck with the darts. I nodded. He duckwalked back to his spot.

I caught a glimpse of Brandenberg sitting with his hand over his mouth. His eyes betrayed the grin hiding back there, the same shit eater from all his billboards. I wondered if it would look the same with no teeth.

Argo was leaning into the group of Japanese men next to him, talking and chopping the air while they looked serious and scanned the crowd. One of them had a cell phone to his ear, hopefully calling in some kind of Shuko-killing army.

At the gate Hollywood produced a hard plastic container.

Brubaker dropped the dart in and closed the cage, turned to wave for the stoppage. "All right, guys, fight!"

"Huh?"

Zombi walked toward me. I stepped right, stalling, pictured myself climbing over the fence and running out of the arena.

Zombi cut me off. I moved left, spotted Gil and Vince on the apron, hands up and out: What the hell? Saw myself yelling at them to throw in the towel, anything to get out of the cage.

My stupid pride wouldn't let me.

Run? Come on.

You know how to get out of here.

Not over. Not around.

Through.

Zombi stepped in front of me. I tore into him like he was a piñata stuffed with strippers. Four punches landed before he knew what was happening. By then he was skating backward, covering up. I chased and bashed him with hooks and straights that split his hands to snap his head back.

He hit the fence and couldn't run anymore. I flurried him with punches, head and body from all angles. He blocked and slipped most of them, tried to counter but paid for it every time he took a hand away from his face.

I dialed back on speed and cranked the power, thudded a right hook against his ribs, and rocked him sideways with a left elbow that splashed into the cut over his eye. Again.

He started to drop.

I followed him down with a left cross to the temple that would've killed a horse. I was smashing him. I was a punch away. He was dead.

Then he earned his nickname.

Zombi dove, hooked my right ankle, and braced it while he drove a shoulder into that knee. I tipped back, tried to roll into a reverse somersault but he kept that ankle pinned and spun around on top of my leg, wrapped it between his thighs, and pulled my ankle into his left armpit.

He fell onto his right side and leaned back, pushed his hips just above my knee to hyperextend the joint. I turned my face into the canvas and roared, my throat allowing only a shredded rasp.

Brubaker crouched next to my head, searching for any sign of a tap or verbal submission. I bit into my mouthguard. Zombi's neck was right there, begging for a rear naked choke. I moved an inch toward it and felt my knee twang, pop. I backed off and Zombi dug in deeper.

I watched my left hand come across to tap his shoulder, submit. Commanded it to stop. It kept going.

Crossed over my chest, on the way down, palm open, fingers spread.

Stop.

It did not.

I tried something else. Closed the fingers into a fist and let the arm go, gave it all the speed it wanted to tap.

And I did tap.

Tapped a looping hook into Zombi's left ear hard enough to bounce his head off the canvas. Once, twice, again. He didn't appreciate it. Scooted away out of arm's reach and had to curl toward my knee, let it bend the right way.

The relief made me roar again. I punched him in the head once more and got my left foot against his spine, pushed and stomped and pulled my right leg until he was wrapped around my shin, ankle.

I flashed on Vince, back at the gym doing sadistic puppet work with my feet, ankles crackling while toes weathervaned around the room.

Between the sweat and blood I was slippery enough to yank the foot out of Zombi's armpit. Got to my feet and rushed in to butcher him. My right knee wouldn't bend. Zombi dodged, rolled, stood, and ran to regroup.

When he squared up I closed in. Looked past the swelling and blood into his eyes.

He was scared.

The bell rang.

———

"Sit," Gil said.

I shook my head, kept pacing in front of the stool, thumping along on my stiff right leg. "Moving target." I grabbed his shirt and pulled him with me.

Hollywood stood in one spot and wiped me off when I walked by.

Gil said, "You can't think about Shuko now."

"Maybe he followed Eddie out."

"Yes, they can handle it. You try to handle both fights, you'll lose the one you're in. Zombi's in front of you now."

I pushed Shuko and his blowgun and swords away, looked across the cage; Zombi's corner looked like a trauma unit. "He's breaking."

"Jesus, you sound like shit. Looking great, though. He doesn't want any more punches. How's that knee?"

"Fine."

"Woody."

"Hurts like a motherfucker."

"He knows so get it away from him. He's gonna keep his distance and look for a way in to wrap you up. Use your feet and your jab. Don't leave anything hanging out to dry."

Vince put an arm around my shoulder. "Those elbows are massacring him. Keep it up but don't bring 'em past your centerline. He's waiting on that, trying to push it all the way past and going for an arm triangle. So bring 'em back as fast as they come out."

"Got it."

"And don't let him sugar foot you again. Don't pounce for the kill 'less you know for damn sure he's on his dying breath."

"Okay."

"Gil, this guy sounds like my aunt Vera."

Gil dumped some water down my neck. "You could do this all day, but you only get five more minutes of fun." He saw the look in my eye. "Less?"

"Less."

He smiled. "Nap time for Zombi."

———

The cutman did a brilliant job sealing Zombi up, but he had to know his art was temporary.

The crowd cheered our last round, ready for it to be as good as the first two. I planned for better and much shorter. Came out in a left lead to protect my right leg, felt like dragging a telephone pole. Zombi walked forward in a slower, heavier version of his first-round self, flat-footed with no head movement.

I stepped toward him. He slid back and shifted right, staying out of reach. I cut him off and chased with a hook, missed. Cracked a short left kick into his inner thigh. His hands dropped to grab it but didn't get there in time. I put a right cross over his ear and watched the blood roll out of that cut, saw his knees buckle.

I forgot about my cracked throat and dead leg. Everything slowed down. The threat in front of me was almost eliminated—a little push and he'd go over the edge. I tunneled in on his head, threw a left jab and dove forward, whipped a right elbow with so much bad intent it deserved a reality show.

Zombi dropped. Before the elbow hit.

He ducked under and stuck his head behind my right shoulder, hooked his right arm around my neck, and clamped his hands together between my shoulder blades. Stepped around, squeezed, and drove his head up, trying to choke me with my right arm. Just like Vince said he would.

I shoved my right arm away with my left, got a little space, and turned away from him.

Gil and Vince harmonized over the crowd: "No."

Zombi slithered around and jumped onto my back, wrapped

his left arm under my chin and left leg around my waist, folded his right knee over that ankle to lock me in a body triangle.

He squished my guts and tried to choke me with the left arm while he pulled his right arm out and over my shoulder. I caught that wrist with both hands like it was a cobra lunging for my face—let it go and he'd trap his left hand in his right elbow, sink the rear naked choke, and make me tap or pass out.

I pushed his wrist away. Zombi sawed his forearm across my neck and somebody poured hot broken glass down my throat. I could hear him breathing behind my ear, snuffling through the blood dripping off his face onto me.

He released the body triangle long enough to stomp my right knee. When I tipped that way he ripped his wrist free and locked the choke.

I spun to shake him off.

Saw Brandenberg clapping his thin, tan hands.

Argo reaching out to the Japanese men, congratulating them.

Black crept in at the corners. In the darkness Shuko's shadow crouched, waited.

I fell forward fast.

Picking up speed.

Smashed my face into the canvas, felt Zombi shudder when his forehead crunched against the floor, bounced, thudded again.

His legs loosened. I pushed to my knees.

Zombi squeezed the choke harder, crushed my neck, and forced trapped blood out of my torn face. The scar tissue beneath my left eyebrow had exploded—a flap of it sagged down and covered that eye. Blood splashed onto the mat. I dove into it, all the strength I had left and all of Zombi's weight focused on our faces as I tried to drive them through the floor.

The world was red.

Somewhere Brubaker yelled, "Stop. It's over."

The arm came away from my throat. I sucked air, letting the blood pound back into my head and find the leaks. Crawled out from under Zombi. Rose to my knees and wiped the sweat and blood out of my good eye, looked at him facedown on the canvas.

Out cold.

———

The cutmen couldn't keep up with the damage. Two more came in from cageside and each one took half of a face.

Hollywood and another guy worked on me. I didn't let the second one close until I'd held him at arm's length and rolled my right eye at him to make sure he wasn't Shuko; he was a pudgy Hispanic guy who didn't welcome scrutiny.

"Might sting." He doused my face before tucking my eyebrow up and holding it there like a tailor while he slapped butterfly bandages everywhere and finished with half a dozen wraps of tape all the way around my head.

Hollywood pulled Gil in. "Boy needs the emergency room and a plastic surgeon."

Gil pushed a lip out. "Tits look fine to me."

I scanned the crowd. Argo and his Yakuza guests were gone. Brandenberg's seat was empty. Eddie and Burch and Vanessa were probably already on a jet.

Zombi was still on the mat when Brubaker raised my hand.

CHAPTER 21

I WALKED THE SAME AISLE EDDIE AND BURCH HAD SPRINTED, kept scanning for Shuko. The crowd cheered my passage, patted me on the shoulders, and showed everybody what came back on their palms. Their night was off to a good start.

The hallway was filling up with event staff and fight crews. Gil and Vince hustled ahead to find somebody to look at my eyebrow with professionalism instead of morbid curiosity.

Argo wandered into my path with his hands in his pockets. He was alone and relaxed. "Well, that was a setback."

"Probably not the word Zombi would use."

"They won't give up. He's not the only fighter they have."

"Any heavyweights?"

"Not right now."

"Then I don't give a shit."

"Helluva fight. If it makes you feel any better, I bet a couple grand on you just in case."

"I don't believe you."

He pulled the stub out.

I tore it up. "Now I feel better." Walked away, left him there blinking.

Robbie waited outside the door to our room, stared at the dead leg and the bandages crusting on my head. "Congrats, man."

"Thanks."

Gil walked over with a stack of towels and a first-aid kit, started pulling the tape off my wrists to get the gloves off.

Robbie poked a thumb at the door. "Sorry. I told 'em not to go in."

"Who?"

"Some assholes."

It was alarming how many people fit the criteria. I opened the door.

Brandenberg sat on the couch with his legs crossed, bobbing a loafer and showing eight inches of silk sock. He was clipping his fingernails and didn't look up. "Come on in."

I told Gil, "Leave 'em on."

He let go of my wrist. "You need a doctor."

"Right now I just don't need any witnesses."

He knew not to argue. "Don't break your hands."

"Five minutes." I stepped in and shut the door.

Brandenberg said, "You can't be serious about assaulting me. I'd own your great-grandchildren."

"My word against yours."

"A whimper against thunder."

The bathroom door was closed. Somebody coughed inside and spat. Brandenberg's pet cops?

"How'd you get back here?"

"Never ask a person like me a question like that. Shows you're stupid. *Why* am I back here—now that's a decent question."

I locked the door. "You're not getting Vanessa back."

"She's my property. And what I do with her is none of your fucking business. But that's not why I'm here. Our friend Shuko is handling that." Brandenberg checked a thin platinum watch. "They ought to be having a nice conversation by now."

"Bullshit."

He shrugged. "You want to debate facts, go to church. I'd be goddamn delighted to take you to Shuko, let you watch him play with your friends before he starts in on you. But I'm here because my business partner thinks you're worth keeping alive."

The bathroom door opened and Lou Gerrone walked out.

———

The room whirled. I pried my left eye open to make sure this was happening.

"Should see your face," Lou said. He looked decent for a dead guy, maybe even less pasty but still drooping a hound dog mug under that receding hairline. Tight slacks and a wrinkled suit coat over an open-collared shirt. "Almost as good as when you stuck your head in the RV and saw me sitting there with my guts hanging out. Took everything for me to keep still, not lose my shit."

"What the fuck is going on?"

"Look, this is what you need to know. Eddie's dead or good as. Shareholders are gonna want somebody with experience to step in, and that's me. The contract we drew up names me president of the co-promotion, not hard to stretch that into full control."

"Eddie never signed that."

"He will when Shuko asks him nice."

"You don't have to kill him."

"Hey, I don't wanna kill anybody. I just want Warrior." Lou presented Brandenberg. "All the killing, blood feud shit comes from here. Guy hears I want Eddie's company. Next thing I know I'm retiring and sitting in a pool of corn syrup with a busted sword sticking out of me."

I said to Brandenberg, "Those were your guys at the RV lot."

"Shuko was there with his little blowpipe. My boys didn't like taking orders from a Jap, let me tell you."

"Burch put a few out of their misery."

"Ah, Mr. Burch. Shuko said he'd work on Eddie first, make Burch watch. Failure's the worst pain a soldier can feel."

"Where are they?"

"Slow down," Lou said. "Bottom line, I'm your new boss. I got big ideas and you're part of them. Gonna work with the Yakuza, not be stupid and fight it like Eddie, get Warrior into Japan. The Russians are interested too."

"Tell me where."

"I'll tell you," Brandenberg said.

Lou stepped between us. "Hold on."

"Shuko wants him to know." Brandenberg studied his nails, folded his hands. "You know he'll get to this idiot anyway. Why waste any time or money on him?"

"I'll handle Shuko," Lou said. "Woody, come on. I'll have the heavyweight belt around your waist in two fights. I'll pull Gil's other fighters in, give 'em a few cans to kick around. If they can't handle that, we'll work it."

It was tempting. No more dangling and twitching from Eddie's puppet strings. Roth and Terence would have their shots and the other guys would at least get a taste. The carrot Lou waved was fat and juicy.

Then Brandenberg brought out the whip. "I can see you're vacillating and I have things to do. So know this. You say no, I'll tell you where Shuko is. When he's done with you I'll hand him a ticket to Brazil so he can visit Marcela, be the last face she sees. Then I'll rezone Gil's property and yank that staph factory of a gym out from under him. So say yes. If your ignorant pride won't let you, just fucking nod."

I stared at him, everything slow enough I could feel the expansion of my chest with each heartbeat. "I'm the ignorant one?"

Brandenberg realized what was about to happen. Too late.

"You're the two who thought it was a good idea to get locked in a room with me."

"You won't lay a finger on me," Brandenberg said.

"That's true." I grabbed Lou by his belt and collar, picked him up, and smashed him into Brandenberg's wide-open mouth.

———

Their blood looked the same, but you could tell who the scattered teeth had come from. In the first ten seconds Brandenberg told me a couple dozen times where Shuko had taken Eddie and Burch. Even gave me directions.

It made sense and his story didn't change—even when his pitch did—and after that we didn't have much to talk about. I left them tangled and dripping off the couch, still breathing and probably dreaming about head-on collisions with freight trains.

I grabbed fresh clothes and shoes, checked the hallway. Gil was there with a bucket of coffee. I shut the door before he caught a glimpse. "Those guys really went at it."

"Just give me your goddamn hands." He ignored the fresh

blood while he cut the gloves off, squeezed my fingers and hands to make sure nothing was broken.

I started walking away from the arena entrance, pulling Gil down the concrete hallway. There were a few people rushing past; everybody else was prepping in the rooms or in the arena for whichever fight had the crowd jumping above us.

I dropped the shirt over my head and hopped into the jeans, stomped into the shoes while I searched the inner wall. There were stacks of chairs, tables, black plywood partitions, rolling carts crammed with painting supplies.

"What are we looking for?" Gil said.

"Shuko has Eddie and Burch."

"You're sure? I saw them run out."

"Straight to him." I stopped.

The door was solid gray metal, all sorts of warning stickers about maintenance personnel only, high voltage, moving machinery.

Nothing about Yakuza assassins.

The door was unlocked. The room inside was small and lined with electrical panels that gave off a deep hum I felt more than heard. It had a concrete floor and an opening in the left wall leading to a steel grate staircase that dropped into darkness.

"You're not going down there," Gil said.

I stepped inside. "Sorry."

"All right, then you're not going down there alone."

He was in deep enough already, and I didn't need to worry about him getting a dart or a sword in his neck.

"Sorry again." I shoved him back and slammed the door, threw a massive dead bolt that Shuko hadn't used.

He wanted me to follow him.

Gil thumped the door and yelled something, sounded like,

"Eddie's not worth it."

That was possible. But the ripple effect of doing nothing—Shuko tortures Eddie and Burch, finds Vanessa, finishes the tattoo so he can rip it apart.

Maybe what's left of Lou ends up running Warrior; I'm out and Gil's blackballed.

And Shuko comes for me anyway, just for blood feud grins.

I sank into the dark stairway.

"He's not worth it."

The echoes followed me down.

Shuko probably thought he was giving me a tough choice—die now or die later. Drawing me into whatever deviant squatter's lair he'd set up so we could fight in the dark, tooth and claw, blood and spit.

What he didn't understand: he wasn't pulling me into a trap.

He was inviting me home.

——

The stairs were steep and narrow. They made a ninety-degree turn to the right and dropped into a space lit by a bank of buzzing fluorescents. I looked at the mess on the floor.

Burch's gun. Stripped, mangled, springs and rods bent and twisted. If I had a gunsmith and two weeks, maybe it would be useful.

The walls were covered in more panels that sprouted thick bands of conduit, all of it stretching toward a black gap in the wall where it rolled around the corners and kept going. I stepped into the passageway, walls close enough to touch with my elbows at my sides.

Something crunched against the floor. Glass. I looked up, could barely see the ghost of another light bank floating near the ceiling. Between me groping through high voltage and the glass eggshells he'd scattered, Shuko had himself a nice early-warning system.

Or he could be two feet in front of me.

I threw a left kick just in case, hit nothing, and felt my right knee buckle. Felt a little stupid too, but me and the pipes made a pact not to tell anybody about it.

I stopped and held my breath, listened for anyone else's. No good. My ears were still ringing from the strikes and chokes Zombi had dished out.

With one eye swollen shut my depth perception was way off—not sure it made a difference in the blackness, but I didn't like having a built-in blind spot. Shapes skimmed through the darkness, darts and faces and swinging pipes.

I moved forward, felt the floor pull me. Had to lean back on my heels to stay balanced. The concrete was sloped, angling down into the bowels of the arena. Good news was I didn't have to worry about the subfloors under the casino. No way those were connected to an area with lock-and-key access only. So I got to search one huge dark nest of tunnels instead of two.

Neat.

I inched ahead, one hand on the wall and one stretched out, waving and waiting to brush against flesh.

Touched fabric instead.

I grabbed, pulled, and lifted my left knee into his face. He was light. My right knee buckled again, and I toppled forward into him, realized no one was there. Just a jacket hanging from the ceiling.

It was wet. Sticky.

I felt the silk lining, found sewn-in pouches and straps: Dorian's custom work that let Burch carry an arsenal without advertising.

I dropped the jacket and moved on, crunching more glass. Somewhere along the way I braced my arms against the conduit on both sides to make sure I couldn't get turned around. I checked over my shoulder and saw more blackness. The light and stairs were swallowed up.

I kept going.

Twenty minutes later, maybe an hour, a week, I could see the outlines of pipes and panels. There was light somewhere ahead. I fought the urge to run—Shuko would plan for that, wait for me to drop my guard and sprint, and that's when the dart would come.

I crept on, didn't see the hallway that angled off ninety degrees to the right until I was in the intersection. Some sections of the conduit stayed straight and ran along the ceiling and wall into more darkness. Others bent the corner and took the new passageway fifty feet toward a room that flashed and died in flickering light.

Something hung in the entrance.

Putting my back as close to the wall as I could, I edged toward the room. A single fluorescent tube burbled and pinged in the middle of the square ceiling. The rest were shards on the floor. Racks of blinking LEDs and dials and switches lined the walls behind steel mesh doors with padlocks. I'd need three years of school just to know what the hell this room was for.

I leaned through the opening and checked the corners.

Empty.

There was another hallway across the space, a black maw the

flickering light couldn't pierce.

I turned, finally got a good look at what was hanging in the doorway but didn't touch it. Light flashed on a tuft of blue hair wrapped in wire, a shiny red coin of scalp still attached.

———

I moved faster.

Eddie and Burch were bleeding, giving up Vanessa, and Shuko was leaving things to make me slow down and stop. Trying to hold me up or make me a stationary target. Either way it was working.

I thumped on my dead leg through the room into the black space on the far wall and braced for the impact with Shuko or whatever he carried.

I wanted this over with. Fuck the chase. Get me into the fight. Nobody there.

Glass crunched under my feet. The walls were smooth concrete, no pipes or conduit. The floor was angled up toward the surface. I leaned into it and climbed. Three steps later the flickering light was lost behind me, dumping me into a pitch-black chute.

I sped up. Pulled air in through my ragged throat and opened wide to roar Shuko's name, tell him I didn't care if he knew I was coming. I started to exhale when I heard a scream.

I froze, felt my hair arch away from my body.

The scream was guttural, shameless. No gender, just something that knew it was about to die. It came from somewhere ahead, above.

My feet didn't want to go toward it. No part of me did. Every cell in my body tried to turn and run. I fought the current and pressed forward. The scream faded but I could still hear it, knew

I would forever.

However long that would be.

A white horizontal line sliced across at eye level. I ducked, noticed it was ahead of me, not moving. I climbed. It dropped until the floor leveled out and the line became a crack at the bottom of a closed door.

The scream had come from the other side.

The door was unlocked.

———

All the lights were working in the room, a space about twenty feet square. Each concrete wall had a door, all closed. The low ceiling was more poured concrete with exposed galvanized strut, with just the lights hanging off it. No idea what the area used to be, but Shuko had turned it into his playroom.

He'd probably found it the day we met in the parking lot. Crept down here and started nesting, knowing we'd all have to come to the arena eventually. There was a thin sleeping pad unrolled on my left next to a five-gallon bucket of dirty water.

In the far right corner a tarp was spread on the floor and up the wall. It sagged with chunks of brown and red, some of them crusty while others glistened. Burch was faceup on the tarp, his shirt torn open. Shuko had made a dozen shallow cuts over his ribs up into his armpit. Blood still trickled out.

Two angry pink and purple splotches on his chest showed where the darts had hit. Whatever recipe Shuko had dipped them in, it was making Burch's skin blister.

Eddie's eyes were closed but he was breathing. Tacky ribbons of blood ran down his face from the mini scalping Shuko had given him. He was tied to the thing in the middle of the room, sitting on the floor with his back against it and his forehead duct-taped so he would have to look at Burch.

The thing in the middle of the room kicked on. I skidded back into the door I'd come through, felt the sudden flood of sweat suck my shirt tight. It squatted there, humming and vibrating, making Eddie's blood-matted hair tremble. An orange extension cord ran from it through the crack under the door across the room.

Somebody in the building above me was missing a box freezer.

I put it in the corner of my good eye so it could crouch and chuckle. There was a tiny video camera on a thin tripod aimed at Burch and the tarp. It was running. When I stepped into the room to swat the thing over, I saw a flat LCD tablet on top of the freezer.

It showed Burch's body live and in HD. There was a control panel ghosted in the corner of the screen: arrows, plus and minus, Record, Stop. Shuko could be anywhere in the room and see what the camera was recording, turn it, zoom in. Make sure it caught what he was doing to the person on the tarp.

The tarp rustled.

Burch screamed, a louder and higher version of what I'd heard in the passageway.

I dropped next to him. "Where is he?" The words shredded my throat.

His eyes fluttered, showed white. "Vanessa."

"He went to get her?"

"I think I told him."

"Doesn't matter. Where?"

He squirmed. Fresh blood welled out of the slices. "Penthouse."

"You kept her in the fucking casino?"

"Close to me."

"And him." I took a breath. Not the time for lectures. "Hold on. I'll come back."

"No."

"No?"

"Bringing her here."

A door opened somewhere deep in one of the passageways. Impossible to tell which direction.

"He'll make me watch," Burch said. The cords on his neck looked ready to snap. He was killing himself trying to get up. Tears slipped out of his eyes.

The door boomed shut. Then a high-pitched sound again and again over a deep hum, getting louder. Closer.

Screams? No, squeaks.

Wheels.

I stood up and spun, trying to watch every door. Backed into an empty corner and wedged my shoulder in. Was only a little more obvious than a battleship in a kitchen sink.

Shuko rolled closer.

Fuck me.

———

Silence.

No more doors banging or wheels squeaking. Shuko was coming in quietly.

I watched the doors and waited. Held my breath and fought the urge to yell, thrash.

The door to the left of the one I'd used shifted a fraction of an inch, then nothing. I was doubting it had moved at all when it blew open and Shuko sidestepped through with a short sword, landed in the corner on his bedroll, and braced himself for me.

He scanned the room, scowling in blue coveralls and a baseball cap that shadowed his eyes. The side of his jaw was a swollen, mottled bruise from where I'd caught him with the elbow. Fresh blood coated the right side of his neck from deep furrows carved under that ear; Vanessa had fought back.

Shuko leaned around for a peek at Eddie and Burch, slid the foot-long blade into a sheath he had sticking out of a thigh pocket. Chucked the hat onto his bed and walked through the doorway into darkness. Came back pushing a trash bin tipped on a dolly with two wheels.

He closed the door and flipped the hinged lid off the bin. Reached in and pulled a handful of blonde hair up. He smiled at Burch. "Look who joined us. You need to make room."

Shuko let the hair slide between his fingers and drop. He stepped over to the tarp and bent to grab Burch's legs, then stood and looked straight into the camera.

His eyes popped and he turned to grab the tablet controller.

The one I had in my hands.

I dropped it and drove up out of the freezer. Don't know what made me happier—the shock on his face or getting the hell out of the freezer-bathtub-tomb—but I howled about it all and hit Shuko with a left uppercut that wedged under his chin and stretched him, lifted, sailed him up and back.

He tipped in midair and landed on the back of his head and shoulders. His knees followed, forked around his face and kept him going in a backward somersault until he thumped against the door next to the tarp.

I jumped out of the freezer and landed on Eddie's legs. He moaned. I pounced toward Shuko, planning to save my knuckles and use the door to finish him off. I was reaching over him to grab the handle when he rolled toward me and came up with the short sword flashing.

I sprang back. My right knee locked and I tripped over Eddie again.

He stirred. "Muh."

I grabbed the camera and tripod out of Burch's corner, swung and hit Shuko in the shoulder as he rose. Sounded like I'd smacked him with a handful of dry spaghetti—the damn thing weighed only five pounds. I spun it and jabbed the legs at him. He ducked and stepped to his left toward the door I'd come through.

Keeping the open freezer between us, I moved right, got to the trash bin. Vanessa was stuffed inside, eyes rolling. She saw me and her face crumpled. She tried to reach up but couldn't move her arms, hands flapping like seaweed.

"You're safe," I said.

"No, she's not." It sounded garbled, thick. Shuko's jaw was broken in at least one place. It sagged away from his head, his bottom teeth jutting out toward me. Blood and spit fell out. He smiled and I heard the bones creak.

"Burch, get up."

Shuko snorted. "Yeah, Burch. Come and play." He looked at him, then back at me. "Guess not."

"Nice bruise."

"Lucky. Coward's move."

"Said the assassin. I was waiting in the cage for you, chicken-shit. Thought you were gonna come in there and try to chop my head off in front of everybody."

"Too quick."

"Yeah, honorable too. Like your daddy."

The grin twitched. His jaw clicked and grated while he got it back. "You come here, I get all the time I want. Keep you in your little box." White vapor welled out of the freezer. "Let you hear what I'm doing to your friends."

"You want to hear what we did to your brothers?"

The smile left for good. "You shouldn't talk. Now I know something's wrong with your throat. Your right knee isn't working. And this freezer scares you almost as much as I do. You're giving me more than I need to kill you."

"Your clan's good at sneaking around, huh? Sticking people when they aren't looking, like I tagged you. Not so good face-to-face, though. Surprised you didn't all starve to death a couple centuries ago. Assassins. Shoulda been practice dummies. You're much better at dying than killing."

He pointed the sword at me over the freezer, his eyes black and dead.

"Yeah, I've seen it all night. Problem is, I've looked into actual dead eyes. Watched the light go out. Yours don't come close. Too jumpy, too much sickness wriggling around in there." I collapsed the tripod, held it across my chest like a pugil stick. "Now let's stop fucking around and give you some real ones."

I was ready for him to shoot around the freezer, blade dancing. Instead he reached into his coveralls and took out the blowgun.

I dropped the tripod and yelled something, slammed the freezer into his legs, shoved it and Eddie across the floor, and pinned Shuko against the door behind him. Braced the freezer with my legs and reached across for the blowgun.

Shuko flicked the blade out and I pulled back, almost lost the tips of my fingers. He brought the blowgun up and I cracked him with the freezer lid, knocking him sideways. Again. Not much momentum but it was heavy.

Shuko's coveralls flapped open, revealing a row of plastic test tubes in elastic loops over his chest. Each one had a long steel dart with a red tuft. He blocked the lid with his left forearm—a stalemate, but I'd take it as long as that blowgun hand was busy. He lunged forward as far as he could to stab me in the face.

I rocked back, had to move my left leg away from the freezer to keep from falling.

He slashed down across my right thigh, jeans and flesh parting to let blood run out.

I yanked that leg away, couldn't help it. Put my hands on the freezer to keep Shuko pinned but he didn't care.

His left hand was free. He brought the blowgun away from the lid.

I ducked. The freezer wasn't tall enough. I stared into the black tunnel and heard Shuko draw a sharp breath. He exhaled in a quick burst, the air puffing out the side of his mouth.

I looked past the blowgun. Shuko's broken jaw wouldn't let him make a seal.

He tried again, the air leaking out between his bloody lips and teeth.

"Well," I said. I grabbed the blowgun, slammed him with the lid again. He stabbed at my chest. I caught his wrist, clamped on it with both hands, and pulled. Stretched him until I felt and heard his shoulder clunk out of its socket.

I peeled the sword out of his hand and dropped it behind me. Kept him stretched tight with my left hand and slammed a right straight into his chest.

Plastic shattered. Shuko hissed in my face.

Hit him again. The coveralls were thick canvas. I could barely feel the shards of plastic through it—Shuko seemed to feel them just fine.

Again. Drove the plastic into his chest.

Again. Needed to get the darts into his blood. Wouldn't take much.

Shuko grunted.

I hit him again.

He spasmed. His eyes rolled back and foam shot out of his nose. I let go. He tipped forward into the freezer. I dragged it and him and Eddie into the middle of the room. Hauled Shuko all the way over, dropped him faceup into the bottom of the freezer. He was jerking and drumming his feet.

I slammed the lid.

Extended the camera tripod and wedged it between the top of the freezer and the low ceiling.

Found Shuko's duct tape and wrapped it around my thigh.

Looked around the room: Burch, Eddie, and Vanessa, all unconscious or close enough, needing medical attention. I limped through door number one—the last door Shuko ever used—to find a fucking elevator.

CHAPTER 22

I STOLE SHUKO'S HAT TO COVER THE BLOODY BANDAGE around my head, told Vanessa we were going for a ride, and rolled her in the trash can through a maze to a freight elevator that opened into a small warehouse with a set of overhead doors.

Ignored those and took her down the long service hallway that ringed the arena, found the door closest to Eddie's private garage. The fights were over. I saw two people far away with heads down over brooms or phones; nobody gave a shit about a guy pushing garbage around.

The hot night air tasted beautiful. I punched the code into the garage and eased Vanessa down the slope to the limo.

Repeated the process with Eddie and Burch, spread everybody on the floor of Eddie's limo so they could mumble and squawk and sweat. Found Eddie's phone and called Gil. Told him what I needed, gave him the code to the garage, and passed out across the front seat.

———

"Woody."

Gil tugged on my foot. Maybe for the first time, maybe the fiftieth.

He and Denny stood next to the limo. Denny wore a purple kimono and leaned to one side to support the weight of his tackle box of herbs and acupuncture supplies.

I sat up and regretted it immediately—somebody lit a short fuse in my eyebrow that led to a block of C-4 in my brain. Standing up would help. My right knee buckled, and the slash across that thigh had a tight lace of pain over a constant aching thud.

Gil hooked my arm. "The hell you doing? Sit down."

I tried to do it slowly, pretending I had a choice.

Denny leaned in, looked at everything. "I can fix that."

"I need stitches."

"Right, let's put more holes in you. Stitches. We'll see. What happened to your throat? Don't answer. I have a tea and a soup, but you can't have them together."

"Backseat."

Denny set his tackle box down and opened the back door. "Hello? Somebody get me a pallet of white sage. Wow." He ducked into the driver's door. "Same guy did this?"

"Same guy."

"Different toxin, though, yes?"

I shrugged.

"Yes," he said. "This one feels softer, not as runny. He had them captive?"

"Yes."

"Mm. Didn't want to deal with the mucus."

Gil said, "Where is he now?"

"Gone."

He nodded, put a hand on my head.

I asked Denny, "You can help them?"

"Starting now, but we'll need more room. Auras are a mess back there, all tangled up."

"Get in."

———

We went to Eddie's place. Made three stacks of mats and blankets on the gym floor, spread out plenty of towels and buckets.

Sunday afternoon Eddie perked up enough to call the Warrior offices and slur about taking a vacation, then hand me the phone so I could hang up on a voice saying, "Is this a joke?"

He passed out again before I could tell him about his hair.

Best for everybody.

Argo called that night. "How's your face?"

"Tolerable."

"Listen, your two biggest fans, the ones paid you a visit after the fight."

Lou Gerrone and Brandenberg. "Yeah."

"My clients visited them in the hospital. Nasty accident they were in. Point is, nobody's happy about them going freelance. They're going to behave."

"Good."

He paused. "Any word from our friend?"

Shuko was the Yakuza's monster; let them clean up his mess. I sure as hell didn't want to. "I know where he's staying. Your clients want him?"

"I think they'd appreciate that. Closure is healthy."

I replayed the lid slamming shut. "I love closure." Told him where the freezer was. "My prints aren't on any of it."

"Who cares?" He hung up.

Gil stopped by with food and whatever Denny needed. He dabbed his finger into the mush Denny kept smearing over my eyebrow and thigh, sniffed it. One time was enough.

———

Saturday morning, a week after the Zombi fight, Burch and Vanessa were gone.

Denny shrugged. "He asked if they were safe for travel. I said yes."

"Where?"

"Where memories can't follow."

"Hope they sell guns there."

Eddie was a shambling pile of whine. Denny and I agreed this was normal behavior for him, no cause for concern. It was Sunday before he could string together two related sentences. I was busy pushing chunks of banana into his cheeks and not smiling when his eyes opened.

"Woody."

"Don't talk with your mouth full."

"Hey, you hear from your girl?"

"Every day."

"What's she think?"

"About what? I didn't tell her about this and don't plan to. Just the fight. She was happy for me." Happy I'd won, called me an idiot for the way I'd done it.

"No, the event."

"Eddie, shut up."

"The big deal I been working on. Shit, must have dreamed I told you. Warrior's going international. We're storming Brazil. You're on the card."

Brazil.

Marcela.

END OF ROUND 2

THE COMPLETE WOODSHED WALLACE SERIES

SUCKERPUNCH

HOOK AND SHOOT

ANACONDA CHOKE

OTHER BOOKS BY JEREMY BROWN

FIND > FIX > FINISH

SHOW NO TEETH

AKON'S MISSION

FIGHT CARD: THE KALAMAZOO KID

CRIME FILES: BODY OF EVIDENCE

CRIME FILES: SHADOW OF DOUBT

ABOUT THE AUTHOR

Jeremy Brown is a novelist working in many genres, including crime thrillers, murder mysteries, and military thrillers. He has worked as a narrative designer and lead writer for a massively popular video game and enjoys kettlebells, stockpiling firewood, and using coffee as a delivery system for cream. He lives in Michigan with his wife, sons, and various animals.

For more information and to sign up for the

Reader Club, please visit

JEREMYWBROWN.COM

www.ingramcontent.com/pod-product-compliance
Lightning Source LLC
Chambersburg PA
CBHW021216250626
47155CB00008B/2822